"It has been suggested that most of the effective and skillfully written Western fiction has been produced by men who, like Frederic Remington in the field of Western art, have been outsiders 'looking in'—careful observers who have synthesized what they saw, what they read and what they were told into a viable and convincing whole. . . . But the books that ring truest about the West have come out of men who, as did cowboy artist Charlie Russell, could work from the inside out—either because they were participants or because they were people of talent who became spiritually and emotionally involved with the frontier. . . .

"Of the participant group, the best all-around writer was Eugene Manlove Rhodes. . . . More satisfyingly recognized during his own lifetime was Stewart Edward White, a vigorous storyteller who knew his Western backgrounds thoroughly. . . . Of those writing Western fiction today, none is more consistently effective on a high-performance level than Jack Schaefer. . . . Stephen Crane qualified as an observer of rather than a participant in the Western scene if any writer ever did."

—from the Introduction

DON WARD, editor of this volume, has been an authority on Western Americana for many years and has edited many anthologies of Western fact and fiction.

GREAT SHORT

AMERICAN

NOVELS OF THE WEST

Edited, with introduction, by
DON WARD

COLLIER BOOKS
NEW YORK, N.Y.

A Collier Books Original

First Edition 1962

Collier Books is a division of The Crowell-Collier Publishing Company

ACKNOWLEDGMENTS

Paso por Aqui—Copyright 1926 by The Curtis Publishing Company; renewed 1954 by May D. Rhodes. Reprinted by permission of and arrangement with Houghton Mifflin Company, the authorized publisher.

The Rawhide—Copyright, 1907, 1935, by Stewart Edward White. Reprinted by permission of the Estate of Stewart Edward White.

The Kean Land—Copyright © 1956 by Jack Schaefer. Reprinted by permission of and arrangement with Houghton Mifflin Company, the authorized publishers.

Library of Congress Catalog Card Number: A62-8716

Contents

Introduction

DON WARD

THE WESTERN NOVEL stands in critical disrepute generally. That it does so is understandable even as it is unjustifiable. Although the percentage of trash written and published in the Western-fiction field is probably no higher than in any other, it might easily seem to be. Sensible evaluation has been thwarted by the tendency of most critics to brand all Western fiction, automatically, as unimportant or worse. One weighty survey of United States literature from 1890 on included the comment that "Wild western novels have come as a flood from such writers as Rex Beach, James Hopper, Zane Grey, Eugene Manlove Rhodes, Clarence Mulford, George Pattullo and dozens of others."

In addition to the impropriety of labeling Rhodes's books "Wild westerns," the statement is misleading because this author's output, far from being a "flood," was quite limited. Besides, Gene Rhodes was a literary craftsman of extraordinary talent and skill, whereas the work of Zane Grey (mentioned in the same breath, as it were) seldom rose above a crude storytelling level. It is true enough that Clarence Mulford ground out millions of words about a saddle-happy sun-god called Hopalong Cassidy; but George Pattullo, whose short stories often accurately reflected the nature of the range lands and the character of the range riders, published very few books—more nearly a trickle than a "flood." In the same survey, this authority—if we can call him that—had a few kind words to say about Owen Wister, but nothing at all to say about Andy Adams, whose novel, *The Log of a Cowboy,* was *The Virginian's* superior in every category except sales.

J. Frank Dobie, a born and bred Texan noted for his ability to distinguish good from bad in literature, has remarked that the "mass-produced" Western, with its accent on the unreal and the sensational, has made it "extremely difficult for any capable, serious writer in the same field to be taken seriously" and that to write and have published a book of Western fiction is to risk its being labeled "Just Another Western"—something any discriminating reader should avoid as he would the measles. Dobie is on record as believing, however, that this attitude is changing.

There are indeed signs that such a change is coming, although the process has been very slow. The critics who are naturally impressed by such novels as *The Oxbow Incident* and *The Big Sky* still take no notice of the carefully constructed and well-written novels of the late Ernest Haycox or of "Luke Short" (Frederick D. Glidden), whose better efforts have brought to "straight Western" writing respectable heights of craftsmanship. Many of the standard-length Western novels, by these two authors and others, directed at a mass audience and published in slick magazines before their appearance in book form, have been marked by qualities superior to those of some more ambitious and much longer novels of the West that have appeared in the last decade. As Conrad Richter's *The Sea of Grass* effectively demonstrates, a Western novel does not have to rival *Gone With the Wind* in wordage in order to be good.

The "Western novel" as a distinct category in American fiction began, in one sense, in 1902 with the publication of *The Virginian* by Owen Wister. More precisely, *The Virginian* was the first widely read and highly praised sustained work of fiction in which the protagonist was a cowboy. Works of fiction with Western-frontier settings antedated Wister's book by many years. Even before Bret Harte's successful and popular tales of the Gold Rush, there had appeared Charles Webber's *Tales of the Southern Border,* sentimental yarning about the Texas frontier, published in 1853. *John Brent,* by Theodore Winthrop, appearing in 1862, told about vaqueros on a California rancho. Mary Hallock Foote's magazine stories about the West were admired by Wister and may have influenced him. The then unknown Emerson Hough wrote a novel about cowboys in 1900.

The spate of paper-covered "dime novels" in the latter decades of the nineteenth century did its bit to discourage any serious interest in the possibility of a true Western literature; indeed, they gave birth to a Never-Never West that later on was revived and nurtured by scores of pulp magazines, a flood of print that dried to a trickle under the combined onslaught of "comic" books and television. The dime-novel heroes often were outsized versions of such real-life frontier characters as Kit Carson, W. F. Cody, Wild Bill Hickok and Billy the Kid; but the pulp-magazine authors generally disdained history, preferring to create such whole-cloth range-gods as Mulford's Hopalong Cassidy and Max Brand's "Silvertip."

The first element of realism introduced into any Western fiction appeared in 1883 with the publication of E. W. Howe's *The Story of a Country Town*. This story of a boy growing up on the prairie was bleak and gloomy, picturing frontier society as notably short on love, kindliness or understanding. Howe went on to write other books, but none of them had the power of *Country Town*. His successor was Hamlin Garland, who added another element of realism by making a deliberate effort to reproduce the prairie settlers' dialect in the talk of his characters. Garland's chief work dealt with the farmers of the prairie-plains, but he also produced a volume of cowboy fiction, *They of the High Trails*, which includes stories of merit.

Gentler and more idealistic than Garland's books were Willa Cather's novels of the prairie farm lands, *O Pioneers* and *My Antonia*. Distressed by the growth of industrialization and what she regarded as its great ills, Miss Cather overlooked the crudenesses and disadvantages of the pastoral-agricultural past, but her best work has an inner glow and a quiet strength that have made it last. *Death Comes for the Archbishop* is regarded by many as the finest novel about the times of Kit Carson, and her "Neighbor Rosicky," published in 1932, is an admirable short work.

Most notable of all the pioneer-farmer novels is *Giants in the Earth,* by O. E. Rolvaag, the story of a family of Norwegian immigrants struggling to make a living on the South Dakota prairie. No novel of the cattle kingdom has matched its tragic power. In comparison, even Richter's *Sea of Grass* and A. B. Guthrie's *These Thousand Hills* seem a bit pale, although each can stand by itself as a solid achievement in rangeland fiction. Perhaps Mari Sandoz's *Slogum House* comes closer to Rolvaag's epic in spirit and feeling, but Miss Sandoz's otherwise praiseworthy novel is burdened by an unsatisfactory ending.

The truth is that there have been fewer outstanding novels dealing with the cattle country than with almost any other phase of our frontier history. The mountain men have been superbly recorded by Steward Edward White in *The Long Rifle,* by Harvey Fergusson in *Grant of Kingdom,* and by A. B. Guthrie, Jr., in *The Big Sky.* The overland pioneers have been equally well delineated in such fine books as *The Way West,* by Guthrie, Emerson Hough's *The Covered Wagon,* Ernest Haycox's *The Earthbreakers,* and *The Travels of Jamie McPheeters,* by Robert Lewis Taylor. The Guthrie and Taylor novels, incidentally, brought Pulitzer prizes to their authors. It is significant that Guthrie's cattle-country novel, *These Thousand Hills,* lacks the robust fullness of his books about the mountain men and the pioneers; and Ernest Haycox, who turned out a score of highly readable standard Westerns about cattle range and cow town, eschewed such a setting for his single big novel, turning instead to the Oregon settlers.

The trail drives have furnished material for a number of good books about cowboys doing a special kind of job. Towering above all others is *The Log of a Cowboy,* by Andy Adams, published in 1903. Frank Dobie has compared it to *Moby Dick,* saying that "if all the literature pertaining to trailing were destroyed, we could still get a conception of trailing cattle from Andy Adams"; and Walter Prescott Webb, pronouncing the book "destined to become a classic," has praised it for its "simple beauty of style," its "pellucid clarity" and its "verisimilitude." In the form of a detailed description of the driving of a herd of Longhorns from the Rio Grande to Montana, *The Log of a Cowboy* provides an unforgettable picture of the drovers in the saddle, around the campfire, and having their infrequent flings in the trail-town fleshpots. It is life transmuted into art by a master's touch; and Adams, although he tried in several subsequent books, was never able to equal the performance.

Another notable novel of the cattle trails was Emerson Hough's *North of 36,* which appeared a score of years after Adams's masterpiece. It achieved a greater popularity than Adams's book did, but it was inferior to *Log* both stylistically and in the degree of its authenticity. Many years earlier, Hough had written a serious novel about life on the ranch and in the cow town that treated its subject in an adult way—*The Girl at the Halfway House,* which preceded Wister's *The Virginian* by two years.

1902 saw the publication of an above-average Western novel by Frances McElrath, called *The Rustler;* it was based on the Johnson County range war and told the story of a Texas cowboy who went wrong after an Eastern girl turned him down. A forceful melodrama, it might have scored a wider success had not Wister's long novel, *The Virginian,* been brought out the same year.

Wister, a Harvard-educated Philadelphian, took a Western trip in 1882, liked it, and returned to Wyoming in 1891. He began to write stories about a cowboy character, and in 1898 they appeared as chapters in an episodic novel, *Lin McLean.* In 1900 he had a volume of short stories published, and two years later *The Virginian* bombshell burst.

The novel went through sixteen printings in its first year, and it is still in print. Artfully constructed to appeal to Eastern readers, *The Virginian* featured a schoolmistress heroine who possessed the advantages of breeding and culture that were virtually all the personal assets that its gallant hero lacked—offered him by the osmosis of love. The book presented the ideal figure of the range rider: strong, valiant, honest, loyal, shrewd and virile;

and its enormous success helped bring about the tide of popular fiction about the cowboy and the cattle ranges that ever since then has flowed and ebbed, but mainly flowed.

Following Wister, then, the deluge. . . . After Bower's *Chip of the Flying U* (1905), Spearman's *Whispering Smith* (1906), Mulford's *Bar-20* (1907), and Raine's *Bucky O'Connor* (1910), the separate items became more and more difficult to keep track of. Among their authors were the incredibly prolific and numbingly successful Zane Grey and the even more prolific and almost as successful Frederick Faust, who wrote Westerns under the by-line "Max Brand" and several other pseudonyms.

As Dobie has remarked, most of this vast output "betrayed rather than revealed life." Of course, most of it was written to entertain casual readers, not to present the writer's view of a world (except, perhaps accidentally); and intelligent evaluation of any written work has to start with what that work is trying to do. In more recent years, trends toward greater realism and a measure of dimension in characterization have become apparent even in the standard Western; but, on the whole, the pageant of frontier fiction has always had its bright spots.

It has been suggested that most of the effective and skillfully written Western fiction has been produced by men who, like Frederic Remington in the field of Western art, were outsiders "looking in"—careful observers who synthesized what they saw, what they read and what they were told into a viable and convincing whole. One such writer was Ernest Haycox. But the books that ring truest about the West have come from men who, like cowboy-artist Charlie Russell, could work from the inside out—either because they were participants, like Andy Adams or Stewart Edward White, or because they were people of talent who became spiritually and emotionally involved with the frontier, like Wister or George Pattullo.

Of the participant group, the best all-around writer was Eugene Manlove Rhodes. A cowboy and a ranch man for a quarter of a century, Rhodes wrote about the land (southwestern New Mexico) and the people (its inhabitants, Anglo- and Spanish-American and Indian) that he knew and loved. His books, Bernard DeVoto once remarked, "are the only body of fiction devoted to the cattle kingdom which is both true to it and written by an artist in prose." As W. H. Hutchinson, Rhodes's biographer and bibliographer, has put it: "the people and the land of six New Mexico counties . . . are preserved for all time in the clear amber of his joyous, dancing, illuminated prose."

Striking as Rhodes's style is, the warmth and spirit that shine in and through his stories are just as important. The best of the customs and traditions of the frontier, its truest philosophy, inhere in the fabric of his stories. Rhodes's characters, or most of them anyway, are decent and kindly and strongly individualistic, and their talk is vivacious and witty. At first one thinks the author must have created all of them out of thin air, patterning each one more or less on himself, only to discover that a good many of them were based on range men whom Rhodes had known. (He often used their real names in his stories, too—Pat Garrett appearing as Pat Garrett in "Paso Por Aqui," for example.)

Considering all this, plus the facts that he plotted soundly and filled his stories with the fibers of life, it would be pleasant to be able to record that Rhodes enjoyed a substantial success. Such was not the case. Much that he wrote was published in the *Saturday Evening Post,* but his book sales never reached a point satisfying to either author or publisher. That was due in part to the fact that, willy nilly, his books were publicized (if at all) as Western thrillers and reviewed as Western thrillers. Discriminating readers who would have enjoyed them never opened one, on the mistaken ground that they were mere horse operas; and the run of Western fans, used to reading something quite different, were apt to find them strangely fibrous and chewy—something like eating Longhorn steaks after you have been raised on a diet of hamburger.

Rhodes's followers may disagree as to which novel of

his is the best, but more often than not "Paso por Aqui" receives support in any such discussion—and fortunately for our purposes, it is of short-novel length.

More satisfyingly recognized during his own lifetime was Stewart Edward White, a vigorous storyteller who knew his Western backgrounds thoroughly, being as much a woodsman, plainsman or horseman as any of his characters. His most widely known and justly renowned work was the Andy Burnett saga, a tetralogy composed of *The Long Rifle, Ranchero, The Folded Hills* and *Stampede.* The best of his cattle-range stories were collected in the volume titled *Arizona Nights,* which includes our selection "The Rawhide." White once referred to this as his "most coherent" piece of work.

Of those writing Western fiction today, none is more consistently effective than Jack Schaefer. One of the "outside-in" group, Schaefer no doubt is better known today than he otherwise would be because of the phenomenal success of the movie based on his first novel, *Shane,* which has become a minor film classic. His limited output has included a number of remarkable short stories in addition to our short novel, "The Kean Land," which originally appeared as a two-part serial in *Collier's.*

Stephen Crane qualified as an observer of, rather than participant in, the Western scene if any writer ever did. Crane spent a few months of his tragically brief life on a trip through the West that resulted not only in the classic "The Bride Comes to Yellow Sky"—which Hollywood, with every evidence of loving care made into a little gem of a movie, surprising all of us—but also in "The Blue Hotel," our fourth selection. Hard to classify by length alone, it is too long to be included in most short-story anthologies, although its structure may cause some to question its status as a short novel. Nevertheless its merit is such as to justify some arbitrariness in classification, which the editor hereby confesses. As has been remarked by many, the story is flawed by the moralizing afterword, but it is truly a memorable one.

If any literary genre should be judged by its best examples, as no doubt it should, it is hoped that the short Western novels here presented have been well selected. They have been, in any event, carefully selected; and the editor's judgment has been fortified by opinions offered by those whose authority in the Western-fiction field outshines his own. Nevertheless, only he made the choices, and on them he stands—for this volume, anyway.

DON WARD

PASO POR AQUI

AT THE AGE of twelve, Eugene Manlove Rhodes, Nebraska-born, moved to New Mexico with his parents. The year was 1881. In the ensuing quarter century, Gene Rhodes was a freight-line swamper and teamster, a guide, a miner, a road builder, a horse wrangler, a cowboy, and a small rancher. In 1906, he came East to settle in Apalachin, New York, the home of his wife, May Davison. It was twenty years before Rhodes returned to his "home range" for a visit, but time never dimmed his love for the New Mexico that looms so large in his stories.

Although his formal schooling was scanty, Rhodes was a voracious reader and early began to write, at first mostly poetry. In 1902, *Out West* magazine carried a short story of his, for which he was paid ten dollars. Subsequently, about sixty of his short stories appeared in various magazines. There were, in addition, fourteen novels or novelettes, most of which were serialized in the *Saturday Evening Post* before being published in book form.

"Paso por Aqui," which appeared as a two-parter in the *Post,* was paired with another short Rhodes novel in a book titled *Once in the Saddle;* it came out in 1927 and is now a collector's item. "Paso por Aqui" is also to be found in the omnibus volume *The Best Novels and Stories of Eugene Manlove Rhodes* (1949). Simple in plot, its strength lies in its depiction of the gallantly generous spirit of the range rider, a recurrent, convincingly presented theme in Rhodes's writing.

In deference to his expressed wish, Gene Rhodes was buried in his beloved San Andres mountains; his grave now is marked by a bronze memorial plaque that bears the legend:

Paso por Aqui
Eugene Manlove Rhodes
Jan. 19, 1869—June 27, 1934

Paso por Aqui

EUGENE MANLOVE RHODES

1

EXCEPTIONS ARE so inevitable that no rule is without them—except the one just stated. Neglecting fractions, then, not to insult intelligence by specifying the obvious, trained nurses are efficient, skillful, devoted. It is a noble calling.

Nevertheless, it is notorious that the official uniform is of reprehensible charm. This regulation is variously explained by men, women and doctors. "No fripperies, curlicues and didos—bully!" say the men. "Ah! Yes! But why? Artful minxes!" say the women, who should know best. "Cheerful influence in the sickroom," say the doctors.

Be that as it may, such uniform Jay wore, spotless and starched, crisp and cool; Jay Hollister, now seated on the wide portico of the Alamogordo Hospital; not chief nurse, but chief ornament, according to many, not only of that hospital but of the great railroad which maintained it. Alamogordo was a railroad town, a new town, a ready-made and highly painted town, direct from Toyland.

Ben Griggs was also a study in white—flannels, oxfords and panama; a privileged visitor who rather over-stepped his privileges; almost a fixture in that pleasant colonnade.

"Lamp of life," said Ben, "let's get down to brass tacks. You're homesick!"

"Homesick!" said Jay scornfully. "Homesick! I'm heartsick, bankrupt, shipwrecked, lost, forlorn—here in this terrible country, among these dreadful people. "Homesick? Why, Ben, I'm just damned!"

"Never mind, heart's delight," said Ben the privileged. "You've got me."

Miss Hollister seemed in no way soothed by this reassuring statement. "Your precious New Mexico! Sand!"

she said. "Sand, snakes, scorpions; wind, dust, glare and heat; lonely, desolate and forlorn!"

"Under the circumstances," said Ben, "you could hardly pay me a greater compliment. 'Whither thou goest, I will go,' and all that. Good girl! This unsolicited tribute—"

"Don't be a poor simpleton," advised the good girl. "I shall stick it out for my year, of course, since I was foolish enough to undertake it. That is all. Don't you make any mistakes. These people shall never be my people."

"No better people on earth. In all the essentials—"

"Oh, who cares anything about essentials?" cried Jay impatiently—voicing, perhaps, more than she knew. "A tin plate will do well enough to eat out of, certainly, if that is what you mean. I prefer china, myself. I'm going back where I can see flowers and green grass, old gardens and sundials."

"I know not what others may say," observed Ben grandly, "but as for me, you take the sundials and give me the sun. Right here, too, where they climb for water and dig for wood. Peevish, my fellow townsman, peevish, waspy, crabbed. You haven't half enough to do. In this beastly climate people simply will not stay sick. They take up their bed and beat it, and you can't help yourself. Nursing is a mere sinecure." His hands were clasped behind his head, his slim length reclined in a steamer chair, feet crossed, eyes half closed, luxurious. "Ah, idleness!" he murmured. "Too bad, too bad! You never were a grouch back home. Rather good company, if anything."

Ben's eyes were blue and dreamy. They opened a trifle wider now, and rolled slowly till they fell upon Miss Hollister, bolt upright and haughty in her chair, her lips pressed in a straight line. She regarded him sternly. He blinked, his hands came from behind his head, he straightened up and adjusted his finger tips to meet with delicate precision. "But the main trouble, the fount and origin of your disappointing conduct is, as hereinbefore said, homesickness. It is, as has been observed, a nobler pang than indigestion, though the symptoms are of striking similarity. But nostalgia, more than any other feeling, is fatal to the judicial faculties, and I think, my dear towny, that when you look at this fair land, your future home, you regard all things with a jaundiced eye."

"Oh-h!" gasped Jay, hotly indignant. "Look at it yourself! Look at it!"

The hospital was guarded and overhung by an outer colonnade of cottonwoods; she looked through a green archway across the leagues of shimmering desert, somber, wavering and dim; she saw the long bleak range beyond, saw-toothed and gray; saw in the midway levels the unbearable brilliance of the White Sands, a wild dazzle and tumult of light, a blinding mirror with two score miles for diameter.

But Ben's eyes widened with delight, their blue darkened to a deeper blue of exultation, not to be feigned.

"More than beautiful—fascinating," he said.

"Repulsive, hateful, malignant, appalling!" cried Jay Hollister bitterly. "The starved, withered grass, the parched earth, the stunted bushes—miserable, hideous—the abomination of desolation!"

"Girl, by all good rights I ought to shut your wild, wild mouth with kisses four—that's what I orter do—elocutin' that way. But you mean it, I guess." Ben nodded his head sagely. "I get your idea. Blotched and leprous, eh? Thin, starved soil, poisoned and mildewed patches—thorns and dwarfed scrub, red leer of the sun. Oh, *sí!* Like that bird in Browning? Hills like giants at a huntin' lay—the round squat turret—all the lost adventures, my peers—the Dark Tower, weird noises just offstage, increasin' like a bill, I mean a bell—increasin' like a bell, fiddles a-moanin', 'O-o-o-h-h-h! What did you do-o-o with your summer's wa-a-a-ges? So this is Paris!' Yes, yes, but why not shed the second-hand stuff and come down to workaday?"

"Ben Griggs," said Miss Hollister with quiet and deadly conviction, "you are absolutely the most blasphemous wretch that ever walked in shoe leather. You haven't anything even remotely corresponding to a soul."

"When we are married," said Ben, and paused, reflecting. "That is, if I don't change my mind—"

"Married!" said Miss Hollister derisively. "When! You!" Her eyes scorned him.

"Woman," said Ben, "beware! You make utter confusion with the parts of speech. You make mere interjections of pronouns, prepositions and verbs and everything. You use too many shockers. More than that—mark me, my lass—isn't it curious that no one has ever thought to furnish printed words with every phonograph record of a song? Just a little sheet of paper—why, it needn't cost more than a penny apiece at the outside. Then we could know what it was all about."

"The way you hop from conversational crag to crag," said Jay, "is beyond all praise."

"Oh, well, if you insist, we can go back to our marriage again."

"My poor misguided young friend," said Jay, "make no mistakes. I put up with you because we played together when we were kids, and because we are strangers here in a strange land, townies together—"

Ben interrupted her. "Two tawny townies twisting twill together!" he chanted happily, beating slow time with a gentle finger. "Twin turtles twitter tender twilight twaddle. Twice twenty travelers—"

"Preposterous imbecile!" said Jay, dimpling nevertheless adorably. "Here is something to put in your little book. Jay Hollister will never marry an idler and a wastrel. Why, you're not even a ne'er-do-well. You're a do-nothing, net."

"All the world loves a loafer," Ben protested. "Still, as Alice remarked, if circumstances were different they would be quite otherwise. If frugal industry—"

"There comes your gambler friend," said Jay coldly.

"Who, Monte? Where?" Ben turned eagerly.

"Across the street. No, the other way." Though she fervently disapproved of Monte, Jay was not sorry for the diversion. It was daily more difficult to keep Ben in his proper place, and she had no desire to discuss frugal industry.

"Picturesque rascal, what? Looking real pleased about

something too. Say, girl, you've made me forget something I was going to tell you."

"He is laughing to himself," said Jay.

"I believe he is, at that." Ben raised his voice. "Hi,
Monte! Come over and tell us the joke."

2

Monte's mother had known him as Rosalio Marquez.
The overname was professional. He dealt Monte wisely
but not too well. He was nearing thirty-five, the easiest
age of all; he was slender and graceful; he wore blue
serge and a soft black hat, low crowned and wide
brimmed. He carried this hat in his hand as he came up
the steps. He bowed courteously to Jay, with murmured
greetings in Spanish, soft syllables of lingering caress;
he waved a friendly salute to Ben.

"Yes, indeed," said Ben. "With all my heart. Your
statement as to the beauty of the day is correct in every
particular, and it affords me great pleasure to indorse an
opinion so just. But, after all, dear heart, that is hardly
the point, is it? The giddy jest, the merry chuckles—
those are the points on which we greatly desire informa-
tion."

Monte hesitated, almost imperceptibly, a shrewd ques-
tioning in his eyes.

"Yes, have a chair," said Jay, "and tell us the joke."

"Thees is good, here, thank you," said Monte. He sat
on the top step and hung the black hat on his knee; his
face lit up with soft low laughter. "The joke? Oh, eet ees
upon the sheriff, Jeem Hunter. I weel tell eet."

He paused to consider. In his own tongue Monte's
speech sounded uncommonly like a pack of firecrackers
lit at both ends. In English it was leisured, low and
thoughtful. The unslurred vowels, stressed and piquant,
the crisp consonants, the tongue-tip accents—these things
combined to make the slow caressing words into something rich and colorful and strange, all unlike our own
smudged and neutral speech. The customary medium of

the Southwest between the two races is a weird and law-less hodge-podge of the two tongues—a barbarous lingua franca.

As Miss Hollister had no Spanish, Monte drew only from his slender stock of English; and all unconsciously he acted the story as he told it.

"When Jeem was a leetle, small boy," said Monte, his hand knee-high to show the size in question, "he dream manee times that he find thoss marbles—oh, many mar-bles! That mek heem ver' glad, thees nize dream. Then he get older"—Monte's hand rose with the sheriff's ma-turity—"and sometime he dream of find money lak thoss marble. And now Jeem ees grown and sheriff—an' las' night he come home, ver' late, ver' esleepy. I weel tell you now how eet ees, but Jeem he did not know eet. You see, Melquiades, he have a leetle, litla game." He glanced obliquely at Miss Hollister, his shoulders and down-drawn lips expressed apology for the little game, and tolerance for it. "Just neeckles and dimes. An' some fellow he go home weener, and there ees hole een hees pocket. But Jeem he do not know. *Bueno,* Jeem has been to Tularosa, Mescalero, Fresnal, all places, to leef word to look out for thees fellow las' week what rob the bank at Belen, and he arrive back on a freight train las' night, mebbe so about three in the morning—oh, veree tired, ver' esleepy. So when he go up the street een the moon-light he see there a long streeng of neeckels and dimes under hees feet." Without moving, Monte showed the homeward progress of that drowsy man and his faint surprise. "So Jeem, he laugh and say, 'There ees that dream again.' And he go on. But bimeby he steel see thoss neeckels, and he peench heemself, so—and he feel eet." Monte's eyes grew round with astonishment. "And he bend heemself to peek eet, and eet ees true money, and not dreaming at all! Yais. He go not back, but on ahead he peek up one dollar seexty-five cents of thees neeckels and dimes."

"I hadn't heard of any robbery, Monte," said Ben. "What about it?"

"Yes, and where is Belen?" said Jay. "Not around here, surely. I've never heard of the place."

"Oh, no—*muy lejos*—a long ways. Belen, what you call Bethlehem, ees yonder this side of Albuquerque, a leetle. I have been there manee times, but not estraight—round about." He made a looping motion of his hand to illustrate. "Las Vegas, and then down, or by Las Cruces, and then up. Eet is hundred feefty, two hundred miles in estraight line—I do not know."

"Anybody hurt?" asked Ben.

"Oh, no—no fuss! Eet ees veree funnee. Don Numa Frenger and Don Nestor Trujillo, they have there beeg estore to sell all theengs, leetle bank, farms, esheep ranch, freighting for thoss mines, buy wool and hides—all theengs for get the monee what ees there een thees place. And las' week, maybe Friday, Saturday, Nestor he ees go to deenair, and Numa Frenger ees in the estore, *solito*.

"Comes een a customer, *un colorado*—es-scusa me, a redhead. He buy tomatoes, cheese, crackers, sardines, sooch things, and a nose bag, and he ask to see shotgun. Don Numa, he exheebit two, three, and thees red he peek out nize shotgun. So he ask for shells, bird-eshot, buck-eshot, and he open the buck-eshot and sleep two shells een barrel, and break eet to throw out thoss shell weeth extractor, and sleep them een again. 'Eet work fine!' he say. 'Have you canteen?'

"Then Numa Frenger he tek long pole weeth hook to get thoss canteen where eet hang from the *viga,* the r-rafter, the beams. And when he get eet, he turn around an' thees estranger ees present thees shotgun at hees meedle.

" 'Have you money een your esafe?' say the *estranjero,* the estr-ranger. And Numa ees bite hees mouth. 'Of your kindness,' say the customer, 'weel you get heem? I weel go weeth you.'

"So they get thees money from the esafe. And thees one weel not tek onlee the paper money. 'Thees gold an' seelver ees so heav-ee,' he tell Numa Frenger. 'I weel not bozzer.' Then he pay for those theengs of which he mek purchase an' correc' Don Numa when he mek meestake in the *adición,* and get hees change back. And then he say to Numa, 'Weel you not be so good to come to eshow me wheech ees best road out from thees town to the ford of the reever?' And Numa, he ees ge-nash hees teeth, but there ees no *remedio.*

"And so they go walking along thees lane between the orchards, these two togezzer, and the leetle bir-rds esing een the *árboles*—thees red fellow laughing and talkin' weeth Numa, ver' gay—leading hees horse by the bridle, and weeth the shotgun een the crook of hees arm. So the people loog out from the doors of their house and say, 'Ah! Don Numa ees diverrt heemself weeth hees friend.'

"And when they have come beyond the town, thees fellow ees mount hees horse. 'For your courtesy,' he say, 'I thank you. At your feet,' he say. 'Weeth God!' And he ride off laughing, and een a leetle way he hoss hees shotgun een a bush, and he ride on to cross the reever eslow. But when Numa Frenger sees thees, he run queeckly, although he ees a ver' fat man, an' not young; he grab thees gun, he point heem, he pull the triggle—Nozzing! He break open the gun to look wizzen side—Nozzing! *O caballeros y conciudadanos!*" Monte threw down the gun; both hands grabbed his black locks and tugged with the ferocity of despair.

"Ah-h! What a lovely cuss word," cried Jay. "How trippingly it goes upon the tongue. I must learn that. Say it again!"

"But eet ees not a bad word, that," said Monte sheepishly. "Eet ees onlee idle word, to feel up. When thees politicos go up an' down, talking nonsense een the nose, when they weesh to theenk of more, then they say with *emoción, 'O caballeros y conciudadanos'*; that ees, 'gentlemen and fellow ceetizens.' No more."

"Well, now, the story?" said Ben. "He crossed the river, going east—was that it?"

"Oh, yes. Well, when Numa Frenger see that thees gun ees emptee, he ees ver' angree man. He ees mos enr-rage heemself for that than for all what gone befor-re. He ees arrouse all Belen, he ees send telegraph to Sabinal, La

Joya, Socorro, San Marcial, ever wheech way, to mek queek the posse, to send queek to the mesa to catch thees man, to mek *proclamación* to pay for heem three thousand dollar of rewar-rd. 'Do not keel heem, I entr-reat you,' say Don Numa. 'Breeng heem back. I want to fry heem.' "

"Now isn't that New Mexico for you?" demanded Jay. "A man commits a barefaced robbery, and you make a joke of it."

Monte pressed the middle finger of his right hand firmly into the palm of his left, pressed as if to hold something there, and looked up under his brows at Miss Hollister.

"Then why do you laugh?" said Monte.

"You win," said Jay. "Go on with the story."

"Well, then," said Monte, "thees fellow he go up on the high plain on thees side of the reever, and he ride east and south by Sierra Montoso, and over the mountains of Los Pinos, and he mek to go over Chupadero Mesa to thoss ruins of Gran Quivira. But he ride onlee *poco á poco,* easalee. And already as posse from La Joya, San Acacia is ride up the Alamillo Cañon, and across the plain." His swift hands fashioned horseman, mountain, mesa and plain. "Page Otero and six, five other men. And they ride veree fast so that already they pass in front of him to the south, and are now before heem on Chupadero, and there they see heem. Eet ees almost sundown.

"*Immediatamente* he turn and go back. And their horses are not so tired lak hees horse, and they spread out and ride fast, and soon they are about to come weethen gunshot weeth the rifle. And when he see eet, thees *colorado* ees ride oopon a reedge that all may see, and he tek that paper money from the nose bag at the head of the saddle and he toss eet up—pouf! The weend is blow gentle and thees money it go joomp, joomp, here, there, een the booshes. Again he ride a leetle way, and again he scatter thees money lak a man to feed the hen een hees yard. So then he go on away, thees red one. And when thees posse come to that place, thees nize money is go hop, hop, along the ground and over the booshes. There ees feefty-dollar beel een the mesquite, there ees twenty-dollar beel een the tar-bush, there ees beels blow by, roll by, slide by. So thees posse ees deesmount heemself to peek heem, *muy enérgico*—lively. And the weend ees come up faster at sundown, *como siempre*. 'Come on!' says Page Otero. 'Come on, thees fellow weel to escape!' Then the posse loog up surprise, and say, 'Who, me?' and they go on to peek up thees monee. So that redhead get clear away thees time."

"Did they get all the money?" asked Ben.

"Numa he say yes. He do not know just how mooch thees bandit ees take, but he theenk they breeng back all, or most nearly all."

"Do they know who he was?" asked Jay.

"Por cierto, no. But from the deescreepcion and hees horse and saddle, they theenk eet ees a cowboy from Quemado, name—I cannot to pr-ronounce thees name, Meester Ben. You say heem. I have eet here een *La Voz del Pueblo."* From a hip pocket he produced a folded newspaper printed in Spanish, and showed Ben the place.

"Ross McEwen—about twenty-five or older, red hair, gray eyes, five feet nine inches—humph!" he returned the paper. "Will they catch him, do you think?"

Monte considered. He looked slowly at the far dim hills; he bent over to watch an inch-high horseman at his feet, toiling through painful immensities.

"The world ees ver' beeg een thees country," he said at last. "I theenk most mebbe not. *Quién sabe?* Onlee thees fellow must have water—and there ees not much water. Numa Frenger ees send now to all places, to Leencoln County, to Jeem Hunter here, and he meks everyone to loog out, to Pat Garrett in Doña Ana Countee, and Pat watches by Parker Lake and the pass of San Agustin; to El Paso, and they watch there most of all that he pass not to Mexico Viejo. Eet may be at some water place they get heem. Or that he get them. He seem lak a man of some enterpr-rize, no?" He rose to go. "But I have talk too much. I mus' go now to my beesness."

"A poor business for a man as bright as you are," said Jay, and sniffed.

"But I geeve a square deal," said Monte serenely. "At your feet, señorita! Unteel then, Meester Ben."

"Isn't he a duck? I declare, it's a shame to laugh at his English," said Jay.

"Don't worry. He gets to hear our Spanish, even if he is too polite to laugh."

"I hate to think of that man being chased for blood money," said Jay. "Hunter and that Pat Garrett you think so much of are keen after that reward, it seems. It is dreadful the way these people here make heroes out of their killers and man hunters."

"Let's get this straight," said Ben. "You're down on the criminal for robbing and down on the sheriff for catching him. Does that sound like sense? If there was no reward offered, it's the sheriff's duty to catch him, isn't it? And if there is a reward, it's still his duty. The reward doesn't make him a man hunter. Woman, you ain't right in your head. And as for Pat Garrett and some of these other old-timers—they're enjoying temporary immortality right now. They've become a tradition while they still live. Do you notice how all these honest-to-goodness old-timers talk? All the world is divided into three parts. One part is old-timers and the other two are not. The most clannish people on earth. And that brings us, by graceful and easy stages, to the main consideration, which I want to have settled before I go. And when I say settled I mean that nothing is ever settled till it is settled right—get me?" He stood up; as Jay rose he took her hands. "If circumstances were otherwise, Jay?"

She avoided his eyes. "Don't ask me now. I don't know, Ben—honest, I don't. You mustn't pester me now. It isn't fair when I'm so miserable." She pulled her hands away.

"Gawd help all poor sailors on a night like this!" said Ben fervently. "Listen, sister, I'm going to work, see? Goin' to fill your plans and specifications, every one, or bust a tug."

"I see you at it," jeered Jay, with an unpleasant laugh. "Work? You?"

"Me. I, myself. A faint heart never filled a spade flush," said Ben. "Going to get me a job and keep it. Lick any man that tries to fire me. Put that in your hope chest. Bye-bye. At your feet!"

As he went down the street his voice floated back to her:

> But now my hair is falling out,
> And down the hill we'll go,
> And sleep together at the foot—
> John Barleycorn, my Jo!

3

A high broad tableland lies east of the Rio Grande, and mountains make a long unbroken wall to it, with cliffs that front the west. This mesa is known locally as El Corredor. It is a pleasing and wholesome country. Zacatón and salt grass are gray green upon the level plain, checkered with patches of bare ground, white and glaring. On those bare patches, when the last rains fell, weeks, months or years ago, an oozy paste filmed over the glossy levels, glazed by later suns, cracking at last to shards like pottery. But in broken country, on ridges and slopes, was a thin turf of buffalo and mesquite grass, curly, yellow and low. There was iron beneath this place and the sand of it was red, the soil was ruddy white, the ridges and the lower hill slopes were granite red, yellowed over with grass. Even the high crowning cliffs were faintly cream, not gray, as limestone is elsewhere. Sunlight was soft and mellow there, sunset was red upon these cliffs. And Ross McEwen fled down that golden corridor.

If he had ridden straight south he might have been far ahead by this time, well on the road to Mexico. But his plan had been to reach the Panhandle of Texas; he had tried easting and failed. Three times he had sought to work through the mountain barrier to the salt plains—a bitter country of lava flow and sinks, of alkali springs, salt springs, magnesia springs, soda springs; of soda lakes, salt lakes, salt marshes, salt creeks; of rotten and crumbling ground, of greasy sand, of chalk that powdered and rose on the lightest airs, to leave no trace that a fugitive had passed this way.

He had been driven back once by posse on Chupadero. Again at night he had been forced back by men who did not see him. He had tried to steal through by the old stage road over the Oscuro, and found the pass guarded; and the last time, today, had been turned back by men that he did not even see. In the mouth of Mockingbird Pass he had found fresh-shod tracks of many horses going east. Mockingbird was held against him.

He could see distinctly, and in one eye-flight, every feature of a country larger than all England. He could look north to beyond Albuquerque, past the long ranges of Manzano, Montoso, Sandia, Oscuro; southward, between h s horse's ears, the northern end of the San Andrés was high and startling before him, blue black with cedar brake and piñon, except for the granite-gold top of Salinas Peak, the great valley of the Jornado del Muerto, the Journey of the Dead, which lay between the San Andrés and the Rio Grande.

And beyond the river was a bright enormous expanse, bounded only by the crest of the dozen ranges that made the crest of the Continental Divide—Dátil, Magdalena, San Mateo, the Black Range, the Mimbres, Florida.

Between, bordering the midway river, other mountain ranges lay tangled: Cuch.llo Negro, Cristobál, Sierra de los Caballos, Doña Ana, Robelero. It was over the summits of these ranges that he saw the Continental Divide.

Here was irony indeed. With that stupendous panorama outspread before h m, he was being headed off, driven, herded! He cocked an eyebrow aslant at the thought, and spoke of it to his horse, who pricked back an ear in attention. He was a honey-colored horse, and his name was Miél, which .s, by .nterpretat on, Honey.

"Wouldn't you almost think, sweetness," said Ross Mc-Ewen in a plaintive drawl, "that there was enough elbow-room here to satisfy every reasonable man? And yet these lads are crowdin' me like a cop after an alley cat."

He sensed that an unusual effort was being made to take him, and he smiled—a little ruefully—at the reflection that the people at Mockingbird might well have been mere chance comers upon their lawful occasions, and with no designs upon him, no knowledge of him. Every man was a possible enemy. He was out of law.

This was the third day of his flight. The man was still brisk and bold, the honey-colored horse was still sturdy, but both lacked something of the sprightly resilience they had brought to the fords of Belen. There had been brief grazing and scant sleep, night riding, doubling and twisting to slip into lonely water holes. McEwen had chosen, as the lesser risk, to ride openly to Prairie Springs. He had found no one there and had borrowed grub for himself and several feeds of corn for the Honey horse. There had been no fast riding, except for the one brief spurt with the posse at Chupadero. But it had been a steady grind, doubly tiresome that they might not keep to the beaten trails. Cross-country traveling on soft ground is rough on horseflesh.

And now they left the plain and turned through tarbush up the long slope to the San Andrés. A thousand ridges and hollows came plunging and headlong against them. And suddenly the tough little horse was tiring, failing.

Halfway to the hill foot they paused for a brief rest. High on their slim lances, banners of yucca blossoms were white and waxen, and wild bees hummed to their homes in the flower stalks of last year; flaunting afar, cactus flowers flamed crimson or scarlet through the black tar-bush.

Long since, McEwen had given up the Panhandle. He planned now to bear far to the southeast, crossing the salt plains below the White Sands to the Guadalupe Mountains, straddling the boundary between the territory and Texas, and so east to the Staked Plains. He knew the country ahead, or had known it ten years before. But there would be changes. There was a new railroad, so he had heard, from El Paso to Tularosa, and so working north toward the states. There would be other things, too—new ranches, and all that. For sample, behind him, just where this long slope merged with the flats, three unexpected windmills, each five miles from the other, had made a line across his path; he had made a weary detour to pass unseen.

The San Andrés made here a twenty-mile offset where they joined the Oscuro, with the huge round mass of Salinas Peak as their mutual corner. Lava Gap, the meeting place of the two ranges, was now directly at his left and ten miles away. The bleak and mile-high walls of it made a frame for the tremendous picture of Sierra Blanca, sixty long miles to the east, with a gulf of nothingness between. Below that nothingness, as McEwen knew, lay the black lava river of the Mal Pais. But Lava Gap was not for him. Unless pursuit was quite abandoned, Lava Gap and Dripping Springs would be watched and guarded. He was fenced in by probabilities.

But the fugitive was confident yet, and by no means at the end of his resources. He knew a dim old Indian trail over a high pass beyond Salinas Peak. It started at Grapevine Spring, Captain Jack Crawford's ranch.

"And at Grapevine," said Ross aloud, "I'll have to buy, beg, borrow or get me a horse. Hope there's nobody at home. If there's anyone there I'll have to get his gun first and trade afterwards. Borrowing horses is not highly recommended, but it beats killing 'em."

To the right and before him the Jornado was hazy, vast and mysterious. To the right and behind him, the lava flow of Pascual sprawled black and sinister in the lowlands; and behind him—far behind him, far below him, a low line of dust was just leaving the central windmill of those three new ranches, a dozen miles away. McEwen watched this dust with some interest while he rolled and lit a cigarette. He drank the last water from his canteen.

"Come on, me bold outlaw," he said, "keep moving. You've done made your bed, but these hellhounds won't let you sleep in it." He put foot to stirrup; he stroked the Honey horse.

"Miél, old man, you tough it out four or five miles more, and your troubles will be over. Me for a fresh horse at Grapevine, come hell or high water. Take it easy. No hurry. Just shuffle along."

The pursuing dust did not come fast, but it came straight his way. "I'll bet a cooky," said Ross sagely, "that some of these gay bucks have got a spyglass. I wonder if that ain't against the rules? And new men throwin' in with them at every ranch. I reckon I would, too, if it wasn't for this red topknot of mine. Why couldn't they meet up with some other redheaded hellion and take him back? Wouldn't that be just spiffin'? One good thing, anyway—I didn't go back to the Quemado country. Some of the boys would sure have got in Dutch, hidin' me out. This is better."

He crossed the old military road that had once gone through Lava Gap to Fort Stanton; he smiled at the shod tracks there; he came to the first hills, pleasingly decorated with bunches of mares—American mares, gentle mares—Corporal Tanner's mares. He picked a bunch with four or five saddle horses in it and drove them slowly up Grapevine Cañon. The Miél horse held up his head and freshened visibly. He knew what this meant. The sun dropped behind the hills. It was cool and fresh in Grapevine. The outlaw took his time. He had an hour or more. He turned for a last look at the north and the cliffs of Oscuro Mountain blazing in the low sun to fiery streamers of red light. You would have seen, perhaps, only a howling wilderness, but this man was to look back, waking and in dream, and to remember that brooding and sunlit silence as the glowing heart of the world. From this place alone he was to be an exile.

"Nice a piece of country as ever laid outdoors," said Ross McEwen. "I've seen some several places where it would be right pleasant to have a job along with a bunch of decent punchers—good grub and all that, mouth organ by the firelight after supper—Or herding sheep."

Grapevine Spring is at the very head of the cañon. To east, south and west the hills rise directly from the corral fences. McEwen drove the mares into the water pen and called loudly to the house. The hail went unanswered. Eagles screamed back from a cliff above him.

"A fool for luck," said McEwen.

He closed the bars, he gave Miél his first installment of water. Then he went to the house. It was unlocked and there was no one there. The ashes on the hearth were cold. He borrowed two cans of beans and some bacon. There was a slender store of corn, and he borrowed one feed of this to make tomorrow's breakfast for the new horse he was soon to acquire. He found an old saddle and he borrowed that, with an old bridle as well; he brought his own to replace them; he lit the little lamp on the table and grinned happily.

"They'll find Miél and my saddle and the light," he said, "and they'll make sure I've taken to the brush."

He went back to the pen; he roped and saddled a saddle-marked brown, broad chested and short coupled, unshod. Shod tracks are too easily followed. Then he scratched his red head and grinned again. The pen was built of poles laid in panels, except at the front; the cedar brake grew to the very sides of it. He went to the back and took down two panels, laying the poles aside; he let the mares drift out there, seeing to it that some of them went around by the house, and the rest on the other side of the pen. It was almost dark by now.

"There," he said triumphantly. "The boys will drive in a bunch of stock when they come, for remounts, and they'll go right on through. Fine mess in the dark. And it'll puzzle them to find which way I went with all these tracks. Time I was gone."

He came back to the watering trough; he washed his hands and face and filled his canteen; he went on where Miél stood weary and huddled in the dusk. His hand was gentle on that drooping neck.

"Miél, old fellow," he said, "you've been one good little horse. *Bueno suerte.*" He led the brown to the bars. "I hate a fool," said Ross McEwen.

He took down the bars and rode into the cedar brush at right angles to the canyon, climbing steadily from the first. It was a high and desperate pass, and branches had

grown across the unused trail; long before he had won
halfway to the summit he heard, far below him, the crash-
ing of horses in the brush, the sound of curses and laughter. The pursuit had arrived at Grapevine.

He topped the summit of that nameless pass an hour
later, and turned down the dark canyon to the east—to
meet grief at once. Since his time a cloud-burst had been
this way. Where there had once been fair footing the
flood had cut deep and wide, and every semblance of
soil had washed away, leaving only a wild moraine, a
loose rubble of rocks and tumbled boulders. But it was
the only way. The hillsides were impossibly steep and
sidelong, glassy granite and gneiss, or treacherous slides
of porphyry. Ross led his horse. Every step was a hazard
in that narrow and darkened place, with crumbling ridge
and pit and jump off, with windrows of smooth round
rock to roll and turn under their feet. It took the better
part of two hours to win through the narrows, perhaps
two miles. The canyon widened then, the hillsides were
lower and Ross could ride again, picking his doubtful
way in the starlight. He turned on a stepladder of hills
to the north, and came about midnight to Dripstone, high
in a secret hollow of the hills. The prodigious bulk of
Salinas loomed mysterious and incredible above him in
the starlight.

He tied the brown horse securely and named him
Porch Climber. He built a tiny fire and toasted strips of
bacon on the coals. Then he spread out his saddle
blankets with hat and saddle for pillow, and so lay down
to untroubled sleep.

4

He awoke in that quiet place before the first stirring
of dawn. A low thin moon was in the sky and the mountains were dim across the east. He washed his eyes out
with water from the canteen. He made a nose bag from
the corn sack and hung it on Porch Climber's brown
head. The Belen nose bag had gone into the discard days
before. He built a fire of twigs and hovered over it while

his precious coffee came to a boil; his coat was thin and the night air was fresh, almost chilly. He smacked his lips over the coffee; he saddled and watered Porch Climber at Dripstone and refilled his canteen there. The horse drank sparingly.

"Better fill up, old-timer," Ross advised him. "You're sure going to need it."

Knuckled ridges led away from Salinas like fingers of a hand. The eastern flat was some large fraction of a mile nearer to sea level than the high plain west of the mountain, and these ridges were massive and steep accordingly. He made his way down one of them. The plain was dark and cold below him; the mountains took shape and grew, the front range of the Rockies—Capitán, Carrizo, Sierra Blanca, Sacramento, with Guadalupe low and dim in the south; the White Sands were dull and lifeless in the midway plain. Bird twitter was in the air. Rabbits scurried through the brush, a quail whirred by and sent back a startled call; crimson streaks shot up the sky, and day grew broad across the silent levels. The cut banks of Salt Creek appeared, wandering away southwest toward the marshes. Low and far against the black base of the Sacramento, white feathers lifted and fluffed, the smoke of the first fires at Tularosa, fifty miles away. Flame tipped the far-off crests, the sun leaped up from behind the mountain wall, the level light struck on the White Sands, glanced from those burnished bevels and splashed on the western cliffs; the desert day blazed over this new half-world.

He had passed a few cows on the ridges, but now, as he came close to the flats, he was suddenly aware of many cattle before him, midges upon the vast plain; more cattle than he had found on the western side of the mountains. He drew rein, instantly on the alert, and began to quarter the scene with a keen scrutiny. At once a silver twinkling showed to northward—the steel fans of a windmill, perhaps six miles out from the foot of the main mountain. His eye moved slowly across the plain. He was shocked to find a second windmill tower six or eight miles south of the first, keeping at the same distance from the hills, and when he made out the faint glimmer of a third, far in the south, he gave way to indignation. It was a bald plain with no cover for the quietly disposed, except a few clumps of soapweed here and there. And this line of windmills was precisely the line of the road to El Paso. Where he had expected smooth going he would have to keep to the roughs; to venture into the open was to court discovery. He turned south across the ridges.

He had talked freely to Miél, but until now he had been reticent with Porch Climber, who had not yet won his confidence. At this unexpected reverse he opened his heart.

"Another good land gone wrong," he said. "I might have known it. This side of Salt Creek is only half-bad cow country, so of course it's all settled up, right where we want to go. No one lives east of Salt Creek, not even sheep herders. And we couldn't possibly make it, goin' on the other side of Salt Creek with all that marsh country and the hell of the White Sands. Why, this is plumb ridiculous!"

He mediated for a while upon his wrongs and then broke out afresh: "When I was here, the only water east of the mountains was the Wildy Well at the corner of the damn White Sands. Folks drove along the road, and when they wanted water they went up in the hills. It's no use to cross over to Tularosa. They'll be waiting for us there. No, sir, we've pointedly got to skulk down through the brush. And you'll find it heavy going, up one ridge and down another, like a flea on a washboard."

Topping the next ridge, he reined back swiftly into a hollow place. He dismounted and peered through a mesquite bush, putting the branches aside to look. A mile to the south two horsemen paced soberly down a ridge— and it was a ridge which came directly from the pass to Grapevine.

"Now ain't them the bright lads?" said the runaway, divided between chagrin and admiration. "What are you going to do with fellows like that? I ask you. I left plain word that I done took to the hills afoot, without the shadow of a doubt. Therefore they reasoned I hadn't. They've coppered every bet. Now that's what I call clear thinkin'. I reckon some of 'em did stay there, but these two crossed over that hell gate at night, just in case.

"I'll tell a man they had a ride where that cloud-burst was. Say, they'll tell their grandchildren about that—if they live that long, which I misdoubt, the way they're carryin' on. This gives me what is technically known as the willies. Hawse," said McEwen, "let's us tarry a spell and see what these hirelin' bandogs are goin' to do now."

He took off the bridle and saddle, he staked Porch Climber to rest and graze while he watched. What the bandogs did was to ride straight to the central windmill, where smoke showed from the house. McEwen awaited developments. Purely from a sense of duty he ate the other can of beans while he waited.

"They'll take word to every ranch," he prophesied gloomily. "Leave a man to watch where there isn't anyone there—take more men along when they find more than one at a well. Wish I was a drummer."

His prognostications were verified. After a long wait, which meant breakfast, a midget horseman rode slowly north toward the first windmill. A little later two men rode slowly south toward the third ranch.

"That's right, spread the news, dammit, and make everybody hate you," said Ross. He saddled and followed them, paralleling their course, but keeping to the cover of the brush.

It was heavy and toilsomegoing, boulders and rocks alternating with soft ground where Porch Climber's feet went through; gravel coarse sand or piled rocks in the washes; tedious twisting in the brush and wearisome windings where a bay of open country forced a detour. He passed by the mouths of Good Fortune, Antelope and Cottonwood canyons, struggling through their dry deltas; he drew abreast of the northern corner of the White Sands. The reflection of it was blinding, yet he found it hard to hold his eyes away. The sun rode high and hot. McEwen consulted his canteen.

More than once or twice came the unwelcome thought that he might take to the hill country, discard Porch Climber and hide by some inaccessible seep or pothole until pursuit died down. But he was a stubborn man, and his heart was set upon Guadalupe; he had an inborn distaste for a diet of chance rabbit and tuna fruit—or, perhaps, slow deer without salt. A stronger factor in his decision—although he hardly realized it—was the horseman's hatred for being set afoot. He could hole in safely; there was little doubt of that. But when he came out of the hole, how then? A man from nowhere, on foot, with no past and no name and a long red beard—that would excite remark. He fingered the stubble on his cheeks with that reflection. Yes, such a man would be put to it to account for himself—and he would have to show up sometime, somewhere. The green cottonwood of Independent Spring showed high on the hill to his right. He held on to the south.

And now he came to the mouth of Sulphur Springs Canyon. Beyond here a great bay of open plain flowed into the hill foot under Kaylor Mountain; and midmost of that bay was another windmill, a long low house, spacious corrals. McEwen was sick of windmills. But this one was close under the mountain, far west of the line of the other ranches and of the El Paso road; McEwen saw with lively interest that his pursuers left the road and angled across the open to this ranch. That meant dinner.

"Honesty," said McEwen with conviction, "is the best policy. Dinnertime for some people, but only noon for me. Early for grub too. . . . And how can these enterprisin' chaps be pursuin' me when they're in front? That isn't reasonable. Who ever heard of deputies goin' ahead and the bandit taggin' along behind. That's not right. It's not moral. I'm goin' around. Besides, if I don't this thing is liable to go on always, just windmills and windmills—to Mexico City—Peru—Chile. I'm plumb tired of windmills. Porch Climber," said McEwen, "have you got any gift of speed? Because, just as soon as these two sheriff men get to that ranch and have time to go in the house, you and me are going to drift out quiet and unostentatious across the open country till we hit the banks of the Salt Marsh. And if these fellows look out and see us you've just got to run for it. And they can maybe get fresh horses too. But if they don't see us we'll be right. We'll drift south under cover of the bank and get ahead of 'em while they stuff their paunches."

Half an hour later he turned Porch Climber's head to the east, and rode sedately across the smooth plain, desiring to raise no dust. Some three miles away, near where he crossed the El Paso road, grew a vigorous motte of mesquite trees. Once beyond that motte, he kept it lined up between him and the ranch; and so came unseen to where the plain broke away to the great marsh which rimmed the basin of the White Sands.

In the east the White Sands billowed in great dry dunes above the level of the plain, but the western half was far below that level, and waterbound. This was the home of mirages; they spread now all their pomp of palm and crystal lake and fairy hill. McEwen turned south along the margin. Here, just under the bank, the ground was moist, almost wet, and yet firm footing, like a road of hard rubber. He brought Porch Climber to a long-reaching trot, steady and smooth; he leaned forward in his stirrups and an old song came to his lips, unsummoned. He sang it with loving mockery, in a nasal but not unpleasing baritone:

> *They give him his orders at Monroe, Virginia,*
> *Sayin', "Pete, you're way behind ti-ime"*—

"Gosh, it does seem natural to sing when a good horse is putting the miles behind him," said McEwen. "This little old brown pony is holdin' up right well, too, after all the grief in the roughs this mawnin'."

> *He looked round then to his black, greasy fireman,*
> *"Just shovel in a little more co-o-oal,*
> *And when we cross that wide old maounting,*
> *You can watch old Ninety-Seven roll!"*

"Hey, Porch Climber! You ain't hardly keepin' time. Peart up a little! Now, lemme see. Must be about twenty mile to the old Wildy Well. Wonder if I'll find any more new ranches between here and there? Likely. Hell of a country, all cluttered up like this!"

> *It's a mighty rough road from Lynchburg to Danville,*
> *And a line on a three-mile gra-ade;*
> *It was on that grade that he lo-ost his av'rage,*
> *And you see what a jump he made!*

He rejoined the wagon road where the White Sands thrust a long and narrow arm far to the west. The old road crossed this arm at the shoulder, a three-mile speedway. Out on the sands magic islands came and went and rose and sank in a misty sea. But in the south, where the road climbed again to the plain, was the inevitable windmill—reality and no mirage.

McEwen followed the road in the posture of a man who had nothing to fear. He had outridden the rumor of his flight; he could come to this ranch with a good face. But he reined down to a comfortable jog. Those behind might overtake him close enough to spy him here in this naked place. Jaunting easily, nearing the ranch where he belonged, a horseman was no object of suspicion, but a man in haste was a different matter.

There was no one at the ranch. The water was brackish and flat, but the two wayfarers drank thankfully. He could see no signs that any horses were watering there; he made a shrewd guess that the boys had taken the horses and gone up into the mountains for better grass and sweet water, or perhaps to get out of sight of the White Sands, leaving the flats to the cattle.

"Probably they just ride down every so often to oil the windmill," he said. "Leastways, I would. Four hundred square miles of lookin'-glass, three hundred and sixty-four days a year—no, thank you! My eyes are most out now."

J. B. was branded on the gate posts of the corral, and on the door. There was canned stuff on a shelf and a few baking-powder biscuits, old and dry. He took a can of salmon and filed it for future reference.

"No time for gormandizin' now," he said. He stuffed the stale biscuits into his pocket to eat on the road.

"There's this much about bread," said McEwen, "I can take it or I can leave it alone. And I've been leaving it alone for several days now."

A pencil and a tablet lay on the table. His gray eyes went suddenly a-dance with impish light. He tore out a page and wrote a few words of counsel and advice.

> *Hey, you J. B. waddies: Look out for a fellow with red hair and gray eyes. Medium-sized man. He robbed the bank at Belen, and they think he came this way. Big reward offered for him. Two thousand, I hear. But I don't know for certain. Send word to the ranches up north. I will tell them as far south as Organ.*
>
> JIM HUNTLEY

He hung this news-letter on a nail above the stove.

"There!" he said. "If them gay jaspers that are after me had any sense at all, they'd see it was no use to go any further, and they'd stay right here and rest up. But they won't. They'll say, 'Hey, this is the way he went—here's some more of the same old guff! But how ever did that feller get down here without us finding any tracks? You can see what a jump he made.' I don't want to be ugly," said McEwen, "but I've got to cipher up some way to shake loose from these fellows. I want to go to sleep. Now who in hell is Jim Huntley?"

Time for concealment was past. From now on he must set his hope on speed. He rode down the big road boldly and, for a time, at a brisk pace; he munched the dry biscuits and washed them down with warm and salty water from his canteen.

There was no room for another ranch between here and Wildy's Well. Wildy's was an old established ranch. It was among the possibilities that he might hit here upon some old acquaintance whose failing sight would not note his passing, and who would give him a fresh horse. He was now needing urge of voice and spur for Porch Climber's lagging feet. It sat in his mind that Wildy was dead. His brows knitted with the effort to remember. Yes, Wildy had been killed by a falling horse. Most likely, though, he would find no one living at the well. Not too bad, the water of Wildy's Well—but they would be in the hills with the good grass.

The brown horse was streaked with salt and sweat; he dragged in the slow sand. Here was a narrow broken country of rushing slopes, pinched between the White Sands and the mountains. The road wound up and down in the crowding brush; the footing was a coarse pebbly sand of broken granite from the crumbling hills. Heat waves rose quivering, the White Sands lifted and shuddered to a blinding shimmer, the dream islands were wavering, shifting and indistinct, astir with rumor. McEwen's eyes were dull for sleep, red rimmed and swollen from glare and alkali dust. The salt water was bitter in his belly. The stubble on his face was gray with powdered dust and furrowed with sweat stains; dust was in his nostrils and his ears, and the taste of dust was in his mouth. Porch Climber plowed heavily. And all at once McEwen felt a sudden distaste for his affair.

He had a searching mind and it was not long before he found a cause. That damn song. Dance music. There were places where people danced, where they would dance tonight. There was a garden in Rutherford—

5

There was no one at Wildy's Well, no horses there and no sign that any horses were using there. McEwen drank deep of the cool sweet water. When Porch Climber had his fill, McEwen plunged arms and head into the trough. Horse and man sighed together; their eyes met in comfortable understanding.

"Feller," said McEwen, "it was that salt water, much as anything else, that slowed you up, I reckon. Yuh was sure sluggish. And yuh just ought to see yourself now! Nemmine, that's over." He took down his rope, and cut off a length, the spread of his arms. He untwisted this length to three strands, soaked these strands in the trough, wrung them out and knotted them around his waist. He eyed the cattle that had been watering here. They had retreated to the far side at his coming and were now waiting impatiently. "Been many a long year since I've seen any Durham cattle," said McEwen. "Everybody's got white-face stuff now. Reckon they raise these for El Paso market. No feeder will buy 'em, unless with a heavy cut in the price."

He hobbled over and closed the corral gate. Every bone of him was a separate ache. A faint breeze stirred; the mill sails turned lazily; the gears squeaked a protest. Ross looked up with interest.

"That was right good water," he said. "Guess you've earned a greasing." He climbed the tall tower. Wildy's Well dated from before the steel windmill; this was massive and cumbersome, a wooden tower, and the wheel itself was of wood. After his oiling Ross scanned the north with an anxious eye. There was no dust. South by east, far in the central plain, dim hills swam indeterminate through the heat haze—Las Cornudas and Heuco. South by west, gold and rose, the peaks of the Organs peered from behind the last corner of the San Andrés. He searched the north again. He could see no dust—but he could almost see a dust.

He shook his head. "Them guys are real intelligent," he said. "I'm losin' my av'rage." He clambered down with some celerity, and set about what he had to do.

He tied the severed end of his rope to the saddle horn, tightened the cinches, swung into the saddle and shook out a loop. Hugging the fence, the cattle tore madly around the corral in a wild cloud of dust. McEwen rode with them on an inner circle, his eye on a big roan steer, his rope whirling in slow and measured rhythms. For a moment the roan steer darted to the lead; the loop shot out, curled over and tightened on both forefeet; Porch Climber whirled smartly to the left; the steer fell heavily. Ross swung off; as he ran, he tugged at the hogging string around his waist. Porch Climber dragged valiantly, Ross ran down the rope, pounced on the struggling steer, gathered three feet together and tied them with the hogging string. These events were practically simultaneous.

McEwen unsaddled the horse. "I guess you can call it

a day," he said. He opened the gate and let the frightened cattle run out. "Here," he said, "is where I make a spoon or spoil a horn." He cut a thong from a saddle string and tied his old plow handle .45 so that it should not jolt from the scabbard. He made a tight roll of the folded bridle, that lonely can of salmon and his coat, with his saddle blanket wrapped around all; he tied these wordly goods securely behind the cantle. He uncoupled the cinches and let out the quarter straps to the last hole.

The tied steer threshed his head madly, bellowing wild threats of vengeance. McEwen carried the saddle and placed it at the steer's back, where he lay. He found a short and narrow strip of board, like a batten, under the tower; and with this, as the frantic roan steer heaved and threshed in vain efforts to rise, he poked the front cinch under the struggling body, inches at a time, until at last he could reach over and hook his fingers into the cinch ring. Before he could do this he was forced to tie the free foot to the three that were first tied; it had been kicking with so much fury and determination that the task could no be accomplished. Into the cinch ring he tied the free end of his rope, bringing it up between body and tied feet; he took a double of loose rope around his hips, dug his heels into the sand and pulled manfully every time the steer floundered; and so, at last and painfully, drew the cinch under until the saddle was on the steer's back and approximately where it should be. Then he put in the latigo strap, taking two turns, and tugged at the latigo till the saddle was pulled to its rightful place. At every tug the roan steer let out an agonized bawl. Then he passed the hind cinch behind the steer's hips and under the tail, drawing it up tightly so that the saddle could not slip over the steer's withers during the subsequent proceedings.

McEwen stood up and mopped the muddy sweat from his face; he rubbed his aching back. He filled his canteen at the trough, drank again and washed himself. He rolled a smoke; he lashed the canteen firmly to the saddle forks. Porch Climber was rolling in the sand. McEwen took him by the forelock and led him through the open gate.

"If you should ask me," he said, "this corral is a spot

where there is going to be trouble, and no place at all for you." He looked up the north road. Nothing in sight.

He went back to the steer. He hitched up his faded blue overalls, tightened his belt and squinted at the sun; he loosened the last-tied foot and coiled the rope at the saddle horn. Then he eased gingerly into the saddle. The steer made lamentable outcry, twisting his neck in a creditable attempt to hook his tormentor; the free foot lashed out madly. But McEwen flattened himself and crouched safely, with a full inch of margin; the steer was near to hooking his own leg and kicking his own face and he subsided with a groan. McEwen settled himself in the saddle.

"Are ye ready?" said McEwen.

"Oi am!" said McEwen.

"Thin go!" said McEwen, and pulled the hogging string.

The steer lurched sideways to his feet, paused for one second of amazement, and left the ground. He pitched, he plunged, he kicked at the stirrups, he hooked at the rider's legs, he leaped, he ran, bawling his terror and fury to the sky; weaving, lunging, twisting, he crashed sidelong into the fence, fell, scrambled up in an instant. The shimmy was not yet invented. But the roan steer shimmied, and he did it nobly; man and saddle rocked and reeled. Then, for the first time, he saw the open gate and thundered through it, abandoning all thought except flight.

Shaken and battered, McEwen was master. The man was a rider. To use the words of a later day, he was "a little warm, but not at all astonished." Yet he had not come off scot-free. When they crashed into the fence he had pulled up his leg, but had taken an ugly bruse upon the hip. The whole performance, and more particularly the shimmy feature, had been a poor poultice for aching bones.

Worse than all, the canteen had been crushed between fence and saddle. The priceless water was lost.

His hand still clutched the hogging string; he had no wish to leave that behind for curious minds to ponder upon. Until his mount slowed from a run to a pounding trot, he made no effort to guide him, the more because the steer's chosen course was not far from the direction in which McEwen wished to go. Wildy's Well lay at the extreme southwestern corner of the White Sands, and McEwen's thought was to turn eastward. He meant to try for Luna's Wells, the old stage station in the middle of the desert, on the road which ran obliquely from Organ to Tularosa.

When time was ripe McEwen leaned over and slapped his hat into the steer's face, on the right side, to turn him to the left and to the east.

The first attempt at guidance, and the fourth attempt, brought on new bucking spells. McEwen gave him time between lessons; what he most feared was that the roan would "sull," or balk, refusing to go farther. When the steer stopped, McEwen waited until he went on of his own accord; when his progress led approximately toward McEwen's goal, he was allowed to go his own way unmolested. McEwen was bethorned, dragged through mesquite bushes, raked under branches; his shirt was beribboned and torn. But he had his way at last. With danger, with infinite patience and with good judgment, he forced his refractory mount to the left and ever to the left, and so came at last into a deep trail which led due east. Muttering and grumbling, the steer followed the trail.

All this had taken time, but speed had also been a factor. When McEwen felt free to turn his head only a half circle of the windmill fans showed above the brush. Wildy's Well was miles behind them.

"Boys," said McEwen, "if you follow me this time, I'll say you're good!"

The steer scuffed and shambled, taking his own gait; he stopped often to rest, his tongue hung out, foam dripped from his mouth. McEwen did not urge him. The way led now through rotten ground and alkali, now through chalk that powdered and billowed in dust; deep trails, channeled by winds at war. As old trails grew too deep for comfort the stock had made new ones to parallel the old; a hundred paths lay side by side.

McEwen was a hard case. A smother of dust was about

him, thirst tormented him, his lips were cracked and bleeding, his eyes sunken, his face fallen in; and weariness folded him like a garment.

"Slate water is the best water," said McEwen.

They came from chalk and brush into a better country; poor indeed, and starved, but the air of it was breathable. The sun was low and the long shadows of the hills reached out into the plain. And now he saw, dead in front, the gleaming vane and sails of a windmill. Only the top—the fans seemed to touch the ground—and yet it was clear to see. McEwen plucked up heart. This was not Luna's. Luna's was far beyond. This was a new one. If it stood in a hollow place—and it did—it could not be far away. Water!

For the first time McEwen urged his mount, gently, and only with the loose and raveled tie string. Once was enough. The roan steer stopped, pawed the ground and proclaimed flat rebellion. For ten minutes, perhaps, McEwen sought to overrule him. It was no use. The roan steer was done. He took down his rope. With a little loop he snared a pawing and rebellious forefoot. He pulled up rope and foot with all his failing strength, and took a quick turn on the saddle horn. The roan made one hop and fell flat-long. McEwen tied three feet, though there was scant need for it. He took off the saddle, carried it to the nearest thicket and raised it, with pain, into the forks of a high soapweed, tucking up latigos and cinches. With pain; McEwen, also, was nearly done.

"My horse gave out on me. I toted my saddle a ways, but it was too heavy, and I hung it up so the cows couldn't eat it," he said, in the tone of one who recites a lesson.

He untied the steer, then came back hotfoot to his soapweed, thinking that the roan might be in a fighting humor. But the roan was done. He got unsteadily to his feet, with hanging head and slavering jaws; he waited for a little and moved slowly away.

"Glad he didn't get on the prod." said McEwen. "I sure expected it. That was one tired steer. He sure done me a good turn. Guess I'd better be strollin' into camp."

It was a sorry strolling. A hundred yards—a quarter—a half—a mile. The windmill grew taller; the first night breeze was stirring, he could see the fans whirl in the sun. A hundred yards—a quarter—a mile! An hour was gone. The shadows overtook him, passed him; the hills were suddenly very close and near, notched black against a crimson sky. Thirst tortured him, the windmill beckoned, sunset winds urged him on. He came to the brow of the shallow dip in which the ranch lay, he saw a little corral, a water pen, a long dark house beyond; he climbed into the water pen and plunged his face into the trough.

The windmill groaned and whined with a dismal clank and grinding of dry gears. Yet there was a low smoke over the chimney. How was this? The door stood open. Except for the creaking plaint of the windmill, a dead quiet hung about the place, a hint of something ominous and sinister. Stumbling, bruised and outworn, McEwen came to that low dark door. He heard a choking cough, a child's wailing cry. His foot was on the threshold.

"What wrong? *Qué es?*" he called.

A cracked and feeble voice made an answer that he could not hear. Then a man appeared at the inner door; an old man, a Mexican, clutching at the wall for support.

"El garrotillo," said the cracked voice. "The strangler —diphtheria."

"I am here to help you," said McEwen.

6

Of what took place that night McEwen had never afterward any clear remembrance, except of the first hour or two. The drone of bees was in his ears, and a whir of wings. He moved in a thin, unreal mist, giddy and light-headed, undone by thirst, weariness, loss of sleep —most of all by alkaline and poisonous dust, deep in his lungs. In the weary time that followed, though he daily fell more and more behind on sleep and rest, he was never so near to utter collapse as on this first interminable night. It remained for him a blurred and distorted vision of the dreadful offices of the sickroom; of sickening odors; of stumbling from bed to bed as one sufferer or another shook with paroxysms of choking.

Of a voice, now far off and now clear, insistent with counsel and question, direction and appeal; of lamplight that waned and flared and dwindled again; of creak and clank and pounding of iron on iron in horrible rhythm, endless, slow, intolerable. That would be the windmill. Yes, but where? And what windmill?

Of terror, and weeping, and a young child that screamed. That woman—why, they had always told him grown people didn't take diphtheria. But she had it, all right. Had it as bad as the two youngsters, too. She was the mother, it seemed. Yes, Florencio had told him that. Too bad for the children to die. . . . But who the devil was Florencio? The windmill turned dismally—clank and rattle and groan.

That was the last one choking now—Felix. Swab out his throat again. Hold the light. Careful. That's it. Burn it up. More cloth, old man. Hold the light this way. There, there, *pobrecito!* All right now. . . . Something was lurking in the corners, in the shadows. Must go see. Drive it away. What's that? What say? Make coffee? Sure. Coffee. Good idea. Salty coffee. Windmill pumpin' salt water. Batter and pound and squeal. Round and round. Round and round. Round and round. . . . Tell you what. Goin' to grease that damn windmill. Right now. . . . Huh? What's that? Wait till morning? All right. All ri'. Sure.

His feet were leaden. His arms minded well enough, but his hands were simply wonderful. Surprisin' skillful, those hands. How steady they were to clean membranes from little throats. Clever hands! They could bring water to these people, too, lift them up and hold the cup and not spill a drop. They could sponge off hot little bodies when the children cried out in delirium. Wring out rag, too! Wonnerful hands! Mus' call people's 'tention to these hands sometime. There, there, let me wash you some more with the nice cool water. Now, now—nothing will hurt you. Uncle Happy's goin' to be right here, takin care of you. Now, now—go to sleep—go-o to sleep!

But his feet were so big, so heavy and so clumsy, and

his legs were insubordinate. Specially the calves. The calf
of each leg, where there had once been good muscles of
braided steel, was now filled with sluggish water of inferior quality. That wasn't the worst either. There was a
distinct blank place, a vacuum, something like the bead in
a spirit level, and it shifted here and there as the water
sloshed about. Wonder nobody had ever noticed that.

Must be edgin' on toward morning. Sick people are
worst between two and four, they say. And they're all
easier now, every one. Both kids asleep—tossin' about.
And now the mother was droppin' off. Yes, sir—she's
goin' to sleep. What did the old man call her? Estefanía.
Yes—Est'fa'—

He woke with sunlight in his eyes. His arm sprawled
before him on a pine table and his head lay on his arm.
He raised up, blinking, and looked around. This was the
kitchen, a sorry spectacle. The sickroom lay beyond an
open door. He sat by that door, where he could see into
the sickroom.

They were all asleep. The woman stirred uneasily and
threw out an arm. The old man lay huddled on a couch
beyond the table.

McEwen stared. The fever had passed and his head
was reasonably clear. He frowned, piecing together remembered scraps from the night before. The old man was
Florencio Telles, the woman was the wife of his dead son,
these were his grandchildren. Felix was one. Forget the
other name. They had come back from a trip to El Paso
a week ago, or some such matter, and must have brought
the contagion with them. First one came down with the
strangler, then another. Well poisoned with it, likely. Have
to boil the drinking water. This was called Rancho Per-
dido—the Lost Ranch. Well named. The old fellow spoke
good English.

McEwen was at home in Spanish, and, from what he
remembered of last night, the talk had been carried on in
either tongue indifferently. What a night!

He rose and tiptoed out with infinite precaution. The
wind was dead. He went to the well and found the oil; he
climbed up and drenched the bearings and gears. He was

surprised to see how weak he was and how sore; and for the first time in his life he knew the feeling of giddiness and was forced to keep one hand clutched tightly to some support as he moved around the platform—he, Ross McEwen.

When he came back the old man met him with finger on lip. They sat on the warm ground, where they could keep watch upon the sickroom, obliquely, through two doors; just far enough away for quiet speech to be unheard.

"Let them sleep. Every minute of sleep for them is so much coined gold. We won't make a move to wake them. And how is it with you, my son, how is it with you?"

"Fine and fancy. When I came here last night I had a thousand aches, and now I've only got one."

"And that one is all over?"

"That's the place. Never mind me. I'll be all right. How long has this been going on?"

"This is the fifth day for the oldest boy, I think. He came down with it first, Demetrio. We thought it was only a sore throat at first. Maybe six days. I am a little mixed up."

"Should think you would be. Now listen. I know something about diphtheria. Not much, but this for certain. Here's what you've got to do, old man: Quick as they wake up in there, you go to bed and stay in bed. You totter around much more and you're going to die. There's your fortune told, and no charge for it."

"Oh, I'm not bad. I do not cough hard. The strangler never hurts old people much." So he said, but every word was an effort.

"Hell, no, you're not bad. Just a walkin' corpse, tha's all. You get to bed and save your strength. When any two of 'em are chokin' to death at once that'll be time enough for you to hobble out and take one of them off my hands. Do they sleep this long, often?"

"Oh, no. This is the first time. They are always better when morning comes, but they have not all slept at the same time, never before. My daughter, you might say, has not slept at all. It has been grief and anxiety with her as much as the sickness. They will all feel encouraged now, since you've come. If it please God, we'll pull them all through."

"Look here!" said McEwen. "It can't be far to Luna's Well. Can't I catch up a horse and lope over there after awhile—bring help and send for a doctor?"

"There's no one there. Francisco Luna and Casimiro both have driven their stock to the Guadalupe Mountains, weeks ago. It has been too dry. And no one uses the old road now. All travel goes by the new way, beyond the new railroad."

"I found no one at the western ranches yesterday," said McEwen.

"No. Everyone is in the hills. The drought is too bad. There is no one but you. The nearest help is Alamogordo —thirty-five miles. And if you go there some will surely die before you get back. I have no more strength. I will be flat on my back this day."

"That's where you belong. I'll be nurse and cook for this family. Got anything to cook?"

"Not much. Frijoles, jerky, bacon, flour, a little canned stuff and dried peaches."

McEwen frowned. "It is in my mind they ought to have eggs and milk."

"When the cattle come to water you can shut up a cow and a calf—or two of them—and we can have a little milk tonight. I'll show you which ones. As I told you last night, I turned out the cow I was keeping up, for fear I'd get down and she would die here in the pen."

"Don Florencio, I'm afraid I didn't get all you told me last night," said McEwen thoughtfully. "I was wild as a hawk, I reckon. Thought that windmill would certainly drive me crazy. Fever."

The old man nodded. "I knew, my son. It galled my heart to make demands on you, but there was no remedy. It had to be done. I was at the end of my strength. Little Felix, if not the other, would surely have been dead by now except for the mercy of God which sent you here."

McEwen seemed much struck by this last remark. He cocked his head a little to one side painfully, for his neck was stiff; he pursed his lip and held it between finger and thumb for a moment of meditation.

"So that was it!" he said. "I see! Always heard tell that God moves in a mysterious way His wonders to perform. I'll tell a man He does!"

A scanty breakfast, not without gratitude; a pitiful attempt at redding up the hopeless confusion and disorder. The sick woman's eyes followed McEwen as he worked. A good strangling spell all around, including the old man, then a period of respite. McEwen buckled on his gun and brought a hammer and a lard pail to Florencio's bed.

"If you need me, hammer on this, and I'll come a-running. I'm going out to the corral and shoot some beef tea. You tell me about what milk cows to shut up."

Don Florencio described several milk cows. "Any of them. Not all are in to water any one day. Stock generally come in every other day, because they get better grass at a distance. And my brand is T T—for my son Timoteo, who is dead. You will find the cattle in poor shape, but if you wait awhile you may get a smooth one."

McEwen nodded. "I was thinking that," he said. "I want some flour sacks. I'll hang some of the best up under the platform on the windmill tower, where the flies won't bother it."

They heard a shot later. A long time afterward he came in with a good chunk of meat, and set about preparing beef tea. "I shut up a cow to milk," he said. "A lot of saddle horses came in and I shut them up. Not any too much water in the tank. After while the cattle will begin bawling and milling around if the water's low. That will distress our family. Can't have that. So I'll just harness one onto the sweep of the horse power, slip on a blindfold and let him pump. You tell me which ones will work."

The old man described several horses.

"That's O. K." said McEwen. "I've got two of them in the pen. Your woodpile is played out. Had to chop down some of your back pen for firewood."

He departed to start the horse power. Later, when beef

tea had been served all around, he came over and sat by Flarencio's bed.

"You have no drop or grain of medicine of any kind," he said, "and our milk won't be very good when we get it, from the looks of the cows—not for sick people. So, everything being just as it is, I didn't look for brands. I beefed the best one I could find, and hung the hide on the fence. Beef tea, right this very now, may make all the difference with our family. Me, I don't believe there's a man in New Mexico mean enough to make a fuss about it under the circumstances. But if there's any kick, there's the hide and I stand back of it. So that'll be all right. The brand was D W."

"It is my very good friend, Dave Woods, at San Nicolas. That will be all right. Don David is *muy simpático*. Sleep now, my son, sleep a little while you may. It will not be long. You have a hard night before you."

"I'm going up on the rising ground and set a couple of soapweeds afire," said McEwen at dark. "Thaty'll make a big blaze and somebody might take notice. I'll hurry right back. Then I'll light some more about ten o'clock and do it again tomorrow night. Someone will be sure to see it. Just once, they might not think anything. But if they see a light in the same place three or four times, they might look down their nose and scratch their old hard heads—a smart man might. Don't you think so?"

"Why, yes," said Florencio; "it's worth trying."

"Those boys are not a bit better that they was. And your daughter is worse. We don't want to miss a bet. Yes, and I'll hold a blanket before the fire and take it away and put it back, over and over. That ought to help people guess that it is a signal. Only—they may guess that it was meant for someone else."

"Try it," said Florencio. "It may work. But I am not sure that our sick people are not holding their own. They are no better, certainly, even with your beef-tea medicine. But we can't expect to see a gain, if there is a gain, for days yet. And so far, they seem worse every night and then better every morning. The sunlight cheers them up at first, and then the day gets hot and they seem worse again. Try your signals, by all means. We need all the help there is. But if you could only guess how much less alone I feel now than before you came, good friend!"

"It must have been plain hell!" said the good friend.

"Isn't there any other one thing we can do?" demanded McEwen the next day, cudgeling his brains. It had been a terrible night. The little lives fluttered up and down; Estefanía was certainly worse; Florencio, though he had but few strangling spells, was very weak—the aftermath of his earlier labors.

"Not one thing. My poor ghost, no man could have done more. There is no more to do."

"But there is!" McEwen fairly sprang up, wearied as he was. "We have every handicap in the world, and only one advantage. And we don't use that one advantage. The sun has a feud with all the damn germs there is; your house is built for shade in this hot country. I'm going to tote all of you out in the sun with your bedding, and keep you there a spell. And while you're there I'll tear out a hole in the south end of your little old adobe wall and let more sunlight in. After the dust settles enough I'll bring you back. Then we'll shovel on a little more coal, and study up something else. And tonight we'll light up our signal fires again. Surely someone will be just fool enough to come out and see what the hell it's all about."

Hours later, after this program had been carried out, McEwen roused from a ten-minute sleep and rubbed his fists in his eyes.

"Are you awake, Don Florencio?" he called softly.

"Yes, my son. What is it?"

"It runs in my mind," said McEwen, "that they burn sulphur in diphtheria cases. Now, if I was to take the powder out of my cartridges and wet it down, let it get partly dry and make a smudge with it—a little at a time— There's sulphur in gunpowder. We'll try that little thing." He was already at work with horseshoe pinchers, twisting out the bullet. He looked up eagerly. "Haven't any tar, have you? To stop holes in your water troughs."

"*Hijo,* you shame me. There is a can of piñon pitch, that I use for my troughs, under the second trough at the upper end. I never once thought of that."

"We're getting better every day," said McEwen joyfully. "We'll make a smoke with some of that piñon wax, and we'll steep some of it in boiling water and breathe the steam of it; we'll burn my wet powder, and when that's done, we'll think of something else; and we'll make old bones yet, every damn one of us! By gollies, tomorrow between times I'm goin' to take your little old rifle and shoot some quail."

"Between times? Oh, Happy!"

"Oh, well, you know what I mean—just shovel on a little more coal—better brag than whine. Hi, Estafanía— hear that? We've dug up some medicine. Yes, we have. Ask Don Florencio if we haven't. I'm going after it."

But as he limped past the window on his way to the corral he heard the sound of a sob. He paused midstep, thinking it was little Felix. But it was Estafanía.

"*Madre de Dios, ayudale su enviado!*"

He tiptoed away, shamefaced.

7

Sleeping on a very thin bed behind a very large boulder, two men camped at the pass of San Agustin; a tall young man and a taller man who was not so young. The very tall man was Pat Garrett, sheriff of Doña Ana, sometime sheriff of other counties.

The younger man was Clint Llewellyn, his deputy, and their camp was official in character. They were keeping an eye out for that Belen bandit, after prolonged search elsewhere.

"Not but what he's got away long ago," said Pat, in his quiet drawling speech, "but just in case he might possibly double back this way."

It was near ten at night when Pat saw the light on the desert. He pointed it out to Clint. "See that fire out there? Your eyes are younger than mine. Isn't it sinking down and then flaring up again?"

"Looks like it is," said Clint. "I saw a fire there—or two of 'em, rather—just about dark, while you took the horses down to water."

"Did you?" said Pat. He stroked his mustache with a large slow hand. "Looks to me like someone was trying to attract attention."

"It does, at that," said Clint. "Don't suppose somebody's had a horse fall with him and got smashed, do you?"

"Do you know," said Pat slowly, "that idea makes me ache, sort of? One thing pretty clear. Somebody wants someone to do something for somebody. Reckon that's us. Looks like a long ride, and maybe for nothing. Yes. But then we're two long men. Where do you place that fire, Clint?"

"Hard to tell. Close to Luna's Wells, maybe."

"Too far west for that," said Garrett. "I'd say it was Lost Ranch. We'll go ask questions anyway. If we was layin' out there with our ribs caved in or our leg broke —Let's go!"

That is how they came to Lost Ranch between three and four the next morning. A feeble light shone in the window. Clint took the horses to water, while Garrett went on to the house. He stopped at the outer door. A man lay on a couch within, a man Garrett knew—old Florencio. Folded quilts made a pallet on the floor, and on the quilts lay another man, a man with red hair and a red stubble of beard. Both were asleep. Florencio's hand hung over the couch, and the stranger's hand held to it in a tight straining clasp. Garrett stroked his chin, frowning.

Sudden and startling, a burst of strangled coughing came from the room beyond and a woman's sharp call.

"Hijo!" cried Florencio feebly, and pulled the hand he held. "Happy! Wake up!" The stranger lurched to his feet and staggered through the door. "Yes, Felix, I'm coming. All right, boy! All right now! Let me see. It won't hurt. Just a minute, now."

Garrett went into the house.

"Clint," said Pat Garrett, "there's folks dyin' in there,

and a dead man doin' for them. You take both horses and light a rag for the Alamogordo Hospital. Diphtheria. Get a doctor and nurses out here just as quick as God will let them come." Garrett was pulling the saddle from his horse as he spoke. "Have 'em bring grub and everything. Ridin' turn about, you ought to make it tolerable quick. I'm stayin' here, but there's no use of your comin' back. You might take a look around Jarilla if you want to, but use your own judgment. Drag it, now. Every minute counts."

A specter came to the doorway. "Better send a wagon-load of water," it said as Clint turned to go. "This well is maybe poisoned. Germs and such."

"Yes, and bedding, too," said Clint. "I'll get everything and tobacco. So long!"

"Friend," said Pat, "you get yourself to bed. I'm takin' on your job. Your part is to sleep."

"Yes, son," Florencio's thin voice quavered joyously. *"Duerme y descansa.* Sleep and rest. Don Patricio will do everything."

McEwen swayed uncertainly. He looked at Garrett with stupid and heavy eyes. "He called you Patricio. You're not Pat Nunn, by any chance?"

"Why not?" said Garrett.

McEwen's voice was lifeless. "My father used to know you," he said drowsily. He slumped over on his bed.

"Who was your father?" said Garrett.

McEwen's dull and glassy eyes opened to look at his questioner. "I'm no credit to him," he said. His eyes closed again.

"Boil the water!" said McEwen.

"He's asleep already!" said Pat Garrett. "The man's dead on his feet."

"Oh, Pat, there was never one like him!" said Florencio. He struggled to his elbow, and looked down with pride and affection at the sprawling shape on the pallet. "Don Patricio, I have a son in my old age, like Abrahán!"

"I'll pull off his boots," said Pat Garrett.

Garrett knelt over McEwen and shook him vigorously. "Hey, fellow, wake up. You, Happy—come alive! Snap out of it! Most sundown, and time you undressed and went to bed."

McEwen set up at last, rubbing his eyes. He looked at the big, kindly face for a little in some puzzlement. Then he nodded.

"I remember you now. You sent your pardner for the doctor. How's the sick folks?"

"I do believe," said Pat, "that we're going to pull 'em through—every one. You sure had a tough lay."

"Yes. Doctor come?"

"He's in sight now—him and the nurses. That's how come me to rouse you up. Fellow, I hated to wake you when you was going so good. But with the ladies comin', you want to spruce yourself up a bit. You look like the wrath of God!"

McEwen got painfully to his feet and wriggled his arms experimentally.

"I'm just one big ache," he admitted. "Who's them fellows?" he demanded. Two men were industriously cleaning up the house; two men that he had never seen.

"Them boys? Monte, the Mexican, he's old Florencio's nephew. Heard the news this mawnin', and comes boilin' out here hell-for-leather. Been here for hours. The other young fellow came with him. Eastern lad. Don't know him, or why he came. Say, Mr. Happy, you want to bathe those two eyes of yours with cold water, or hot water, or both. They look like two holes burned in a blanket. Doc will have to give you a good jolt of whisky too. Man, you're pretty nigh ruined!"

"I knew there was something," said Mr. Happy. "Got to get me a name. And gosh, I'm tired! I'm a good plausible liar, most times, but I'll have to ask you to help out. Andy Hightower—how'd that do? Knew a man named Alan Hightower once, over on the Mangas."

"Does he run cattle over there now somewhere about Quemado?"

"Yes," said McEwen.

"I wouldn't advise Hightower," said Garrett.

"My name," said McEwen, "is Henry Clay."

Doctor Lamb, himself the driver of the covered spring wagon reached Lost Ranch at sundown. He brought with him two nurses, Miss Mason and Miss Hollister, with Lida Hopper, who was to be cook; also, many hampers and much bedding. Dad Lucas was coming behind, the doctor explained, with a heavy wagon loaded with water and necessaries. Garrett led the way to the sickroom.

Monte helped Garrett unload the wagon and care for the team; Lida Hopper prepared supper in the kitchen.

Mr. Clay had discreetly withdrawn, together with the other man. They were out in the corral now, getting acquainted. The other man, it may be mentioned, was none other than Ben Griggs; and his discretion was such that Miss Hollister knew nothing of his presence until the next morning.

Mr. Clay, still wearied, bedded down under the stars, Monte rustling the credentials for him. When Dad Lucas rolled in, the men made camp by the wagon.

"Well, doctor," said Garrett, "how about the sick? They going to make it?"

"I think the chances are excellent," said the doctor. "Barring relapse, we should save every one. But it was a narrow squeak. That young man who nursed them through —why, Mr. Garrett, no one on earth could have done better, considering what he had to do with. Nothing, practically, but his two hands."

"You're all wrong there, doc. He had a backbone all the way from his neck to the seat of his pants. That man," said Garrett, "will do to take along."

"Where is he, Mr. Garrett? And what's his name? The old man calls him 'son,' all the boys call him 'Uncle Happy.' What's his right name?"

"Clay," said Garrett. "He's dead to the world. You won't see much of him. A week of sleep is what he needs. But you remind me of something. If you will allow it I would like to speak to all of you together. Just a second.

Would you mind asking the nurses to step in for a minute or two, while I bring the cook?"

"Certainly," said Doctor Lamb.

"I want to ask a favor of all of you," said Garrett, when the doctor had ushered in the nurses. "I won't keep you. I just want to declare myself. Some of you know me, and some don't. My name is Pat Garrett, and I am the sheriff of Doña Ana County, over west. But for reasons that are entirely satisfactory to myself, I would like to be known as Pat Nunn, for the present. That's all. I thank you."

"Of course," said Doctor Lamb, "if it is to serve the purpose of the law—"

"I would not go so far," said Garrett. "If you put it that my purpose is served, you will be quite within the truth. Besides, this is not official. I am not sheriff here. This ranch is just cleverly over the line and in Otero County. Old Florencio pays taxes in Otero. I am asking this as a personal favor, and only for a few days. Perfectly simple. That's all. Thank you."

"Did you ask the men outside?"

"No. I just told them," said Mr. Pat Nunn. "It would be dishonorable for a lady to tip my hand; for a man it would be plumb indiscreet."

"Dad Lucas," said the doctor, "is a cynical old scoundrel, and a man without principle, and swivel tongued besides."

"He is all that you say, and a lot more that you would never guess," said Garrett, "but if I claimed to be Humpty Dumpty, Dad Lucas would swear that he saw me fall off of the wall." He held up his two index fingers, side by side. "Dad and me, we're like that. We've seen trouble together —and there is no bond so close. Again, one and all, I thank you. Meetin's adjourned."

Lost Ranch was a busy scene on the following day. A cheerful scene, too, despite the blazing sun, the parched desert and the scarred old house. Reports from the sickroom were hopeful. The men had spread a tarpaulin by the wagon, electing Dad Lucas for cook. They had salvaged a razor of Florencio's and were now doing mightily with it. Monte and Ben Griggs, after dinner, were to take Dad's team and Florencio's wagon to draw up a jag of mesquite roots. In the meantime Monte dragged up stop-gap firewood by the saddle horn, and Ben kept the horse power running in the water pen. Keeping him company, Pat Garrett washed Henry Clay's clothes. More accurately, it was Pat Nunn who did this needed work with grave and conscientious thoroughness.

"Henry Clay and me, after bein' in the house so long," said Mr. Nunn, "why, we'll have to boil up our clothes before we leave, or we might go scattering diphtheria hither and yonder and elsewhere."

"But how if you take it yourselves?"

"Then we'll either die or get well," said Mr. Nunn slowly. "In either case, things will keep juneing along just the same. Henry Clay ain't going to take it, or he'd have it now. It takes three days after you're exposed. Something like that. We'll stick around a little before we go, just in case."

"Which way are you going, Mr. Nunn?" asked Ben.

"Well, I'm going to Tularosa. Old Florencio will have to loan me a horse. Clay too. He's afoot. Don't know where he's going. Haven't asked him. He's too worn out to talk much. His horse played out on him out on the flat somewheres and he had to hang up his saddle and walk in. So Florencio told me. He's goin' back and get his saddle tomorrow."

Miss Mason being on duty, Jay Hollister, having picked up a bite of breakfast, was minded to get a breath of fresh air; and at this juncture she tripped into the water pen where Mr. Nunn and Ben plied their labors.

"And how is the workingman's bride this morning?" asked Ben brightly.

"Great Cæsar's ghost! Ben Griggs, what in the world are you doing here?" demanded Jay with a heightened color.

"Workin'," said Ben, and fingered his blue overalls proudly. "Told you I was goin' to work. Right here is where I'm needed. Why, there are only four of us, not counting you three girls and the doctor, to do what Clay was doing. You should have seen Monte and me cleaning house yesterday."

"Yes?" Jay smiled sweetly. "What house was that?"

"Woman!" said Ben, touched in his workman's pride. "If you feel that way now, you should have seen this house when we got here."

"You're part fool. You'll catch diphtheria."

"Well, what about you? The diphtheria part, I mean. What's the matter with your gettin' diphtheria?"

"That's different. That's a trade risk. That's my business."

"You're my business," said Ben.

Jay shot a startled glance at Mr. Nunn, and shook her head.

"Oh, yes!" said Ben. "Young woman, have you met Mr. Nunn?"

Soap in hand, Mr. Nunn looked up from his task. "Good morning, miss. Don't mind me," he said. "Go right on with the butchery."

"Good morning, Mr. Nunn. Please excuse us. I was startled at finding this poor simpleton out here where he has no business to be. Have I met Mr. Nunn? Oh, yes, I've met him twice. The doctor introduced him once, and he introduced himself once."

Mr. Nunn acknowledged this gibe with twinkling eye. Miss Hollister looked around her, and shivered in the sun. "What a ghastly place!" she cried. "I can't for the life of me understand why anybody should live here. We came through some horrible country yesterday, but this is the worst yet. Honestly, Mr. Nunn, isn't this absolutely the most God-forsaken spot on earth?"

Mr. Nunn abandoned his work for the moment and stood up, smiling. So this was Pat Garrett of whom she had heard so much; the man who killed Billy the Kid. Well, he had a way with him. Jay could not but admire the big square head, the broad spread of his shoulders and a certain untroubled serenity in his quiet face.

"Oh, I don't know," said Mr. Nunn. "Look there!"

"Where? I don't see anything," said Jay. "Look at what?"

"Why, the bees," said Pat. "The wild bees. They make honey here. Little family of 'em in every sotol stalk; and that old house up there with the end broken in—No, Miss Hollister, I've seen worse places than this."

8

The patients were improving. Old Florencio, who had been but lightly touched, mended apace. He had suffered from exhaustion and distress quite as much as from disease itself. Demetrio and little Felix gained more slowly, and Estefanía was weakest of all.

The last was contrary to expectation. As a usual thing, diphtheria goes hardest with the young. But all were in a fair way to recover. Doctor Lamb and Dad Lucas had gone back to town. Dad had returned with certain comforts and luxuries for the convalescents.

Jay Hollister, on the morning watch, was slightly annoyed. Mr. Pat Garrett and the man Clay were leaving, it seemed, and nothing would do but that Clay must come to the sickroom for leave-taking. Quite naturally, Jay had not wished her charges disturbed. Peace and quiet were what they needed. But Garrett had been insistent, and he had a way with him. Oh, well! The farewell was quiet enough and brief enough on Clay's part, goodness knows, but rather fervent from old Florencio and his daughter-in-law. That was the Spanish of it, Jay supposed. Anyhow, that was all over and the disturbers were on their way to Tularosa.

Relieved by Miss Mason, Jay went in search of Ben Griggs to impart her grievance, conscious that she would get no sympathy there, and queerly unresentful of that lack. He was not to be seen. She went to the kitchen.

"Where's that trifling Ben, Lida?"

"H'm? I'm sure I don't know, Miss Jay. That Mexican went up on top of the house just now. He'll know, likely."

Jay climbed the rickety ladder, stepped on the adobe parapet and so down to the flat roof. Monte sat on the farther wall, looking out across the plain so intently that he did not hear her coming.

"Do you know where Ben is?" said Jay.

Monte came to his feet. "Oh, yais! He is weeth the Señor Lucas to haul wood, Mees Hollister. Is there what I can do?"

"What are we going to do about water?" said Jay. "There's only one barrel left. Of course we can boil the well water, but it's horrible stuff."

"*Prontamente*—queekly. All set. Ben weel be soon back, and here we go, Ben and me, to the spreeng of San Nicolas." He pointed to a granite peak of the San Andrés. "There at thees peenk hill yonder."

"What, from way over there?"

"Eet ees closest, an' ver' sweet water, ver' good."

Jay looked and wondered, tried to estimate the void that lay between, and could not even guess. "What a dreadful country! How far is it?"

"Oh, twent-ee miles. *Es nada.* We feel up by sundown and come back in the cool stars."

"Oh, do sit down," said Jay, "and put on your hat. You're so polite you make me nervous. I shouldn't think you'd care much about the cool," said Jay, "the way you sit up here, for pleasure, in the broiling sun."

"Plezzer? Oh, no!" said Monte. "Look!" He turned and pointed. "No, not here, not close by. Mebbe four, three miles. Look across thees bare spot an' thees streep of mesquite to thees long chalk reedge; and now, beyond thees row and bunches of yuccas. You see them now?"

Jay followed his hand and saw, small and remote, two horsemen creeping black and small against the infinite recession of desert. She nodded.

"Eet ees with no joy," said Monte, "that I am to see the las' of *un caballero valiente*—how do you say heem? —of a gallan' gentleman—thees redhead."

"You are not very complimentary to Mr. Garrett," said Jay.

"Oh, no, no, no—you do not unnerstand!" Monte's eyes narrowed with both pity and puzzlement. He groped visibly for words. "*Seguramente, siempre,* een all ways Pat

Garrett ees a man complete. Eet is known. But thees young fellow—he ees play out the streeng—*pobrecito!* Oh, Mees Jay, eet ees a bad spread! Es-scusame, please, Mees Hollister. I have not the good words—onlee the man talk."

"Oh, he did well enough—but why not?" said Jay. "What else could he do? There has been something all the time that I don't understand. Danger from diphtheria? Nonsense. I am not a bit partial to you people out here. Perhaps you know that. But I must admit that danger doesn't turn you from anything you have set your silly heads to do. Of course Mr. Clay had to work uncommonly hard, all alone here. But he had no choice. No; it's something else, something you have kept hidden from me all along. Why all the conspiracy and the pussyfoot mystery?"

"Eet was not jus' lak that, mees. Not *conjuración* exactlee. But everee man feel for heemself eet ees ver good to mek no talk of thees theeng" For once Monte's hands were still. He looked off silently at the great bare plain and the little horsemen dwindling in the distance. "I weel tell you, then," he said at last. "Thees *cosa* are bes' not spoken, and yet eet ees right for you shall know. Onlee I have not those right words. Ben, he shall tell you when he come.

"Eet ees lak thees, Mees Jay. Ver' long ago—yais, before not any of your people is cross over the Atlantic Ocean—my people they are here een thees country and they go up and down to all places—yais, to *las playas de mar,* to the shores of the sea by California. And when they go by Zuñi and by thees rock El Morro, wheech your people call—I have forget that name. You have heard heem?"

"Yes," said Jay. "Inscription Rock. I've read about it."

"*Sí, sí!* That ees the name. Well, eet ees good camp ground, El Morro, wood and water, and thees gr-reat cleef for shade and for shelter een estr-rong winds. And here some fellow he come and he cry out, '*Adiós, el mundo!* What lar-rge weelderness ees thees! And me, I go now eento thees beeg lonesome, and perhaps I shall not to r-return! *Bueno, pues,* I mek now for me a gravestone!' And so he mck on that beeg rock weeth hees dagger, *'Pasó por aquí, Don Fulano de Tal'*—passed by here, Meester So-and-So—weeth the year of eet. And after heem come others to El Morro—so few, so far from Spain. They see what he ees write there, and they say, *'Con razón!'*—eet ees weeth reason to do thees. An' they also mek eenscreepción, *'Pasó por aquí'*—and their names, and the year of eet."

His hand carved slow letters in the air. His eye was proud.

"I would not push my leetleness upon thees so lar-rge world, but one of thees, Mees Hollister—oh, not of the great, not of the first—he was of mine, my ver' great, great papa. So long ago! And he mek also *'Pasó por aquí, Salvador Holguin.'* I hear thees een the firelight when I am small fellow. And when I am man-high I mek veesit to thees place and see heem."

His eyes followed the far horseman, now barely to be seen, a faint moving blur along the north.

"And thees fellow, too, thees redhead, he pass this way, *Pasó por aquí*"—again the brown hand wrote in the air— "and he mek here good and not weeked. But, before that —I am not God!" Lips, shoulders, hands, every line of his face disclaimed that responsibility. "But he is thief, I theenk," said Monte. "Yais, he ees thees one—Mack-Yune?—who rob the bank of Numa Frenger las' week at Belen. I theenk so."

Jay's eyes grew round with horror, her hand went to her throat. "Not arrested?"

For once Monte's serene composure was shaken. His eyes narrowed, his words came headlong.

"Oh, no, no, no! You do not unnerstan'. Ees eemposevilly, what you say! Pat Garrett ees know nozzing, he ees fir-rm r-resolve to know nozzing. An' thees Mack-Yune, he ees theenk *por verdad* eet ees Pat Nunn who ride weeth heem to Tularosa. He guess not one theeng that eet ees the sheriff. Pat Garrett he go that none may deesturb or moless' heem. Becows, thees young fellow ees tek eshame for thees bad life, an' he say to heemself, 'I weel arize and go to my papa'."

She began to understand. She looked out across the desert and the thorn, the white chalk and the sand. Sun dazzle was in her eyes. These people! Peasant, gambler, killer, thief—She felt the pulse pound in her throat.

"And een Tularosa, all old-timers, everee man he know Pat Garrett. Not lak thees Alamogordo, new peoples. And when thees old ones een Tularosa see Meester Pat Garrett mek good-by weeth hees friend at the tr-rain, they will theenk nozzing, say nozzing. *Adiós!*"

He sat sidewise upon the parapet and waved his hand to the nothingness where the two horsemen had been swallowed up at last.

"And him the sheriff!" said Jay. "Why, they could impeach him for that. They could throw him out of office."

He looked up, smiling. "But who weel tell?" said Monte. His outspread hands were triumphant. "We are all decent people."

THE RAWHIDE

STEWART EDWARD WHITE (1873–1946), novelist, short-story writer, and travel writer, was unexcelled in the spinning of tales of the outdoors, the rivers and woods, the mountains and plains—"all that goes to make the life of action in the places where action is life," as Joseph Henry Jackson put it. Few writers have known their chosen backgrounds as well as he did or from as intimate first-hand experience, for White was a vigorous outdoorsman, thoroughly at home in the wilds. An impressive succession of books, from the early *Blazed Trail* to the late *Wild Geese Calling,* has earned Stewart Edward White a secure place in the literature of the American frontier.

"The Rawhide," first published in *McClure's* magazine, was the best piece in a book of White's fiction published as *Arizona Nights.* The author always regarded it as his most effectively sustained writing, and in this case it must be conceded that a writer was a good judge of his own creation. The death of his wife, a loss grievously felt by White, turned his thoughts to the other world, and he wrote several books concerned with mysticism, the best of which was *The Unobstructed Universe.* Primarily, however, he will continue to be judged on the basis of his extraordinary tetralogy, *The Saga of Andy Burnett* (mentioned in our Introduction).

The Rawhide

STEWART EDWARD WHITE

Chapter 1

The Passing of the Colt's Forty-Five

THE MAN of whom I am now to tell you came to Arizona in the early days of Chief Cochise. He settled in the Soda Springs Valley, and there persisted in spite of the devastating forays of that Apache. After a time he owned all the wells and springs in the valley, and so, naturally, controlled the grazing on that extensive free range. Once a day the cattle, in twos and threes, in bands, in strings, could be seen winding leisurely down the deep-trodden and converging trails to the water troughs at the home ranch, there leisurely to drink, and then leisurely to drift away into the saffron and violet and amethyst distances of the desert. At ten other outlying ranches this daily scene was repeated. All these cattle belonged to the man, great by reason of his priority in the country, the balance of his even character, and the grim determination of his spirit.

When he had first entered Soda Springs Valley his companions had called him Buck Johnson. Since then his form had squared, his eyes had steadied to the serenity of a great authority, his mouth, shadowed by the mustache and the beard, had closed straight in the line of power and taciturnity. There was about him more than a trace of the Spanish. So now he was known as Señor Johnson, although in reality he was straight American enough.

Señor Johnson lived at the home ranch with a Chinese cook, and Parker, his foreman. The home ranch was of adobe, built with loopholes like a fort. In the obsolescence of this necessity, other buildings had sprung up unfortified. An adobe bunkhouse for the cowpunchers, an adobe blacksmith shop, a long, low stable, a shed, a windmill and pondlike reservoir, a whole system of corrals of different sizes, a walled-in vegetable garden—these gathered to themselves cottonwoods from the moisture of their being, and so added each a little to the green spot in the desert. In the smallest corral, between the stable and the shed, stood a buckboard and a heavy wagon, the only wheeled vehicles about the place. Under the shed were rows of saddles, riatas, spurs mounted with silver, bits ornamented with the same metal, curved short irons for the range branding, long, heavy "stamps" for the corral branding. Behind the stable lay the "pasture," a thousand acres of desert fenced in with wire. There the hardy cowponies sought out the sparse, but nutritious, bunch grass, sixty of them, beautiful as antelope, for they were the pick of Señor Johnson's herds.

And all about lay the desert, shimmering, changing, many-tinted, wonderful, hemmed in by the mountains that seemed tenuous and thin, like beautiful mists, and by the sky that seemed hard and polished like a turquoise.

Each morning at six o'clock the ten cowpunchers of the home ranch drove the horses to the corral, neatly roped the dozen to be "kept up" for that day, and rewarded the rest with a feed of grain. Then they rode away at a little fox trot, two by two. All day long they traveled thus, conducting the business of the range, and at night, having completed the circle, they jingled again into the corral. At the ten other ranches this program had been duplicated. The half-hundred men of Señor Johnson's outfit had covered the area of a European principality. All of it, every acre, every spear of grass, every cactus prickle, every creature on it, practically belonged to Señor Johnson, because Señor Johnson owned the water, and without water one cannot exist on the desert.

This result had not been gained without struggle. The fact could be read in the settled lines of Señor Johnson's face, and the great calm of his gray eye. Indian days drove him often to the shelter of the loopholed adobe ranch house, there to await the soldiers from the Fort, in plain sight thirty miles away on the slope that led to the foot of the Chiricahuas. He lost cattle and some men, but the profits were great, and in time Cochise, Geronimo, and the lesser lights had flickered out in the winds of destiny. The sheep terror merely threatened, for it was soon discovered that with the feed of Soda Springs Valley grew a burr that annoyed the flocks beyond reason, so the bleating scourge swept by forty miles away.

Cattle rustling so near the Mexican line was an easy matter. For a time Señor Johnson commanded an armed band. He was lord of the high, the low, and the middle justice. He violated international ethics, and for the laws of nations he substituted his own. One by one he annihilated the thieves of cattle, sometimes in open fight, but oftener by surprise and deliberate massacre. The country was delivered. And then, with indefatigable energy, Señor Johnson became a skilled detective. Alone, or with Parker, his foreman, he rode the country through, gathering evidence. When the evidence was unassailable he brought offenders to book. The rebranding through a wet blanket he knew and could prove; the earmarking of an unbranded calf until it could be weaned he understood; the paring of hoofs to prevent traveling he could tell as far as he could see; the crafty alteration of similar brands—as when a Mexican changed Johnson's Lazy Y to a Dumbbell Bar—he saw through at a glance. In short, the hundred and one petty tricks of the sneak thief he ferreted out, in danger of his life. Then he sent to Phoenix for a Ranger—and that was the last of the Dumbbell Bar brand, or the Three Link Bar brand, or the Hour Glass brand, or half a dozen others. The Soda Springs Valley acquired a reputation for good order.

Señor Johnson at this stage of his career found himself dropping into a routine. In March began the spring branding, then the corraling and breaking of the wild horses, the summer range riding, the great fall roundup, the shipping of cattle, and the riding of the winter range. This happened over and over again.

You and I would not have suffered from ennui. The roping and throwing and branding, the wild swing and dash of handling stock, the mad races to head the mustangs, the fierce combats to subdue these raging wild beasts to the saddle, the spectacle of the roundup with its brutish multitudes and its graceful riders, the dust and monotony and excitement and glory of the Trail, and especially the hundreds of incidental and gratuitous adventures of bears and antelope, of thirst and heat, of the joy of taking care of one's self—all these would have filled our days with the glittering, charging throng of the unusual.

But to Señor Johnson it had become an old story. After the days of construction the days of accomplishment seemed to him lean. His men did the work and reaped the excitement. Señor Johnson never thought now of riding the wild horses, of swinging the rope coiled at his saddle horn, or of rounding ahead of the flying herds. His inspections were business inspections. The country was tame. The leather chaps with the silver conchas hung behind the door. The Colt's forty-five depended at the head of the bed. Señor Johnson rode in mufti. Of his cowboy days persisted still the high-heeled boots and spurs, the broad Stetson hat, and the fringed buckskin gauntlets.

The Colt's forty-five had been the last to go. Finally one evening Señor Johnson received an express package. He opened it before the undemonstrative Parker. It proved to contain a pocket "gun"—a nickel-plated, thirty-eight-caliber Smith & Wesson "five-shooter." Señor Johnson examined it a little doubtfully. In comparison with the six-shooter it looked like a toy.

"How do you like her?" he inquired, handing the weapon to Parker.

Parker turned it over and over, as a child a rattle. Then he returned it to its owner. "Señor," said he, "if ever you shoot me with that little old gun, and I find it out the same day, I'll just raise hell with you!"

"I don't reckon she'd *injure* a man much," agreed the Señor, "but perhaps she'd call his attention."

However, the "little old gun" took its place, not in Señor Johnson's hip pocket, but inside the front waistband of his trousers, and the old shiny Colt's forty-five, with its "Texas-style" holster, became a bedroom ornament.

Thus, from a frontiersman dropped Señor Johnson to the status of a property owner. In a general way he had to attend to his interests before the cattlemen's association; he had to arrange for the buying and shipping, and the rest was leisure. He could now have gone away somewhere as far as time went. So can a fish live in trees—as far as time goes. And in the daily riding, riding, riding over the range he found the opportunity for abstract thought which the frontier life had crowded aside.

Chapter 2

The Shapes of Illusion

EVERY DAY, as always, Señor Johnson rode abroad over the land. His surroundings had before been accepted casually as a more or less pertinent setting of action and condition. Now he sensed some of the fascination of the Arizona desert.

He noticed many things before unnoticed. As he jingled loosely along on his cow horse, he observed how the animal waded fetlock-deep in the gorgeous orange California poppies, and then he looked up and about, and saw that the rich color carpeted the landscape as far as his eye could reach, so that it seemed as though he could ride on and on through them to the distant Chiricahuas. Only, close under the hills, lay, unobtrusive, a narrow streak of gray. And in a few hours he had reached the streak of gray, and ridden out into it to find himself the center of a limitless alkali plain, so that again it seemed the valley could contain nothing else of importance.

Looking back, Señor Johnson could discern a tenuous ribbon of orange—the poppies. And perhaps ahead a little shadow blotted the face of the alkali, which, being reached and entered, spread like fire until it, too, filled the whole plain, until it, too, arrogated to itself the right of typifying Soda Springs Valley as a shimmering prairie of mesquite. Flowered upland, dead lowland, brush, cactus, volcanic rock, sand, each of these for the time being occupied the whole space, broad as the sea. In the circlet of the mountains was room for many infinities.

Among the foothills Señor Johnson, for the first time, appreciated color. Hundreds of acres of flowers filled the velvet creases of the little hills and washed over the smooth, rounded slopes so accurately in the placing and manner of tinted shadows that the mind had difficulty in believing the color not to have been shaded in actually by free sweeps of some gigantic brush. A dozen shades of pinks and purples, a dozen of blues, and then the flame-reds, the yellows, and the vivid greens. Beyond were the mountains in their glory of volcanic rocks, rich as the tapestry of a Florentine palace. And, modifying all the others, the tinted atmosphere of the Southwest, refracting the sun through the infinitesimal earth motes thrown up constantly by the wind devils of the desert, drew before the scene a delicate and gauzy veil of lilac, of rose, of saffron, of amethyst, or of mauve, according to the time of day.

Señor Johnson discovered that looking at the landscape upside down accentuated the color effects. It amused him vastly suddenly to bend over his saddle horn, the top of his head nearly touching his horse's mane. The distant mountains at once started out into redder prominence; their shadows of purple deepened to the royal color; the rose veil thickened.

"She's the prettiest country God ever made!" exclaimed Señor Johnson with entire conviction.

And no matter where he went, nor into how familiar country he rode, the shapes of illusion offered always variety. One day the Chiricahuas were a tableland; next day a series of castellated peaks; now an anvil; now a saw tooth; and rarely they threw a magnificent suspension bridge across the heavens to their neighbors, the ranges on the west. Lakes rippling in the wind and breaking on the shore, cattle big as elephants or small as rabbits; distances that did not exist and forests that never were, beds of lava along the hills swearing to a cloud shadow, while the sky was polished like a precious stone—these, and many other beautiful and marvelous but empty shows the great desert displayed lavishly, with the glitter and inconsequence of a dream. Señor Johnson sat on his horse in the hot sun, his chin in his hand, his elbow on the pommel, watching it all with grave, unshifting eyes.

Occasionally, belated, he saw the stars, the wonderful desert stars, blazing clear and unflickering, like the flames of candles. Or the moon worked her necromancies, hemming him in by mountains ten thousand feet high through which there was no pass. And then as he rode, the mountains shifted like the scenes in a theater, and he crossed the little sand dunes out from the dream country to the adobe corrals of the home ranch.

All these things, and many others, Señor Johnson now saw for the first time, although he had lived among them for twenty years. It struck him with the freshness of a surprise. Also it reacted chemically on his mental processes to generate a new power within him. The new power, being as yet unapplied, made him uneasy and restless and a little irritable. He tried to show some of his wonders to Parker.

"Jed," said he one day, "this is a great country."

"You know it," replied the foreman.

"Those tourists in their nickel-plated Pullmans call this a desert. Desert, hell! Look at them flowers!"

The foreman cast an eye on a glorious silken mantle of purple, a hundred yards broad. "Sure," he agreed; "shows what we could do if we only had a little water."

And again: "Jed," began the Señor, "did you ever notice them mountains?"

"Sure," agreed Jed.

"Ain't that a pretty color?"

"You bet," agreed the foreman; "now you're talking! I always said they was mineralized enough to make a good prospect."

This was unsatisfactory. Señor Johnson grew more restless. His critical eye began to take account of small details. At the ranch house one evening he, on a sudden, bellowed loudly for Sang, the Chinese servant.

"Look at these!" he roared when Sang appeared.

Sang's eyes opened in bewilderment.

"There, and there!" shouted the cattleman. "Look at them old newspapers and them gun rags! The place is like a cow yard. Why in the name of heaven don't you clean up here!"

"Allee light," babbled Sang; "I clean him."

The papers and gun rags had lain there unnoticed for nearly a year. Señor Johnson kicked them savagely.

"It's time we took a brace here," he growled. "We're livin' like a lot of Oilers."

Chapter 3

The Paper a Year Old

SANG HURRIED OUT for a broom. Señor Johnson sat where he was, his heavy, square brows knit. Suddenly he stooped, seized one of the newspapers, drew near the lamp, and began to read.

It was a Kansas City paper and, by a strange coincidence, was dated exactly a year before. The sheet Señor Johnson happened to pick up was one usually passed over by the average newspaper reader. It contained only columns of little two-and three-line advertisements classified as *Help Wanted, Situations Wanted, Lost and Found,* and *Personal.* The latter items Señor Johnson commenced to read while awaiting Sang and the broom.

The notices were five in number. The first three were of the mysterious newspaper-correspondence type, in which Birdie beseeches Jack to meet her at the fountain; the fourth advertised a clairvoyant. Over the fifth Señor Johnson paused long. It read: *Wanted—By an intelligent and refined lady of pleasing appearance, correspondence with a gentleman of means. Object matrimony.*

Just then Sang returned with the broom and began noisily to sweep up the debris. The rustling of papers aroused Señor Johnson from his reverie. At once he exploded.

"Get out of here, you debased Mongolian!" he shouted. "Can't you see I'm reading?"

Sang fled, sorely puzzled, for the Señor was calm and unexcited and aloof in his everyday habit.

Soon Jed Parker, tall, wiry, hawknosed, deliberate, came into the room and flung his broad hat and spurs into the corner. Then he proceeded to light his pipe and threw the burned match on the floor.

"Been over to look at the Grant Pass range," he announced cheerfully. "She's no good. Drier than cork legs. Th' country wouldn't support three horned toads."

"Jed," quoth the Señor solemnly, "I wisht you'd hang up your hat like I have. It don't look good there on the floor."

"Why, sure," agreed Jed, with an astonished stare.

Sang brought in supper and slung it on the red and white squares of oilcloth. Then he moved the lamp and retired.

Señor Johnson gazed with distaste into his cup. "This coffee would float a wedge," he commented sourly.

"She's no puling infant," agreed the cheerful Jed.

"And this!" went on the Señor, picking up what purported to be plum duff: "Bog down a few currants in dough and call her pudding!"

He ate in silence, then pushed back his chair and went to the window, gazing through its grimy panes at the mountains, ethereal in their evening saffron.

"Blamed Chink," he growled, "why don't he wash these windows?"

Jed laid down his busy knife and idle fork to gaze on his chief with amazement. Buck Johnson, the austere, the aloof, the grimly taciturn, the dangerous, to be thus complaining like a querulous woman!

"Señor," said he, "you're off your feed."

Señor Johnson strode savagely to the table and sat down with a bang. "I'm sick of it," he growled; "this thing will kill me off. I might as well go be a buck nun and be done with it."

With one round-arm sweep he cleared aside the dishes. "Give me that pen and paper behind you," he requested.

For an hour he wrote and destroyed. The floor became littered with torn papers. Then he enveloped a meager result. Parker had watched him in silence. The Señor looked up to catch his speculative eye. His own eye twinkled a little, but the twinkle was determined and sinister, with only an alloy of humor.

"Señor," ventured Parker slowly, "this event sure knocks me hell-west and crooked. If the loco you have culled hasn't paralyzed your speaking parts, would you mind telling me what in the name of heaven, hell, and high water is up?"

"I am going to get married," announced the Señor calmly.

"What!" shouted Parker. "Who to?"

"To a lady," replied the Señor, "an intelligent and refined lady—of pleasing appearance."

Chapter 4

Dreams

ALTHOUGH THE PAPER WAS a year old, Señor Johnson in due time received an answer from Kansas. A correspondence ensued. Señor Johnson enshrined above the big fireplace the photograph of a woman. Before this he used to stand for hours at a time slowly constructing in his mind what he had hitherto lacked—an ideal of woman and of home. This ideal he used sometimes to express to himself and to the ironical Jed.

"It must sure be nice to have a little woman waitin' for you when you come in off'n the desert." Or: "Now, a woman would have them windows just blooming with flowers and white curtains and such truck." Or: "I bet that Sang would get a wiggle on him with his little old cleaning-duds if he had a woman ahead of his jerk line."

Slowly he reconstructed his life, the life of the ranch, in terms of this hypothesized feminine influence. Then matters came to an understanding. Señor Johnson had sent his own portrait. Estrella Sands wrote back that she adored big black beards, but she was afraid of him, he had such a fascinating bad eye, no woman could resist him. Señor Johnson at once took things for granted, sent on to Kansas a preposterous sum of "expense" money and a railroad ticket, and raided Goodrich's store at Willets, a hundred miles away, for all manner of gaudy carpets, silverware, fancy lamps, works of art, pianos, linen, and gimcracks for the adornment of the ranch house. Furthermore, he offered wages more than equal to a hundred miles of desert to a young Irish girl, named Susie O'Toole, to come out as housekeeper, decorator, boss of Sang and another Chinaman, and companion to Mrs. Johnson when she should arrive.

Furthermore, he laid off from the range work Brent Palmer, the most skillful man with horses, and set him to "gentling" a beautiful little sorrel. A side saddle had arrived from El Paso. It was "center-fire," which is to say it had but the single horsehair cinch, broad, tasseled, very genteel in its suggestion of pleasure use only. Brent could be seen at all times of day, cantering here and there on the sorrel, a blanket tied around his waist to simulate the long riding-skirt. He carried also a sulky and evil gleam in his eye, warning against undue levity.

Jed Parker watched these various proceedings sardonically. Once, the baby light of innocence blue in his eye, he inquired if he would be required to dress for dinner. "If so," he went on, "I'll have my man brush up my low-necked clothes."

But Señor Johnson refused to be baited. "Go on, Jed," said he; "you know you ain't got clothes enough to dust a fiddle."

The Señor was happy these days. He showed it by an unwonted joviality of spirit, by a slight but evident unbending of his Spanish dignity. No longer did the splendor of the desert fill him with a vague yearning and uneasiness. He looked upon it confidently, noting its various phases with care, rejoicing in each new development of color and light, of form and illusion, storing them away in his memory so that their recurrence should find him prepared to recognize and explain them. For soon he would have someone by his side with whom to appreciate them. In that sharing he could see the reason for them, the reason for their strange bitter-sweet effects on the human soul.

One evening he leaned on the corral fence, looking toward the Dragoons. The sun had set behind them. Gigantic they loomed against the western light. From their summits, like an aureole, radiated the splendor of the dust-moted air, this evening a deep amber. A faint reflection of it fell across the desert, glorifying the reaches of its nothingness.

"I'll take her out on an evening like this," quoth Señor Johnson to himself, "and I'll make her keep her eye on the ground till we get right up by Running Bear Knob, and then I'll let her look up all at once. And she'll surely enjoy this life. I bet she never saw a steer roped in her life. She can ride with me every day out over the range and I'll show her the busting and the branding and that band of antelope over by the Tall Windmill. I'll teach her to shoot, too. And we can make little pack trips off in the hills when she gets too hot—up there by Deerskin Meadows 'mongst the high peaks."

He mused, turning over in his mind a new picture of his own life, aims, and pursuits as modified by the sympathetic and understanding companionship of a woman. He pictured himself as he must seem to her in his different pursuits. The picturesqueness pleased him. The simple, direct vanity of the man—the wholesome vanity of a straightforward nature-awakened to preen its feathers before the idea of the mate.

The shadows fell. Over the Chiricahuas flared the evening star. The plain, self-luminous with the weird lucence of the arid lands, showed ghostly. Jed Parker, coming out from the lamp-lit adobe, leaned his elbows on the rail in silent company with his chief. He, too, looked abroad. His mind's eye saw what his body's eye had always told him were the insistent notes—the alkali, the cactus, the sage, the mesquite, the lava, the choking dust, the blinding heat, the burning thirst. He sighed in the dim half recollection of past days.

"I wonder if she'll like the country?" he hazarded.

But Señor Johnson turned on him his steady eyes, filled with the great glory of the desert. "Like the country!" he marveled slowly. "Of course! Why shouldn't she?"

Chapter 5

The Arrival

THE OVERLAND DREW INTO WILLETS, coated from engine to observation with white dust. A porter, in strange contrast of neatness, flung open the vestibule, dropped his little carpeted step, and turned to assist someone. A few idle passengers gazed out on the uninteresting, flat frontier town.

Señor Johnson caught his breath in amazement. "God! Ain't she just like her picture!" he exclaimed. He seemed to find this astonishing.

For a moment he did not step forward to claim her, so she stood looking about her uncertainly, her leather suitcase at her feet.

She was indeed like the photograph. The same full-curved, compact little figure, the same round face, the same cupid's-bow mouth, the same appealing, large eyes, the same haze of doll's hair. In a moment she caught sight of Señor Johnson and took two steps toward him, then stopped. The Señor at once came forward.

"You're Mr. Johnson, ain't you?" she inquired, thrusting her little pointed chin forward, and so elevating her baby-blue eyes to his.

"Yes, ma'am," he acknowledged formally. Then, after a moment's pause: "I hope you're well."

"Yes, thank you."

The station loungers, augmented by all the ranchmen and cowboys in town, were examining her closely. She looked at them in a swift side glance that seemed to gather all their eyes to hers. Then, satisfied that she possessed the universal admiration, she returned the full force of her attention to the man before her.

"Now you give me your trunk checks," he was saying, "and then we'll go right over and get married."

"Oh!" she gasped.

"That's right, ain't it?" he demanded.

"Yes, I suppose so," she agreed.

A little subdued, she followed him to the clergyman's house, where, in the presence of Goodrich, the storekeeper, and the preacher's wife, the two were united. Then they mounted the buckboard and drove from town.

Señor Johnson said nothing, because he knew of nothing to say. He drove skillfully and fast through the gathering dusk. It was a hundred miles to the home ranch, and that hundred miles, by means of five relays of horses already arranged for, they would cover by morning. Thus they would avoid the dust and heat and high winds of the day.

The sweet night fell. The little desert winds laid soft fingers on their cheeks. Overhead burned the stars, clear, unflickering, like candles. Dimly could be seen the horses, their flanks swinging steadily in the square trot. Ghostly bushes passed them, ghostly rock elevations. Far, in indeterminate distance, lay the outlines of the mountains. Always, they seemed to recede. The plain, all but invisible, the wagon trail quite so, the depths of space—these flung heavy on the soul their weight of mysticism.

The woman, until now bolt-upright in the buckboard seat, shrank nearer to the man. He felt against his sleeve the delicate contact of her garment and thrilled to the touch. A coyote barked sharply from a neighboring eminence, then trailed off into the long-drawn, shrill howl of his species.

"What was that?" she asked quickly.

"A coyote—one of them little wolves," he explained.

The horses' hoofs rang clear on a hardened bit of the alkali crust, then dully as they encountered again the dust of the plain. Vast, vague, mysterious in the silence of night, filled with strange influences breathing through space like damp winds, the desert took them to the heart of her great spaces.

"Buck," she whispered, a little tremblingly. It was the first time she had spoken his name.

"What is it?" he asked, a new note in his voice.

But for a time she did not reply. Only the contact against his sleeve increased by ever so little. "Buck," she repeated, then all in a rush and with a sob, "Oh, I'm afraid."

Tenderly the man drew her to him.

"There, little girl," he reassured her, his big voice rich and musical. "There's nothing to get scairt of. I'll take care of you. What frightens you, honey?"

She nestled close in his arm with a sigh of half relief. "I don't know," she laughed, but still with a tremble in her tones. "It's all so big and lonesome and strange— and I'm so little."

"There, little girl," he repeated.

They drove on and on. At the end of two hours they stopped. Men with lanterns dazzled their eyes. The horses were changed, and so out again into the night where the desert seemed to breathe in deep, mysterious exhalations like a sleeping beast.

Señor Johnson drove his horses masterfully with his one free hand. The road did not exist, except to his trained eyes. They seemed to be swimming out, out, into a vapor of night with the wind of their going steady against their faces.

"Buck," she murmured, "I'm so tired."

He tightened his arm around her and she went to sleep, half-waking at the ranches where the relays waited, dozing again as soon as the lanterns dropped behind. And Señor Johnson, alone with his horses and the solemn stars, drove on, ever on, into the desert.

By gray of the early summer dawn they arrived.

The girl awakened, descended, smiling uncertainly at Susie O'Toole, blinking somnolently at her surroundings. Susie put her to bed in the little southwest room where hung the shiny Colt's forty-five in its worn leather "Texas-style" holster. She murmured incoherent thanks and sank again to sleep, overcome by the fatigue of unaccustomed traveling, by the potency of the desert air, by the excitement of anticipation to which her nerves had long been strung.

Señor Johnson did not sleep. He was tough, and used to it. He lit a cigar and rambled about, now reading the newspapers he had brought with him, now prowling softly about the building, now visiting the corrals and outbuildings, once even the thousand-acre pasture where his saddle horse knew him and came to him to have its forehead rubbed.

The dawn broke in good earnest, throwing aside its gauzy draperies of mauve. Sang, the Chinese cook, built his fire. Señor Johnson forbade him to clang the risingbell, and himself roused the cowpunchers. The girl slept on. Señor Johnson tiptoed a dozen times to the bedroom door. Once he ventured to push it open. He looked long within, then shut it softly and tiptoed out into the open, his eyes shining.

"Jed," he said to his foreman, "you don't know how it made me feel. To see her lying there so pink and soft and pretty, with her yaller hair all tumbled about and a little smile on her—there in my old bed, with my old gun hanging over her that way—By heaven, Jed, it made me feel almost holy!"

Chapter 6

The Wagon Tire

ABOUT NOON she emerged from the room, fully refreshed and wide awake. She and Susie O'Toole had unpacked at least one of the trunks, and now she stood arrayed in shirtwaist and blue skirt. At once she stepped into the open air and looked about her with considerable curiosity.

"So this is a real cattle ranch," was her comment.

Señor Johnson was at her side, pressing on her with boyish eagerness the sights of the place. She patted the stag hounds and inspected the garden. Then, confessing herself hungry, she obeyed with alacrity Sang's call to an early meal. At the table she ate coquettishly, throwing her birdlike side glances at the man opposite.

"I want to see a real cowboy," she announced, as she pushed her chair back.

"Why, sure!" cried Señor Johnson joyously. "Sang! hi, Sang! Tell Brent Palmer to step in here a minute."

After an interval the cowboy appeared, mincing in on his high-heeled boots, his silver spurs jingling, the fringe of his chaps impacting softly on the leather. He stood at ease, his broad hat in both hands, his dark, level brows fixed on his chief.

"Shake hands with Mrs. Johnson, Brent. I called you in because she said she wanted to see a real cowpuncher."

"Oh, Buck!" cried the woman.

For an instant the cowpuncher's level brows drew together. Then he caught the woman's glance fair. He smiled. "Well, I ain't much to look at," he proffered.

"That's not for you to say, sir," said Estrella, recovering.

"Brent, here, gentled your pony for you," exclaimed Señor Johnson.

"Oh," cried Estrella, "have I a pony? How nice. And it was so good of you, Mr. Brent. Can't I see him? I want to see him. I want to give him a piece of sugar." She fumbled in the bowl.

"Sure you can see him. I don't know as he'll eat sugar. He ain't that educated. Think you could teach him to eat sugar, Brent?"

"I reckon," replied the cowboy.

They went out toward the corral, the cowboy joining them as a matter of course. Estrella demanded explanations as she went along. Their progress was leisurely. The blindfolded pump mule interested her.

"And he goes round and round that way all day without stopping, thinking he's really getting somewhere!" she marveled. "I think that's a shame! Poor old fellow, to get fooled that way!

"It is some foolish," said Brent Palmer, "but he ain't any worse off than a cow pony that hikes out twenty mile and then twenty back."

"No, I suppose not," admitted Estrella.

"And we got to have water, you know." added Señor Johnson.

Brent rode up the sorrel bareback. The pretty animal, gentle as a kitten, nevertheless planted his forefeet strongly and snorted at Estrella.

"I reckon he ain't used to the sight of a woman," proffered the Señor, disappointed. "He'll get used to you. Go up to him soft-like and rub him between the eyes."

Estrella approached, but the pony jerked back his head with every symptom of distrust. She forgot the sugar she had intended to offer him.

"He's a perfect beauty," she said at last, "but, my! I'd never dare ride him. I'm awful scairt of horses."

"Oh, he'll come around all right," assured Brent easily. "I'll fix him."

"Oh, Mr. Brent," she exclaimed, "don't think I don't appreciate what you've done. I'm sure he's really just as gentle as he can be. It's only that I'm foolish."

"I'll fix him," repeated Brent.

The two men conducted her here and there, showing her the various institutions of the place. A man bent near the shed nailing a shoe to a horse's hoof.

"So you even have a blacksmith!" said Estrella. Her guides laughed amusedly.

"Tommy, come here!" called the Señor.

The horseshoer straightened up and approached. He was a lithe, curly-haired young boy, with a reckless, humorous eye and a smooth face, now red from bending over.

"Tommy, shake hands with Mrs. Johnson," said the Señor. "Mrs. Johnson wants to know if you're the blacksmith." He exploded in laughter.

"Oh, Buck!" cried Estrella again.

"No, ma'am," answered the boy directly; "I'm just tacking a shoe on Danger, here. We all does our own blacksmithing."

His roving eye examined her countenance respectfully, but with admiration. She caught the admiration and returned it, covertly but unmistakably, pleased that her charms were appreciated.

They continued their rounds. The sun was very hot and the dust deep. A woman would have known that these things distressed Estrella. She picked her way through the debris; she dropped her head from the burning; she felt her delicate garments moistering with perspiration, her hair dampening; the dust sifted up through the air. Over in the large corral a bronco buster, assisted by two of the cowboys, was engaged in roping and throwing some wild mustangs. The sight was wonderful, but here the dust billowed in clouds.

"I'm getting a little hot and tired," she confessed at last. "I think I'll go to the house."

But near the shed she stopped again, interested in spite of herself by a bit of repairing Tommy had under way. The tire of a wagon wheel had been destroyed. Tommy was mending it. On the ground lay a fresh cowhide. From this Tommy was cutting a wide strip. As she watched he measured the strip around the circumference of the wheel.

"He isn't going to make a tire of that!" she exclaimed incredulously.

"Sure," replied Señor Johnson.

"Will it wear?"

"It'll wear for a month or so, till we can get another from town."

Estrella advanced and felt curiously of the rawhide. Tommy was fastening it to the wheel at the ends only.

"But how can it stay on that way?" she objected. "It'll come right off as soon as you use it."

"It'll harden on tight enough."

"Why?" she persisted. "Does it shrink much when it dries?"

Señor Johnson stared to see if she might be joking. "Does it shrink?" he repeated slowly. "There ain't nothing shrinks more, nor harder. It'll mighty nigh break that wood."

Estrella, incredulous, interested, she could not have told why, stooped again to feel the soft, yielding hide. She shook her head.

"You're joking me because I'm a tenderfoot," she accused brightly. "I know it dries hard, and I'll believe it shrinks a lot, but to break wood—that's piling it on a little thick."

"No, that's right, ma'am," broke in Brent Palmer. "It's awful strong. It pulls like a horse when the desert sun gets on it. You wrap anything up in a piece of that hide and see what happens. Some time you take and wrap a piece around a potato and put her out in the sun and see how it'll squeeze the water out of her."

"Is that so?" she appealed to Tommy. "I can't tell when they are making fun of me."

"Yes, ma'am, that's right," he assured her.

Estrella passed a strip of the flexible hide playfully about her wrists. "And if I let that dry that way I'd be handcuffed hard and fast." she said.

"It would cut you down to the bone," supplemented Brent Palmer.

She untwisted the strip, and stood looking at it, her eyes wide.

"I—I don't know why—" she faltered. "The thought makes me a little sick. Why, isn't it queer? Ugh! it's like a snake!" She flung it from her energetically and turned toward the ranch house.

Chapter 7

Estrella

THE HONEYMOON DEVELOPED and the necessary adjustments took place. The later Señor Johnson had not foreseen, and yet, when the necessity for them arose, he acknowledged them right and proper.

"Course she don't want to ride over to Circle I with us," he informed his confidant, Jed Parker. "It's a long ride, and she ain't used to riding yet. Trouble is I've been thinking of doing things with her just as if she was a man. Women are different. They likes different things."

This second idea gradually overlaid the first in Señor

Johnson's mind. Estrella showed little aptitude or interest in the rougher side of life. Her husband's statement as to her being still unused to riding was distinctly a euphemism. Estrella never arrived at the point of feeling safe on a horse. In time she gave up trying, and the sorrel drifted back to cowpunching. The range work she never understood. As a spectacle it imposed itself on her interest for a week; but since she could discover no real and vital concern in the welfare of cows, soon the mere outward show became an old story.

Estrella's sleek nature avoided instinctively all that interfered with bodily well-being. When she was cool and well-fed and not thirsty, and surrounded by a proper degree of feminine daintiness, then she was ready to amuse herself. But she could not understand the desirability of those pleasures for which a certain price in discomfort must be paid. As for firearms, she confessed herself frankly afraid of them. That was the point at which her intimacy with them stopped.

The natural level to which these waters fell is easily seen. Quite simply, the Señor found that a wife does not enter fully into her husband's workaday life. The dreams he had dreamed did not come true.

This was at first a disappointment to him, of course, but the disappointment did not last. Señor Johnson was a man of sense, and he easily modified his first scheme of married life.

"She'd get sick of it, and I'd get sick of it," he formulated his new philosophy. "Now I got something to come back to, somebody to look forward to. And it's a *woman;* it ain't one of these darn gangle-leg cowgirls. The great thing is to feel you belong to someone, and that someone nice and cool and fresh and purty is waitin' for you when you come in tired. It beats that other little old idee of mine slick as a gun barrel."

So, during this, the busy season of the range riding, immediately before the great fall roundups, Señor Johnson rode abroad all day, and returned to his own hearth as many evenings of the week as he could. Estrella always saw him coming and stood in the doorway to greet him.

He kicked off his spurs, washed and dusted himself, and spent the evening with his wife. He liked the sound of exactly that phrase, and was fond of repeating it to himself in a variety of connections.

"When I get in I'll spend the evening with my wife," "If I don't ride over to Circle I, I'll spend the evening with my wife," and so on. He had a good deal to tell her of the day's discoveries, the state of the range, and the condition of the cattle. To all of this she listened at least with patience. Señor Johnson, like most men who have long delayed marriage, was self-centered without knowing it. His interest in his mate had to do with her personality rather than with her doings.

"What you do with yourself all day today?" he occasionally inquired.

"Oh, there's lots to do," she would answer, a trifle listlessly; and this reply always seemed quite to satisfy his interest in the subject.

Señor Johnson, with a curiously instant transformation often to be observed among the adventurous, settled luxuriously into the state of being a married man. Its smallest details gave him distinct and separate sensations of pleasure.

"I plumb likes it all," he said. "I likes havin' interest in some fool geranium plant, and I likes worryin' about the screen doors and all the rest of the plumb foolishness. It does me good. It feels like stretchin' your legs in front of a good warm fire."

The center, the compelling influence of this new state of affairs, was undoubtedly Estrella, and yet it is equally to be doubted whether she stood for more than the suggestion. Señor Johnson conducted his entire life with reference to his wife. His waking hours were concerned only with the thought of her, his every act revolved in its orbit controlled by her influence. Nevertheless she, as an individual human being, had little to do with it.

Señor Johnson referred his life to a state of affairs he had himself invented and which he called the married state, and to a woman whose attitude he had himself determined upon and whom he designated as his wife. The actual state of affairs—whatever it might be—he did not see; and the actual woman supplied merely the material medium necessary to the reality of his idea. Whether Estrella's eyes were interested or bored, bright or dull, alert or abstracted, contented or afraid, Señor Johnson could not have told you. He might have replied promptly enough—that they were happy and loving. That is the way Señor Johnson conceived a wife's eyes.

The routine of life, then, soon settled. After breakfast the Señor insisted that his wife accompany him on a short tour of inspection. "A little *pasear*," he called it, "just to get set for the day." Then his horse was brought, and he rode away on whatever business called him. Like a true son of the alkali, he took no lunch with him, nor expected his horse to feed until his return. This was an hour before sunset. The evening passed as has been described. It was all very simple.

When the business hung close to the ranch house—as in the bronco busting, the rebranding of bought cattle, and the like—he was able to share his wife's day. Estrella conducted herself dreamily, with a slow smile for him when his actual presence insisted on her attention. She seemed much given to staring out over the desert. Señor Johnson, appreciatively, thought he could understand this. Again, she gave much leisure to rocking back and forth on the low, wide veranda, her hands idle, her eyes vacant, her lips dumb. Susie O'Toole had early proved incompatible and had gone.

"A nice, contented, home sort of a woman," said Señor Johnson.

One thing alone besides the desert, on which she never seemed tired of looking, fascinated her. Whenever a beef was killed for the uses of the ranch, she commanded strips of the green skin. Then, like a child, she bound them and sewed them and nailed them to substances particularly susceptible to their constricting power. She choked the necks of green gourds, she indented the tender bark of cottonwood shoots, she expended an apparently exhaustless ingenuity on the fabrication of mechanical devices whose principle answered to the pulling of the drying rawhide. And always along the adobe fence could be seen a long row of potatoes bound in skin, some of them fresh and smooth and round, some sweating in the agony of squeezing; some wrinkled and dry and little, the last drops of life tortured out of them. Señor Johnson laughed good-humoredly at these toys, puzzled to explain their fascination for his wife.

"They're sure an amusing enough contraption, honey," sair he, "but what makes you stand out there in the hot sun staring at them that way? It's cooler on the porch."

"I don't know," said Estrella helplessly, turning her slow, vacant gaze on him. Suddenly she shivered in a strong physical revulsion. "I don't know!" she cried with passion.

After they had been married about a month Señor Johnson found it necessary to drive into Willets. "How would you like to go, too, and buy some duds?" he asked Estrella.

"Oh!" she cried strangely. "When?"

"Day after tomorrow."

The trip decided, her entire attitude changed. The vacancy of her gaze lifted; her movements quickened; she left off staring at the desert, and her rawhide toys were neglected. Before starting, Señor Johnson gave her a checkbook. He explained that there were no banks in Willets, but that Goodrich, the storekeeper, would honor her signature.

"Buy what you want to, honey," said he. "Tear her wide open. I'm good for it."

"How much can I draw?" she asked, smiling.

"As much as you want to," he replied with emphasis.

"Take care"—she poised before him with the checkbook extended—"I may draw—I might draw fifty thousand dollars."

"Not out of Goodrich," he grinned; "you'd bust the game. But hold him up for the limit, anyway."

He chuckled aloud, pleased at the rare, birdlike coquetry of the woman. They drove to Willets. It took them two days to go and two days to return. Estrella went through the town in a cyclone burst of enthusiasm, saw everything, exhausted everything in two hours. Willets was not a large place. On her return to the ranch she sat down at once in the rocking chair on the veranda. Her hands fell into her lap. She stared out over the desert.

Señor Johnson stole up behind her, clumsy as a playful bear. His eyes followed the direction of hers to where a cloud shadow lay across the slope, heavy, palpable, untransparent, like a blotch of ink.

"Pretty, isn't it, honey?" said he. "Glad to get back?"

She smiled at him her vacant, slow smile. "Here's my checkbook," she said; "put it away for me. I'm through with it."

"I'll put it in my desk," said he. "It's in the left-hand cubbyhole," he called from inside.

"Very well," she replied.

He stood in the doorway, looking fondly at her unconscious shoulders and the pose of her blond head thrown back against the high rocking chair.

"That's the sort of a woman, after all," said Señor Johnson. "No blame fuss about her."

Chapter 8

The Roundup

THIS, AS YOU WELL MAY GATHER, was in the summer routine. Now the time of the great fall roundup drew near. The home ranch began to bustle in preparation.

All through Cochise County were short mountain ranges set down, apparently at random, like a child's blocks. In and out between them flowed the broad, plain-like valleys. On the valley were the various ranges, great or small, controlled by the different individuals of the Cattlemen's Association. During the year an unimportant, but certain, shifting of stock took place. A few cattle of Señor Johnson's Lazy Y eluded the vigilance of his riders to drift over through the Grant Pass and into the ranges of his neighbor; equally, many of the neighbor's steers watered daily at Señor Johnson's troughs. It was a matter of courtesy to permit this, but one of the reasons for the fall roundup was a redistribution to the proper ranges. Each cattle owner sent an outfit to the scene of labor. The combined outfits moved slowly from one valley to another, cutting out the strays, branding the late calves, collecting for the owner of that particular range all his stock, that he might select his marketable beef. In turn each cattleman was host to his neighbors and their men.

This year it had been decided to begin the circle of the roundup at the C O Bar, near the banks of the San Pedro. Thence it would work eastward, wandering slowly in north and south deviation, to include all the country, until the final break-up would occur at the Lazy Y.

The Lazy Y crew was to consist of four men, thirty riding-horses, a chuck wagon, and cook. These, helping others, and receiving help in turn, would suffice, for in the roundup labor was pooled to a common end. With them would ride Jed Parker, to safeguard his master's interests.

For a week the punchers, in their daily rides, gathered in the range ponies. Señor Johnson owned fifty horses which he maintained at the home ranch for everyday riding, two-hundred broken saddle animals, allowed the freedom of the range, except when special occasion demanded their use, and perhaps half a thousand quite unbroken—brood mares, stallions, young horses, broncos, and the like. At this time of year it was his habit to corral all those saddlewise in order to select horses for the round-ups and to replace the ranch animals. The latter he turned loose for their turn at the freedom of the range.

The horses chosen, next the men turned their attention to outfit. Each had, of course, his saddle, spurs, and "rope." Of the latter the chuck wagon carried many extra. That vehicle, furthermore, transported such articles as the blankets, the tarpaulins under which to sleep, the running-irons for branding, the cooking layout, and the men's personal effects. All was in readiness to move for the six weeks' circle, when a complication arose. Jed Parker, while nimbly escaping an irritated steer, twisted the high heel of his boot on the corral fence. He insisted the injury amounted to nothing. Señor Johnson, however, disagreed.

"It don't amount to nothing, Jed," he pronounced after manipulation, "but she might make a good able-bodied injury with a little coaxing. Rest her a week and then you'll be all right."

"Rest her, the devil!" growled Jed; "who's going to San Pedro?"

"I will, of course," replied the Señor promptly. "Didje think we'd send the Chink?"

"I was first cousin to a Yaqui jackass fer sendin' young Billy Ellis out. He'll be back in a week. He'd do."

"So'd the President," the Señon pointed out; "I hear he's had some experience."

"I hate to have you to go," objected Jed. "There's the missis." He shot a glance sideways at his chief.

"I guess she and I can stand it for a week," scoffed the latter. "Why, we're old married folks by now. Besides, you can take care of her."

"I'll try," said Jed Parker, a little grimly.

Chapter 9

The Long Trail

THE ROUNDUP CREW started early the next morning, just about sunup. Señor Johnson rode first, merely to keep out of the dust. Then followed Tom Rich, jogging along easily in the cowpuncher's "Spanish trot," whistling soothingly to quiet the horses, giving a lead to the band of saddle animals strung out loosely behind him. These moved on gracefully and lightly in the manner of the unburdened plains horse, half decided to follow Tom's guidance, half inclined to break to right or left. Homer and Jim Lester flanked them, also riding in a slouch of apparent laziness, but every once in a while darting forward like bullets to turn back into the main herd certain individuals whom the early morning of the unwearied day had inspired to make a dash for liberty. The rear was brought up by Jerky Jones, the fourth cowpuncher, and the four-mule chuck wagon, lost in its own dust.

The sun mounted; the desert went silently through its changes. Wind devils raised straight, true columns of dust six, eight hundred, even a thousand feet into the air. The billows of dust from the horses and men crept and crawled with them like a living creature. Glorious color, magnificent distance, astonishing illusion, filled the world.

Señor Johnson rode ahead, looking at these things. The separation from his wife, brief as it would be, left room in his soul for the heart-hunger which beauty arouses in men. He loved he charm of the desert, yet it hurt him.

Behind him the punchers relieved the tedium of the march, each after his own manner. In an hour the bunch of loose horses lost its early-morning good spirits and settled down to a steady plodding that needed no supervision. Tom Rich led them, now, in silence, his time fully occupied in rolling Mexican cigarettes with one hand. The other three dropped back together and exchanged desultory remarks. Occasionally Jim Lester sang. It was always the same song of uncounted verses, but Jim had a strange fashion of singing a single verse at a time. After a long interval he would sing another.

> *My love is a rider*
> *And broncos he breaks,*
> *But he's given up riding*
> *And all for my sake,*
> *For he found him a horse*
> *And it suited him so*
> *That he vowed he'd ne'er ride*
> *Any other bronco!*

he warbled, and then in the same breath: "Say, boys, did you get onto the *pisano*-looking shorthorn at Willets last week?"

"Nope."

"He sifted in wearin' one of these hard-boiled hats, and carryin' a brogue thick enough to skate on. Says he wants a job drivin' team—that he drives a truck plenty back to St. Louis, where he comes from. Goodrich sets him behind them little pinto cavallos he has. Say! that son of a gun a driver! He couldn't drive nails in a snowbank." An expressive free-hand gesture told all there was to tell of the runaway. "Th' shorthorn landed headfirst in Goldfish Charlie's horse trough. Charlie fishes him out. 'How the devil, stranger,' says Charlie, 'did you come to fall in here?' 'You blamed fool,' says the shorthorn, just cryin' mad. 'I didn't come to fall in here, I come to drive horses.' "

And then, without a transitory pause:

> Oh, my Love has a gun
> And that gun he can use,
> But he's quit his gun fighting
> As well as his booze.
> And he's sold him his saddle,
> His spurs, and his rope,
> And there's no more cowpunching
> And that's what I hope.

The alkali dust, swirled back by a little breeze, billowed up and choked him. Behind, the mules coughed, their coats whitening with the powder. Far ahead in the distance lay the westerly mountains. They looked an hour away, and yet every man and beast in the outfit knew that hour after hour they were doomed, by the enchantment of the land, to plod ahead without apparently getting an inch nearer. The only salvation was to forget the mountains and to fill the present moment full of little things.

But Señor Johnson, today, found himself unable to do this. In spite of his best efforts he caught himself straining toward the distant goal, becoming impatient, trying to measure progress by landmarks—in short, acting like a tenderfoot on the desert, who wears himself down and dies, not from the hardship, but from the nervous strain which he does not know how to avoid. Señor Johnson knew this as well as you and I. He cursed himself vigorously, and began with great resolution to think of something else.

He was aroused from this by Tom Rich, riding alongside. "Somebody coming, Señor," said he.

Señor Johnson raised his eyes to the approaching cloud of dust. Silently the two watched it until it resolved into a rider loping easily along. In fifteen minutes he drew rein, his pony dropped immediately from a gallop to immobility, he swung into a graceful at-ease attitude across his saddle, grinned amiably, and began to roll a cigarette.

"Billy Ellis," cried Rich.

"That's me," replied the newcomer.

"Thought you were down to Tucson?"

"I was."

"Thought you wasn't comin' back for a week yet?"

"Tommy," proffered Billy Ellis dreamily, "when you go to Tucson next you watch out until you sees a little, squint-eyed Britisher. Take a look at him. Then come away. He says he don't know nothin' about poker. Mebbe he don't, but he'll outhold a warehouse."

But here Señor Johnson broke in: "Billy, you're just in time. Jed has hurt his foot and can't get on for a week yet. I want you to take charge. I got a lot to do at the ranch."

"Ain't got my war bag," objected Billy.

"Take my stuff. I'll send yours on when Parker goes."

"All right."

"Well, so long."

"So long, Señor."

They moved. The erratic Arizona breezes twisted the dust of their going. Señor Johnson watched them dwindle. With them seemed to go the joy in the old life. No longer did the long trail possess for him its ancient fascination. He had become a domestic man.

"And I'm glad of it," commented Señor Johnson.

The dust eddied aside. Plainly could be seen the swaying wagon, the loose-riding cowboys, the gleaming, naked backs of the herd. Then the veil closed over them again. But down the wind, faintly, in snatches, came the words of Jim Lester's song:

> *Oh, Sam has a gun*
> *That has gone to the bad,*

Which makes poor old Sammy
Feel pretty damn sad,
For that gun it shoots high
And that gun it shoots low,
And it wabbles about
Like a bucking bronco!

Señor Johnson turned and struck spurs to his willing pony.

Chapter 10

The Discovery

SEÑOR BUCK JOHNSON loped quickly back toward the home ranch, his heart glad at this fortunate solution of his annoyance. The home ranch lay in plain sight not ten miles away. As Señor Johnson idly watched it shimmering in the heat, a tiny figure detached itself from the mass and launched itself in his direction.

"Wonder what's eating him!" marveled Señor Johnson, "—and who is it?"

The figure drew steadily nearer. In half an hour it had approached near enough to be recognized.

"Why, it's Jed!" cried the Señor, and spurred his horse. "What do you mean, riding out with that foot?" he demanded sternly, when within hailing distance.

"Foot, hell!" gasped Parker, whirling his horse alongside. "Your wife's run away with Brent Palmer."

For fully ten seconds not the faintest indication proved that the husband had heard, except that he lifted his bridle hand, and the well-trained pony stopped.

"What did you say?" he asked finally.

"Your wife's run away with Brent Palmer," repeated Jed, almost with impatience.

Again the long pause.

"How do you know?" asked Señor Johnson, then.

"Know, hell! It's been going on for a month. Sang saw

them drive off. They took the buckboard. He heard 'em planning it. He was too scairt to tell till they'd gone. I just found it out. They've been gone two hours. Must be going to make the Limited." Parker fidgeted, impatient to be off. "You're wasting time," he snapped at the motionless figure.

Suddenly Johnson's face flamed. He reached, from his saddle to clutch Jed's shoulder, nearly pulling the foreman from his pony.

"You lie!" he cried. "You're lying to me! It ain't so!"

Parker made no effort to extricate himself from the painful grasp. His cool eyes met the blazing eyes of his chief.

"I wisht I did lie, Buck," he said sadly. "I wisht it wasn't so. But it is."

Johnson's head snapped back to the front with a groan. The pony snorted as the steel bit his flanks, leaped forward, and with head outstretched, nostrils wide, the wicked white of the bronco flickering in the corner of his eye, struck the beeline for the home ranch. Jed followed as fast as he was able.

On his arrival he found his chief raging about the house like a wild beast. Sang trembled from a quick and stormy interrogatory in the kitchen. Chairs had been upset and let lie. Estrella's belongings had been tumbled over. Señor Johnson there found only too sure proof, in the various lacks, of a premeditated and permanent flight. Still he hoped; and as long as he hoped, he doubted, and the demons of doubt tore him to a frenzy. Jed stood near the door, his arms folded, his weight shifted to his sound foot, waiting and wondering what the next move was to be.

Finally, Señor Johnson, struck with a new idea, ran to his desk to rummage in a pigeonhole. But he found no need to do so, for lying on the desk was what he sought—the checkbook from which Estrella was to draw on Goodrich for the money she might need. He fairly snatched it open. Two of the checks had been torn out, stub and all. And then his eye caught a crumpled bit of blue paper under the edge of the desk.

He smoothed it out. The check was made out to bearer and signed Estrella Johnson. It called for fifteen thousand dollars. Across the middle was a great ink blot, reason for its rejection. At once Señor Johnson became singularly and dangerously cool.

"I reckon you're right, Jed," he cried in his natural voice. "She's gone with him. She's got all her traps with her, and she's drawn on Goodrich for fifteen thousand. And *she* never thought of going just this time of month when the miners are in with their dust, and Goodrich would be sure to have that much. That's friend Palmer. Been going on a month, you say?"

"I couldn't say anything, Buck," said Parker anxiously. "A man's never sure enough about them things till afterwards."

"I know," agreed Buck Johnson; "give me a light for my cigarette."

He puffed for a moment, then rose, stretching his legs. In a moment he returned from the other room, the old shiny Colt's forty-five strapped loosely on his hip. Jed looked him in the face with some anxiety. The foreman was not deceived by the man's easy manner; in fact, he knew it to be symptomatic of one of the dangerous phases of Señor Johnson's character.

"What's up, Buck?" he inquired.

"Just going out for a *pasear* with the little horse, Jed."

"I suppose I better come along?"

"Not with your lame foot, Jed."

The tone of voice was conclusive. Jed cleared his throat.

"She left this for you," said he, proffering an envelope. "Them kind always writes."

"Sure," agreed Señor Johnson, stuffing the letter carelessly into his side pocket. He half drew the Colt's from its holster and slipped it back again. "Makes you feel plumb like a man to have one of these things rubbin' against you again," he observed irrelevantly. Then he went out, leaving the foreman leaning, chair tilted, against the wall.

Chapter 11

The Capture

ALTHOUGH he had left the room so suddenly, Señor Johnson did not at once open the gate of the adobe wall. His demeanor was gay, for he was a Westerner, but his heart was black. Hardly did he see beyond the convexity of his eyeballs.

The pony, warmed up by its little run, pawed the ground, impatient to be off. It was a fine animal, clean-built, deep-chested, one of the mustang stock descended from the Arabs brought over by Pizzarro.

But Señor Johnson stood stock-still, his brain absolutely numb and empty. His hand brushed against something which fell to the ground. He brought his dull gaze to bear on it. The object proved to be a black, wrinkled spheroid, baked hard as iron in the sun—one of Estrella's toys, a potato squeezed to dryness by the constricting power of the rawhide. In a row along the fence were others. To Señor Johnson it seemed that thus his heart was being squeezed in the fire of suffering.

But the slight movement of the falling object roused him. He swung open the gate. The pony bowed his head delightedly. He was not tired, but his reins depended straight to the ground, and it was a point of honor with him to stand. At the saddle horn, in its sling, hung the riata, the "rope" without which no cowman ever stirs abroad, but which Señor Johnson had rarely used of late. Señor Johnson threw the reins over, seized the pony's mane in his left hand, held the pommel with his right, and so swung easily aboard, the pony's jump helping him to the saddle. Wheel tracks led down the trail. He followed them.

Truth to tell, Señor Johnson had very little idea of what he was going to do. His action was entirely instinctive. The wheel tracks held to the southwest, so he held to the southwest too.

The pony hit his stride. The miles slipped by. After seven of them the animal slowed to a walk. Señor Johnson allowed him to get his wind, then spurred him on again.

About suppertime he came to the first ranch house. There he took a bite to eat and exchanged his horse for another, a favorite of his, named Button. The two men asked no questions.

"See Mrs. Johnson go through?" asked the Señor from the saddle.

"Yes, about three o'clock. Brent Palmer driving her. Bound for Willets to visit the preacher's wife, she said. Ought to catch up at the Circle I. That's where they'd all spend the night, of course. So long."

Señor Johnson knew now the couple would follow the straight road. They would fear no pursuit. He himself was supposed not to return for a week, and the story of visiting the minister's wife was not only plausible, it was natural. Jed had upset calculations, because Jed was shrewd, and had eyes in his head. Buck Johnson's first mental numbness was wearing away. He was beginning to think.

The night was very still and very dark, the stars very bright in their candlelight glow. The man, loping steadily on through the darkness, recalled that other night, equally still, equally dark, equally starry, when he had driven out from his accustomed life into the unknown with a woman by his side, the sight of whom asleep had made him feel "almost holy." He uttered a short laugh.

The pony was a good one, well equal to twice the distance he would be called upon to cover this night. Señor Johnson managed him well. By long experience and a natural instinct he knew just how hard to push his mount, just how to keep inside the point where too rapid exhaustion of vitality begins.

Toward the hour of sunrise he drew rein to look about him. The desert, till now wrapped in the thousand little noises that make night silence, drew breath in preparation for the awe of the daily wonder. It lay across the world heavy as a sea of lead, and as lifeless; deeply unconscious, like an exhausted sleeper. The sky bent above, the stars paling. Far away the mountains seemed to wait. And then, imperceptibly, those in the east became blacker and sharper, while those in the west became faintly lucent and lost the distinctness of their outline. The change was nothing, yet everything. And suddenly a desert bird sprang into the air and began to sing.

Señor Johnson caught the wonder of it. The wonder of it seemed to him wasted, useless, cruel in its effect. He sighed impatiently, and drew his hand across his eyes.

The desert became gray with the first light before the glory. In the illusory revealment of it Señor Johnson's sharp frontiersman's eyes made out an object moving away from him in the middle distance. In a moment the object rose for a second against the sky line, then disappeared. He knew it to be the buckboard, and that the vehicle had just plunged into the dry bed of an arroyo.

Immediately life surged through him like an electric shock. He unfastened the riata from its sling, shook loose the noose, and moved forward in the direction in which he had last seen the buckboard.

At the top of the steep little bank he stopped behind the mesquite, straining his eyes; luck had been good to him. The buckboard had pulled up, and Brent Palmer was at the moment beginning a little fire, evidently to make the morning coffee.

Señor Johnson struck spurs to his horse and half slid, half fell, clattering, down the steep clay bank almost on top of the couple below.

Estrella screamed. Brent Palmer jerked out an oath, and reached for his gun. The loop of the riata fell wide over him, immediately to be jerked tight, binding his arms tight to his side.

The bronco buster, swept from his feet by the pony's rapid turn, nevertheless struggled desperately to wrench himself loose. Button, intelligent at all rope work, walked steadily backward, step by step, taking up the slack, keeping the rope tight as he had done hundreds of times before when a steer had struggled as this man was struggling now. His master leaped from the saddle and ran forward.

Button continued to walk slowly back. The riata remained taut. The noose held.

Brent Palmer fought savagely, even then. He kicked, he rolled over and over, he wrenched violently at his pinioned arms, he twisted his powerful young body from Señor Johnson's grasp again and again. But it was no use. In less than a minute he was bound hard and fast. Button promptly slackened the rope. The dust settled. The noise of the combat died. Again could be heard the single desert bird singing against the dawn.

Chapter 12

In the Arroyo

SENOR JOHNSON quietly approached Estrella. The girl had, during the struggle, gone through an aimless but frantic exhibition of terror. Now she shrank back, her eyes staring wildly, her hands behind her, ready to flop again over the brink of hysteria.

"What are you going to do?" she demanded, her voice unnatural.

She received no reply. The man reached out and took her by the arm.

And then at once, as though the personal contact of the touch had broken through the last crumb of numbness with which shock had overlaid Buck Johnson's passions, the insanity of his rage broke out. He twisted her violently on her face, knelt on her back, and with the short piece of hard rope the cowboy always carries to "hog-tie" cattle, he lashed her wrists together. Then he arose panting, his square black beard rising and falling with the rise and fall of his great chest.

Estrella had screamed again and again until her face had been fairly ground into the alkali. There she had choked and strangled and gasped and sobbed, her mind nearly unhinged with terror. She kept appealing to him in a hoarse voice, but could get no reply, no indication that he had even heard. This terrified her still more. Brent

Palmer cursed steadily and accurately, but the man did not seem to hear him either.

The tempest had broken in Buck Johnson's soul. When he had touched Estrella he had, for the first time, realized what he had lost. It was not the woman—her he despised. But the dreams! All at once he knew what they had been to him—he understood how completely the very substance of his life had changed in response to their slow soul-action. The new world had been blasted—the old no longer existed to which to return.

Buck Johnson stared at this catastrophe until his sight blurred. Why, it was atrocious! He had done nothing to deserve it! Why had they not left him peaceful in his own life of cattle and the trail? He had been happy. His dull eyes fell on the causes of the ruin.

And then, finally, in the understanding of how he had been tricked of his life, his happiness, his right to well-being, the whole force of the man's anger flared. Brent Palmer lay there cursing him artistically. That man had done it; that man was in his power. He would get even. How?

Estrella, too, lay huddled, helpless and defenseless, at his feet. She had done it. He would get even. How?

He had spoken no word. He spoke none now, either in answer to Estrella's appeals, becoming piteous in their craving for relief from suspense, or in response to Brent Palmer's steady stream of insults and vituperations. Such things were far below. The bitterness and anger and desolation were squeezing his heart. He remembered the silly little row of potatoes sewn in the green hide lying along the top of the adobe fence, some fresh and round, some dripping as the rowhide contracted, some black and withered and very small. A fierce and savage light sprang into his eyes.

Chapter 13

The Rawhide

FIRST OF ALL he unhitched the horses from the buckboard and turned them loose. Then, since he was early trained in Indian warfare, he dragged Palmer to the wagon wheel, and tied him so closely to it that he could not roll over. For, though the bronco buster was already so fettered that his only possible movement was of the jackknife variety, nevertheless he might able to hitch himself along the ground to a sharp stone, there to saw through the rope about his wrists. Estrella her husband held in contempt. He merely supplemented her wrist bands by one about the ankles.

Leisurely he mounted Button and turned up the wagon trail, leaving the two. Estrella had exhausted herself. She was capable of nothing more in the way of emotion. Her eyes tight closed, she inhaled in deep, trembling, long-drawn breaths, and exhaled with the name of her Maker.

Brent Palmer, on the contrary, was by no means subdued. He had expected to be shot in cold blood. Now he did not know what to anticipate. His black, level brows drawn straight in defiance, he threw his curses after Johnson's retreating figure.

The latter, however, paid no attention. He had his purposes. Once at the top of the arroyo he took a careful survey of the landscape, now rich with dawn. Each excresence on the plain his half-squinted eyes noticed, and with instant skill relegated to its proper category of soapweed, mesquite, cactus. At length he swung Button in an easy lope toward what looked to be a bunch of soapweed in the middle distance.

But in a moment the cattle could be seen plainly. Button pricked up his ears. He knew cattle. Now he proceeded tentatively, lifting high his little hoofs to avoid the half-seen inequalities of the ground and the ground's growths, wondering whether he were to be called on to rope or to drive. When the rider had approached to within a hundred feet, the cattle started. Immediately Button understood that he was to pursue. No rope swung above his head, so he sheered off and ran as fast as he could to cut ahead of the bunch. But his rider with knee and rein forced him in. After a moment, to his astonishment, he found himself running alongside a big steer. Button had never hunted buffalo—Buck Johnson had.

The Colt's forty-five barked once, and then again. The steer staggered, fell to his knees, recovered, and finally stopped, the blood streaming from his nostrils. In a moment he fell heavily on his side—dead.

Señor Johnson at once dismounted and began methodically to skin the animal. This was not easy, for he had now way of suspending the carcass nor of rolling it from side to side. However, he was practiced at it and did a neat job. Two or three times he even caught himself taking extra pains that the thin flesh strips should not adhere to the inside of the pelt. Then he smiled grimly, and ripped it loose.

After the hide had been removed he cut from the edge, around and around, a long, narrow strip. With this he bound the whole into a compact bundle, stropped it on behind his saddle, and remounted. He returned to the arroyo.

Estrella still lay with her eyes closed. Brent Palmer looked up keenly. The bronco buster saw the green hide. A puzzled expression crept across his face.

Roughly Johnson loosed his enemy from the wheel and dragged him to the woman. He passed the free end of the riata about them both, tying them close together. The girl continued to moan, out of her wits with terror.

"What are you going to do now, you devil?" demanded Palmer, but received no reply.

Buck Johnson spread out the rawhide. Putting forth his huge strength, he carried to it the pair, bound together like a bale of goods, and laid them on its cool surface. He threw across them the edges, and then deliberately began to wind around and around the huge and unwieldy rawhide package the strip he had cut from the edge of the pelt.

Nor was this altogether easy. At last Brent Palmer understood. He writhed in the struggle of desperation, foaming blasphemies. The uncouth bundle rolled here and there. But inexorably the other, from the advantage of his position, drew the thongs tighter.

And then, all at once, from vituperation the bronco buster fell to pleading, not for life, but for death.

"For God's sake, shoot me!" he cried from within the smothering folds of the rawhide. "If you ever had a heart in you, shoot me! Don't leave me here to be crushed in this vise. You wouldn't do that to a yellow dog. An Injin wouldn't do that, Buck. It's a joke, isn't it? Don't go away an' leave me, Buck. I've done you dirt. Cut my heart out, if you want to; I won't say a word, but don't leave me here for the sun—"

His voice was drowned in a piercing scream, as Estrella came to herself and understood. Always the rawhide had possessed for her an occult fascination and repulsion. She had never been able to touch it without a shudder, and yet she had always been drawn to experiment with it. The terror of her doom had now added to it for her all the vague and premonitory terrors which heretofore she had not understood.

The richness of the dawn had flowed to the west. Day was at hand. Breezes had begun to play across the desert; the wind devils to raise their straight columns. A first long shaft of sunlight shot through a pass in the Chiricahuas, trembled in the dust-moted air, and laid its warmth on the rowhide. Señor Johnson roused himself from his gloom to speak his first words of the episode.

"There, damn you!" said he. "I guess you'll be close enough together now!"

He turned away to look for his horse.

Chapter 14

The Desert

BUTTON was a trusty of Señor Johnson's private animals. He was never known to leave his master in the lurch, and so was habitually allowed certain privileges. Now, instead of remaining exactly on the spot where he was "tied to the ground," he had wondered out of the dry arroyo bed to the upper level of the plains, where he knew certain bunch grasses might be found. Buck Johnson climbed the steep wooded bank in search of him.

The pony stood not ten feet distant. At his master's abrupt appearance he merely raised his head, a wisp of grass in the corner of his mouth, without attempting to move away. Buck Johnson walked confidently to him, fumbling in his side pocket for the piece of sugar with which he habitually soothed Button's sophisticated palate. His hand encountered Estrella's letter. He drew it out and opened it.

> *Dear Buck,* it read, *I am going away. I tried to be good, but I can't. It's too lonesome for me. I'm afraid of the horses and the cattle and the men and the desert. I hate it all. I tried to make you see how I felt about it, but you couldn't seem to see. I know you'll never forgive me, but I'd go crazy here. I'm almost crazy now. I suppose you think I'm a bad woman, but I am not. You won't believe that. It's true though. The desert would make anyone bad. I don't see how you stand it. You've been good to me, and I've really tried, but it's no use. The country is awful. I never ought to have come. I'm sorry you are going to think me a bad woman, for I like you and admire you, but nothing, nothing could make me stay here any longer.* She signed herself simply *Estrella Sands,* her maiden name.

Buck Johnson stood staring at the paper for a much longer time than was necessary merely to absorb the meaning of the words. His senses, sharpened by the stress of the last sixteen hours, were trying mightily to cut to the mystery of a change going on within himself. The phrases of the letter were bald enough, yet they conveyed something vital to his inner being. He could not understand what it was.

Then abruptly he raised his eyes.

Before him lay the desert, but a desert suddenly and miraculously changed, a desert he had never seen before. Mile after mile it swept away before him, hot, dry, suffocating, lifeless. The sparse vegetation was gray with the alkali dust. The heat hung choking in the air like a curtain. Lizards sprawled in the sun, repulsive. A rattlesnake dragged its loathsome length from under a mesquite. The dried carcass of a steer, whose parchment skin drew tight across its bones, rattled in the breeze. Here and there rock ridges showed with the obscenity of so many skeletons, exposing to the hard, cruel sky the earth's nakedness. Thirst, delirium, death, hovered palpable in the wind; dreadful, unconquerable, ghastly.

The desert showed her teeth and lay in wait like a fierce beast. The little soul of man shrank in terror before it.

Buck Johnson stared, recalling the phrases of the letter, recalling the words of his foreman, Jed Parker. *"It's too lonesome for me," "I'm afraid," "I hate it all," "I'd go crazy here," "The desert would make anyone bad," "The country is awful."* And the musing voice of the old cattleman, *"I wonder if she'll like the country!"* They reiterated themselves over and over; and always as refrain his own confident reply, *"Like the country? Sure! Why shouldn't she?"*

And then he recalled the summer just passing, and the woman who had made no fuss. Chance remarks of hers came back to him, remarks whose meaning he had not at the time grasped, but which now he saw were desperate appeals to his understanding. He had known his desert. He had never known hers.

With an exclamation Buck Johnson turned abruptly back to the arroyo. Button followed him, mildly curious, certain that his master's reappearance meant a summons for himself.

Down the miniature cliff the man slid, confidently, without hesitation, sure of himself. His shoulders held squarely, his step elastic, his eye bright, he walked to the fearful, shapeless bundle now lying motionless on the flat surface of the alkali.

Brent Palmer had fallen into a grim silence, but Estrella still moaned. The cattleman drew his knife and ripped loose the bonds. Immediately the flaps of the wet rawhide fell apart, exposing to the new daylight the two bound together. Buck Johnson leaned over to touch the woman's shoulder.

"Estrella," said he gently.

Her eyes came open with a snap, and stared into his, wild with the surprise of his return.

"Estrella," he repeated, "how old are you?"

She gulped down a sob, unable to comprehend the purport of his question. "How old are you, Estrella?" he repeated again.

"Twenty-one," she gasped finally.

"Ah!" said he.

He stood for a moment in deep thought, then began methodically, without haste, to cut loose the thongs that bound the two together.

When the man and the woman were quite freed, he stood for a moment, the knife in his hand, looking down on them. Then he swung himself into the saddle and rode away, straight down the narrow arroyo, out beyond its lower widening, into the vast plains the hither side of the Chiricahuas. The alkali dust was snatched by the wind from beneath his horse's feet. Smaller and smaller he dwindled, rising and falling, rising and falling in the monotonous cow pony's lope. The heat shimmer veiled him for a moment, but he reappeared. A mirage concealed him, but he emerged on the other side of it. Then suddenly he was gone. The desert had swallowed him up.

THE BLUE HOTEL

INFLUENCED STRONGLY by the nineteenth-century Russian novelists and by the French Naturalists, Stephen Crane (1871–1900) won deserved recognition as the earliest American realist among writers of fiction. His best-known novel remains *The Red Badge of Courage,* but *Maggie: A Girl of the Streets* was the first American Naturalistic novel. Crane was subjected to severe attack by those who were disturbed by his realism, but he found strong defenders in William Dean Howells, Hamlin Garland, and others.

"The Blue Hotel" was included in Crane's *The Monster* (1899). Its unflagging realism may be, in a way, pointed up more than otherwise by the afterword (§ 9), which, deplored as it frequently has been, flaws but does not spoil a fine achievement.

The Blue Hotel

STEPHEN CRANE

1

THE PALACE HOTEL at Fort Romper was painted a light blue, a shade that is on the legs of a kind of heron, causing the bird to declare its position against any background. The Palace Hotel, then, was always screaming and howling in a way that made the dazzling winter landscape of Nebraska seem only a gray swampish hush. It stood alone on the prairie, and when the snow was falling the town two hundred yards away was not visible. But when the traveler alighted at the railway station he was obliged to pass the Palace Hotel before he could come upon the company of low clapboard houses which composed Fort Romper, and it was not to be thought that any traveler could pass the Palace Hotel without looking at it. Pat Scully, the proprietor, had proved himself a master of strategy when he chose his paints. It is true that on clear days, when the great transcontinental expresses, long lines of swaying Pullmans, swept through Fort Romper, passengers were overcome at the sight, and the cult that knows the brown-reds and the subdivisions of the dark greens of the East expressed shame, pity, horror, in a laugh. But to the citizens of this prairie town and to the people who would naturally stop there, Pat Scully had performed a feat. With this opulence and splendor, these creeds, classes, egotisms, that streamed through Romper on the rails day after day, they had no color in common.

As if the displayed delights of such a blue hotel were not sufficiently enticing, it was Scully's habit to go every morning and evening to meet the leisurely trains that stopped at Romper and work his seductions upon any man that he might see wavering, gripsack in hand.

One morning, when a snow-crusted engine dragged its long string of freight cars and its one passenger coach to the station, Scully performed the marvel of catching three men. One was a shaky and quick-eyed Swede, with a great shining cheap valise; one was a tall bronzed cowboy, who was on his way to a ranch near the Dakota line; one was a little silent man from the East, who didn't look it, and didn't announce it. Scully practically made them prisoners. He was so nimble and merry and kindly that each probably felt it would be the height of brutality to try to escape. They trudged off over the creaking board sidewalks in the wake of the eager little Irishman. He wore a heavy fur cap squeezed tightly down on his head. It caused his two red ears to stick out stiffly, as if they were made of tin.

At last, Scully, elaborately, with boisterous hospitality, conducted them through the portals of the blue hotel. The room which they entered was small. It seemed to be merely a proper temple for an enormous stove, which, in the center, was humming with godlike violence. At various points on its surface the iron had become luminous and glowed yellow from the heat. Beside the stove Scully's son Johnnie was playing High-Five with an old farmer who had whiskers both gray and sandy. They were quarreling. Frequently the old farmer turned his face toward a box of sawdust—colored brown from tobacco juice—that was behind the stove, and spat with an air of great impatience and irritation. With a loud flourish of words Scully destroyed the game of cards, and bustled his son upstairs with part of the baggage of the new guests. He himself conducted them to three basins of the coldest water in the world. The cowboy and the Easterner burnished themselves fiery red with this water, until it seemed to be some kind of metal-polish. The Swede, however, merely dipped his fingers gingerly and with trepidation. It was notable that throughout this series of small ceremonies the three travelers were made to feel that Scully was very benevolent. He was conferring great favors upon them. He handed the towel from one to another with an air of philanthropic impulse.

Afterward they went to the first room, and, sitting about the stove, listened to Scully's officious clamor at his daughters, who were preparing the midday meal. They reflected in the silence of experienced men who tread carefully amid new people. Nevertheless, the old farmer, stationary, invincible in his chair near the warmest part of the stove, turned his face from the sawdust-box frequently and addressed a glowing commonplace to the strangers. Usually he was answered in short but adequate sentences by either the cowboy or the Easterner. The Swede said nothing. He seemed to be occupied in making furtive estimates of each man in the room. One might have thought that he had the sense of silly suspicion which comes to guilt. He resembled a badly frightened man.

Later, at dinner, he spoke a little, addressing his conversation entirely to Scully. He volunteered that he had come from New York, where for ten years he had worked as a tailor. These facts seemed to strike Scully as fascinating, and afterward he volunteered that he had lived at Romper for fourteen years. The Swede asked about the crops and the price of labor. He seemed barely to listen to Scully's extended replies. His eyes continued to rove from man to man.

Finally, with a laugh and a wink, he said that some of these Western communities were very dangerous; and after his statement he straightened his legs under the table, tilted his head, and laughed again, loudly. It was plain that the demonstration had no meaning to the others. They looked at him wondering and in silence.

2

As the men trooped heavily back into the front room, the two little windows presented views of a turmoiling sea of snow. The huge arms of the wind were making attempts—mighty, circular, futile—to embrace the flakes as they sped. A gate-post like a still man with a blanched face stood aghast amid this profligate fury. In a hearty voice Scully announced the presence of a blizzard. The guests of the blue hotel, lighting their pipes, assented with grunts of lazy masculine contentment. No island of the sea could be exempt in the degree of this little room with its humming stove. Johnnie, son of Scully, in a tone which defined his opinion of his ability as a card-player, challenged the old farmer of both gray and sandy whiskers to a game of High-Five. The farmer agreed with a contemptuous and bitter scoff. They sat close to the stove, and squared their knees under a wide board. The cowboy and the Easterner watched the game with interest. The Swede remained near the window, aloof, but with a countenance that showed signs of an inexplicable excitement.

The play of Johnnie and the gray-beard was suddenly ended by another quarrel. The old man arose while casting a look of heated scorn at his adversary. He slowly buttoned his coat, and then stalked with fabulous dignity from the room. In the discreet silence of all the other men the Swede laughed. His laughter rang somehow childish. Men by this time had begun to look at him askance, as if they wished to inquire what ailed him.

A new game was formed jocosely. The cowboy volunteered to become the partner of Johnnie, and they all then turned to ask the Swede to throw in his lot with the little Easterner. He asked some questions about the game, and, learning that it wore many names, and that he had played it when it was under an alias, he accepted the invitation. He strode toward the men nervously, as if he expected to be assaulted. Finally, seated, he gazed from face to face and laughed shrilly. This laugh was so strange that the Easterner looked up quickly, the cowboy sat intent and with his mouth open, and Johnnie paused, holding the cards with still fingers.

Afterward there was a short silence. Then Johnnie said, "Well, let's get at it. Come on now!" They pulled their chairs forward until their knees were bunched under the board. They began to play, and their interest in the game caused the others to forget the manner of the Swede.

The cowboy was a board-whacker. Each time that he held superior cards he whanged them, one by one, with exceeding force, down upon the improvised table, and took the tricks with a glowing air of prowess and pride that sent thrills of indignation into the hearts of his opponents. A game with a board-whacker in it is sure to become intense. The countenances of the Easterner and the Swede were miserable whenever the cowboy thundred down his aces and kings, while Johnnie, his eyes gleaming with joy, chuckled and chuckled.

Because of the absorbing play none considered the strange ways of the Swede. They paid strict heed to the game. Finally, during a lull caused by a new deal, the Swede suddenly addressed Johnnie: "I suppose there have been a good many men killed in this room." The jaws of the others dropped and they looked at him.

"What in hell are you talking about?" said Johnnie.

The Swede laughed again his blatant laugh, full of a kind of false courage and defiance. "Oh, you know what I mean all right," he answered.

"I'm a liar if I do!" Johnnie protested. The card was halted, and the men stared at the Swede. Johnnie evidently felt that as the son of the proprietor he should make a direct inquiry. "Now, what might you be drivin' at, mister?" he asked. The Swede winked at him. It was a wink full of cunning. His fingers shook on the edge of the board. "Oh, maybe you think I have been to nowheres. Maybe you think I'm a tenderfoot?"

"I don't know nothin' about you," answered Johnnie, "and I don't give a damn where you've been. All I got to say is that I don't know what you're driving at. There hain't never been nobody killed in this room."

The cowboy, who had been steadily gazing at the Swede, then spoke: "What's wrong with you, mister?"

Apparently it seemed to the Swede that he was formidably menaced. He shivered and turned white near the corners of his mouth. He sent an appealing glance in the direction of the little Easterner. During these moments he did not forget to wear his air of advanced pot-valor. "They say they don't know what I mean," he remarked mockingly to the Easterner.

The latter answered after prolonged and cautious reflection. "I don't understand you," he said, impassively.

The Swede made a movement then which announced that he thought he had encountered treachery from the only quarter where he had expected sympathy, if not help. "Oh, I see you are all against me. I see—"

The cowboy was in a state of deep stupefaction. "Say," he cried, as he tumbled the deck violently down upon the board, "say, what are you gittin' at, hey?"

The Swede sprang up with the celerity of a man escaping from a snake on the floor. "I don't want to fight!" he shouted. "I don't want to fight!"

The cowboy stretched his long legs indolently and deliberately. His hands were in his pockets. He spat into the sawdust-box. "Well, who the hell thought you did?" he inquired.

The Swede backed rapidly toward a corner of the room. His hands were out protectingly in front of his chest, but he was making an obvious struggle to control his fright. "Gentlemen," he quavered, "I suppose I am going to be killed before I can leave this house! I suppose I am going to be killed before I can leave this house!" In his eyes was the dying-swan look. Through the windows could be seen the snow turning blue in the shadow of dusk. The wind tore at the house, and some loose thing beat regularly against the clapboards like a spirit tapping.

A door opened, and Scully himself entered. He paused in surprise as he noted the tragic attitude of the Swede. Then he said, "What's the matter here?"

The Swede answered him swiftly and eagerly: "These men are going to kill me."

"Kill you!" ejaculated Scully. "Kill you! What are you talkin'?"

The Swede made the gesture of a martyr.

Scully wheeled sternly upon his son. "What is this, Johnnie?"

The lad had grown sullen. "Damned if I know," he answered. "I can't make no sense to it." He began to shuffle the cards, fluttering them together with an angry snap. "He says a good many men have been killed in this room, or something like that. And he says he's goin' to be killed here too. I don't know what ails him. He's crazy, I shouldn't wonder."

Scully then looked for explanation to the cowboy, but the cowboy simply shrugged his shoulders.

"Kill you?" said Scully again to the Swede. "Kill you? Man, you're off your nut."

"Oh, I know," burst out the Swede. "I know what will happen. Yes, I'm crazy—yes. Yes, of course, I'm crazy—yes. But I know one thing—" There was a sort of sweat of misery and terror upon his face. "I know I won't get out of here alive."

The cowboy drew a deep breath, as if his mind was passing into the last stages of dissolution. "Well, I'm doggoned," he whispered to himself.

Scully wheeled suddenly and faced his son. "You've been troublin' this man!"

Johnnie's voice was loud with its burden of grievance. "Why, good Gawd, I ain't done nothin' to 'im."

The Swede broke in. "Gentlemen, do not disturb yourselves. I will leave this house. I will go away, because"—he accused them dramatically with his glance—"because I do not want to be killed."

Scully was furious with his son. "Will you tell me what is the matter, you young devil? What's the matter, anyhow? Speak out!"

"Blame it!" cried Johnnie in despair, "don't I tell you I don't know? He—he says we want to kill him, and that's all I know. I can't tell what ails him."

The Swede continued to repeat: "Never mind, Mr. Scully; never mind. I will leave this house. I will go away, because I do not wish to be killed. Yes, of course, I am crazy—yes. But I know one thing! I will go away. I will leave this house. Never mind, Mr. Scully; never mind. I will go away."

"You will not go 'way," said Scully. "You will not go 'way until I hear the reason of this business. If anybody has troubled you I will take care of him. This is my house. You are under my roof, and I will not allow any peaceable man to be troubled here." He cast a terrible eye upon Johnnie, the cowboy, and the Easterner.

"Never mind, Mr. Scully; never mind. I will go away.

I do not wish to be killed." The Swede moved toward the door which opened upon the stairs. It was evidently his intention to go at once for his baggage.

"No, no," shouted Scully peremptorily; but the white-faced man slid by him and disappeared. "Now," said Scully severely, "what does this mane?"

Johnnie and the cowboy cried together: "Why, we didn't do nothin' to 'im!"

Scully's eyes were cold. "No," he said, "you didn't?"

Johnnie swore a deep oath. "Why, this is the wildest loon I ever see. We didn't do nothin' at all. We were just sittin' here playin' cards, and he—"

The father suddenly spoke to the Easterner. "Mr. Blanc," he asked, "what has these boys been doin'?"

The Easterner reflected again. "I didn't see anything wrong at all," he said at last, slowly.

Scully began to howl. "But what does it mane?" He stared ferociously at his son. "I have a mind to lather you for this, me boy."

Johnnie was frantic. "Well, what have I done?" he bawled at his father.

3

"I think you are tongue-tied," said Scully finally to his son, the cowboy, and the Easterner; and at the end of this scornful sentence he left the room.

Upstairs the Swede was swiftly fastening the straps of his great valise. Once his back happened to be half turned toward the door, and, hearing a noise there, he wheeled and sprang up, uttering a loud cry. Scully's wrinkled visage showed grimly in the light of the small lamp he carried. This yellow effulgence, streaming upward, colored only his prominent features, and left his eyes, for instance, in mysterious shadow. He resembled a murderer.

"Man! man!" he exclaimed, "have you gone daffy?"

"Oh, no! Oh, no!" rejoined the other. "There are people in this world who know pretty nearly as much as you do—understand?"

For a moment they stood gazing at each other. Upon

the Swede's deathly pale cheeks were two spots brightly crimson and sharply edged, as if they had been carefully painted. Scully placed the light on the table and sat himself on the edge of the bed. He spoke ruminatively "By cracky, I never heard of such a thing in my life. It's a complete muddle. I can't, for the soul of me, think how you ever got this idea into your head." Presently he lifted his eyes and asked: "And did you sure think they were going to kill you?"

The Swede scanned the old man as if he wished to see into his mind. "I did," he said at last. He obviously suspected that this answer might precipitate an outbreak. As he pulled on a strap his whole arm shook, the elbow wavering like a bit of paper.

Scully banged his hand impressively on the footboard of the bed. "Why, man, we're goin' to have a line of ilictric street-cars in this town next spring."

" 'A line of electric street-cars,' " repeated the Swede, stupidly.

"And," said Scully, "there's a new railroad goin' to be built down from Broken Arm to here. Not to mintion the four churches and the smashin' big brick schoolhouse. Then there's the big factory, too. Why, in two years Romper'll be a met-tro-*pol*-is."

Having finished the preparation of his baggage, the Swede straightened himself. "Mr. Scully," he said, with sudden hardihood, "how much do I owe you?"

"You don't owe me anythin'," said the old man, angrily.

"Yes, I do," retorted the Swede. He took seventy-five cents from his pocket and tendered it to Scully; but the latter snapped his fingers in disdainful refusal. However, it happened that they both stood gazing in a strange fashion at three silver pieces on the Swede's open palm.

"I'll not take your money," said Scully at last. "Not after what's been goin' on here." Then a plan seemed to strike him. "Here," he cried, picking up his lamp and moving toward the door. "Here! Come with me a minute."

"No," said the Swede, in overwhelming alarm.

"Yes," urged the old man. "Come on! I want you to come and see a picter—just across the hall—in my room."

The Swede must have concluded that his hour was come. His jaw dropped and his teeth showed like a dead man's. He ultimately followed Scully across the corridor, but he had the step of one hung in chains.

Scully flashed the light high on the wall of his own chamber. There was revealed a ridiculous photograph of a little girl. She was leaning against a balustrade of gorgeous decoration, and the formidable bang to her hair was prominent. The figure was as graceful as an upright sled-stake, and, withal, it was of the hue of lead. "There," said Scully, tenderly, "that's the picter of my little girl that died. Her name was Carrie. She had the purtiest hair you ever saw. I was that fond of her, she—"

Turning then, he saw that the Swede was not contemplating the picture at all, but, instead, was keeping keen watch on the gloom in the rear.

"Look, man!" cried Scully, heartily. "That's the picter of my little gal that died. Her name was Carrie. And then here's the picter of my oldest boy, Michael. He's a lawyer in Lincoln, an' doin' well. I gave that boy a grand eddication, and I'm glad for it now. He's a fine boy. Look at 'im now. Ain't he bold as blazes, him there in Lincoln, an honored an' respicted gintleman! An honored and respicted gintleman," concluded Scully with a flourish. And, so saying, he smote the Swede jovially on the back.

The Swede faintly smiled.

"Now," said the old man, "there's only one more thing." He dropped suddenly to the floor and thrust his hand beneath the bed. The Swede could hear his muffled voice. "I'd keep it under me piller if it wasn't for that boy Johnnie. Then there's the old woman—Where is it now? I never put it twice in the same place. Ah, now come out with you!"

Presently he backed clumsily from under the bed, dragging with him an old coat rolled into a bundle. "I've fetched him," he muttered. Kneeling on the floor, he unrolled the coat and extracted from its heart a large yellow-brown whisky-bottle.

His first maneuver was to hold the bottle up to the light. Reassured, apparently, that nobody had been tampering with it, he thrust it with a generous movement toward the Swede.

The weak-kneed Swede was about to eagerly clutch this element of strength, but he suddenly jerked his hand away and cast a look of horror upon Scully.

"Drink," said the old man affectionately. He had risen to his feet, and now stood facing the Swede.

There was a silence. Then again Scully said: "Drink!"

The Swede laughed wildly. He grabbed the bottle, put it to his mouth; and as his lips curled absurdly around the opening and his throat worked, he kept his glance, burning with hatred, upon the old man's face.

4

After the departure of Scully the three men, with the cardboard still upon their knees, preserved for a long time an astounded silence. Then Johnnie said: "That's the dad-dangedest Swede I ever see."

"He ain't no Swede," said the cowboy, scornfully.

"Well, what is he then?" cried Johnnie. "What is he then?"

"It's my opinion," replied the cowboy deliberately, "he's some kind of a Dutchman." It was a venerable custom of the country to entitle as Swedes all light-haired men who spoke with a heavy tongue. In consequence the idea of the cowboy was not without its daring. "Yes, sir," he repeated. "It's my opinion this feller is some kind of a Dutchman."

"Well, he says he's a Swede, anyhow," muttered Johnnie, sulkily. He turned to the Easterner: "What do you think, Mr. Blanc?"

"Oh, I don't know," replied the Easterner.

"Well, what do you think makes him act that way?" asked the cowboy.

"Why, he's frightened." The Easterner knocked his pipe against a rim of the stove. "He's clear frightened out of his boots."

"What at?" cried Johnnie and the cowboy together.

The Easterner reflected over his answer.

"What at?" cried the others again.

"Oh, I don't know, but it seems to me this man has been reading dime novels, and he thinks he's right out in the middle of it—the shootin' and stabbin' and all."

"But," said the cowboy, deeply scandalized, "this ain't Wyoming, ner none of them places. This is Nebrasker."

"Yes," added Johnnie, "an' why don't he wait till he gits *out West?*"

The traveled Easterner laughed. "It isn't different there even—not in these days. But he thinks he's right in the middle of hell."

Johnnie and the cowboy mused long.

"It's awful funny," remarked Johnnie at last.

"Yes," said the cowboy. "This is a queer game. I hope we don't git snowed in, because they we'd have to stand this here man bein' around with us all the time. That wouldn't be no good."

"I wish pop would throw him out," said Johnnie.

Presently they heard a loud stamping on the stairs, accompanied by ringing jokes in the voice of old Scully, and laughter, evidently from the Swede. The men around the stove stared vacantly at each other. "Gosh!" said the cowboy. The door flew open, and old Scully, flushed and anecdotal, came into the room. He was jabbering at the Swede, who followed him, laughing bravely. It was the entry of two roisterers from a banquet hall.

"Come now," said Scully sharply to the three seated men, "move up and give us a chance at the stove." The cowboy and the Easterner obediently sidled their chairs to make room for the newcomers. Johnnie, however, simply arranged himself in a more indolent attitude, and then remained motionless.

"Come! Git over, there," said Scully.

"Plenty of room on the other side of the stove," said Johnnie.

"Do you think we want to sit in the draught?" roared the father.

But the Swede here interposed with a grandeur of confidence. "No, no. Let the boy sit where he likes," he cried in a bullying voice to the father.

"All right! All right!" said Scully, deferentially. The cowboy and the Easterner exchanged glances of wonder.

The five chairs were formed in a crescent about one side of the stove. The Swede began to talk; he talked arrogantly, profanely, angrily. Johnnie, the cowboy, and the Easterner maintained a morose silence, while old Scully appeared to be receptive and eager, breaking in constantly with sympathetic ejaculations.

Finally the Swede announced that he was thirsty. He moved in his chair, and said that he would go for a drink of water.

"I'll git it for you," cried Scully at once.

"No," said the Swede, contemptuously. "I'll get it for myself." He arose and stalked with the air of an owner off into the executive parts of the hotel.

As soon as the Swede was out of hearing Scully sprang to his feet and whispered intensely to the others: "Upstairs he thought I was tryin' to poison 'im."

"Say," said Johnnie, "this makes me sick. Why don't you throw 'im out in the snow?"

"Why, he's all right now," declared Scully. "It was only that he was from the East, and he thought this was a tough place. That's all. He's all right now."

The cowboy looked with admiration upon the Easterner. "You were straight," he said. "You were on to that there Dutchman."

"Well," said Johnnie to his father, "he may be all right now, but I don't see it. Other time he was scared, but now he's too fresh."

Scully's speech was always a combination of Irish brogue and idiom, Western twang and idiom, and scraps of curiously formal diction taken from the story-books and newspapers. He now hurled a strange mass of language at the head of his son. "What do I keep? What do I keep? What do I keep?" he demanded, in a voice of thunder. He slapped his knee impressively, to indicate that he himself was going to make reply, and that all should heed. "I keep a hotel," he shouted. "A hotel, do you mind? A guest under my roof has sacred privileges. He is to be intimidated by none. Not one word shall he hear that would prijudice him in favor of goin' away. I'll not have it. There's no place in this here town where they can say they iver took in a guest of mine because he was afraid to stay here." He wheeled suddenly upon the cowboy and the Easterner. "Am I right?"

"Yes, Mr. Scully," said the cowboy, "I think you're right."

"Yes, Mr. Scully," said the Easterner, "I think you're right."

5

At six-o'clock supper, the Swede fizzed like a fire-wheel. He sometimes seemed on the point of bursting into riotous song, and in all his madness he was encouraged by old Scully. The Easterner was encased in reserve; the cowboy sat in wide-mouthed amazement, forgetting to eat, while Johnnie wrathily demolished great plates of food. The daughters of the house, when they were obliged to replenish the biscuits, approached as warily as Indians, and, having succeeded in their purpose, fled with ill-concealed trepidation. The Swede domineered the whole feast, and he gave it the appearance of a cruel bacchanal. He seemed to have grown suddenly taller; he gazed, brutally disdainful, into every face. His voice rang through the room. Once when he jabbed out harpoon-fashion with his fork to pinion a biscuit, the weapon nearly impaled the hand of the Easterner, which had been stretched quietly out for the same biscuit.

After supper, as the men filed toward the other room, the Swede smote Scully ruthlessly on the shoulder. "Well, old boy, that was a good, square meal." Johnnie looked hopefully at his father; he knew that shoulder was tender from an old fall; and, indeed, it appeared for a moment as if Scully was going to flame out over the matter, but in the end he smiled a sickly smile and remained silent. The others understood from his manner that he was admitting his responsibility for the Swede's new viewpoint.

Johnnie, however, addressed his parent in an aside.

"Why don't you license somebody to kick you down-stairs?" Scully scowled darkly by way of reply.

When they were gathered about the stove, the Swede insisted on another game of High-Five. Scully gently deprecated the plan at first, but the Swede turned a wolf-ish glare upon him. The old man subsided, and the Swede canvassed the others. In his tone there was always a great threat. The cowboy and the Easterner both remarked indifferently that they would play. Scully said that he would presently have to go to meet the 6.58 train, and so the Swede turned menacingly upon Johnnie. For a moment their glances crossed like blades, and then John-nie smiled and said, "Yes, I'll play."

They formed a square, with the little board on their knees. The Easterner and the Swede were again partners. As the play went on, it was noticeable that the cowboy was not board-whacking as usual. Meanwhile, Scully, near the lamp, had put on his spectacles and, with an appear-ance curiously like an old priest, was reading a newspaper. In time he went out to meet the 6.58 train, and, despite his precautions, a gust of polar wind whirled into the room as he opened the door. Besides scattering the cards, it chilled the players to the marrow. The Swede cursed frightfully. When Scully returned, his entrance disturbed a cozy and friendly scene. The Swede again cursed. But presently they were once more intent, their heads bent forward and their hands moving swiftly. The Swede had adopted the fashion of board-whacking.

Scully took up his paper and for a long time remained immersed in matters which were extraordinarily remote from him. The lamp burned badly, and once he stopped to adjust the wick. The newspaper, as he turned from page to page, rustled with a slow and comfortable sound. Then suddenly he heard three terrible words: "You are cheatin'!"

Such scenes often prove that there can be little of dra-matic import in environment. Any room can present a tragic front; any room can be comic. This little den was now hideous as a torture-chamber. The new faces of the men themselves had changed it upon the instant The Swede held a huge fist in front of Johnnie's face, while the latter looked steadily over it into the blazing orbs of his accuser. The Easterner had grown pallid; the cowboy's jaw had dropped in that expression of bovine amazement which was one of his important mannerisms. After the three words, the first sound in the room was made by Scully's paper as it floated forgotten to his feet. His spectacles had also fallen from his nose, but by a clutch he had saved them in air. His hand, grasping the spectacles, now remained poised awkwardly and near his shoulder. He stared at the card-players.

Probably the silence was while a second elapsed. Then, if the floor had been suddenly twitched out from under the men they could not have moved quicker. The five had projected themselves headlong toward a common point. It happened that Johnnie, in rising to hurl himself upon the Swede, had stumbled slightly because of his curiously instinctive care for the cards and the board. The loss of the moment allowed time for the arrival of Scully, and also allowed the cowboy time to give the Swede a great push which sent him staggering back. The men found tongue together, and hoarse shouts of rage, appeal, or fear burst from every throat. The cowboy pushed and jostled feverishly at the Swede, and the Easterner and Scully clung wildly to Johnnie; but through the smoky air, above the swaying bodies of the peace-compellers, the eyes of the two warriors ever sought each other in glances of challenge that were at once hot and steely.

Of course the board had been overturned, and now the whole company of cards was scattered over the floor, where the boots of the men trampled the fat and painted kings and queens as they gazed with their silly eyes at the war that was waging above them.

Scully's voice was dominating the yells. "Stop now! Stop, I say! Stop, now—"

Johnnie, as he struggled to burst through the rank formed by Scully and the Easterner, was crying, "Well, he says I cheated! He says I cheated! I won't allow no

man to say I cheated! If he says I cheated, he's a————
————!"

The cowboy was telling the Swede, "Quit, now! Quit, d'ye hear——"

The screams of the Swede never ceased: "He did cheat! I saw him! I saw him——"

As for the Easterner, he was importuning in a voice that was not heeded: "Wait a moment, can't you? Oh, wait a moment. What's the good of a fight over a game of cards? Wait a moment——"

In this tumult no complete sentences were clear. "Cheat"—"Quit"—"He says"—these fragments pierced the uproar and rang out sharply. It was remarkable that, whereas Scully undoubtedly made the most noise, he was the least heard of any of the riotous band.

Then suddenly there was a great cessation. It was as if each man had paused for breath; and although the room was still lighted with the anger of men, it could be seen that there was no danger of immediate conflict, and at once Johnnie, shouldering his way forward, almost succeeded in confronting the Swede. "What did you say I cheated for? What did you say I cheated for? I don't cheat, and I won't let no man say I do!"

The Swede said, "I saw you! I saw you!"

"Well," cried Johnnie, "I'll fight any man what says I cheat!"

"No, you won't," said the cowboy. "Not here."

"Ah, be still, can't you?" said Scully, coming between them.

The quiet was sufficient to allow the Easterner's voice to be heard. He was repeating, "Oh, wait a moment, can't you? What's the good of a fight over a game of cards? Wait a moment!"

Johnnie, his red face appearing above his father's shoulder, hailed the Swede again. "Did you say I cheated?"

The Swede showed his teeth. "Yes."

"Then," said Johnnie, "we must fight."

"Yes, fight," roared the Swede. He was like a demoniac.

"Yes, fight! I'll show you what kind of a man I am! I'll show you who you want to fight! Maybe you think I can't fight! Maybe you think I can't! I'll show you, you skin, you card-sharp. Yes, you cheated! You cheated! You cheated!"

"Well, let's go at it, then, mister," said Johnnie, coolly.

The cowboy's brow was beaded with sweat from his efforts in intercepting all sorts of raids. He turned in despair to Scully. "What are you goin' to do now?"

A change had come over the Celtic visage of the old man. He now seemed all eagerness; his eyes glowed.

"We'll let them fight," he answered, stalwartly. "I can't put up with it any longer. I've stood this damned Swede till I'm sick. We'll let them fight."

6

The men prepared to go out of doors. The Easterner was so nervous that he had great difficulty in getting his arms into the sleeves of his new leather coat. As the cowboy drew his fur cap down over his ears his hands trembled. In fact, Johnnie and old Scully were the only ones who displayed no agitation. These preliminaries were conducted wthout words.

Scully threw open the door. "Well, come on," he said. Instantly a terrific wind caused the flame of the lamp to struggle at its wick, while a puff of black smoke sprang from the chimney-top. The stove was in mid-current of the blast, and its voice swelled to equal the roar of the storm. Some of the scarred and bedabbled cards were caught up from the floor and dashed helplessly against the farther wall. The men lowered their heads and plunged into the tempest as into a sea.

No snow was falling, but great whirls and clouds of flakes, swept up from the ground by the frantic winds, were streaming southward with the speed of bullets. The covered land was blue with the sheen of an unearthly satin, and there was no other hue save where, at the low, black railway station—which seemed incredibly distant— one light gleamed like a tiny jewel. As the men floundered into a thigh-deep drift, it was known that the Swede was bawling out something. Scully went to him, put a hand on his shoulder, and projected an ear. "What's that you say?" he shouted.

"I say," bawled the Swede again, "I won't stand much show against this gang. I know you'll all pitch on me."

Scully smote him reproachfully on the arm. "Tut, man!" he yelled. The wind tore the words from Scully's lips and scattered them far alee.

"You are all a gang of—" boomed the Swede, but the storm also seized the remainder of this sentence.

Immediately turning their backs upon the wind, the men had swung around a corner to the sheltered side of the hotel. It was the function of the little house to preserve here, amid this great devastation of snow, an irregular V-shape of heavily encrusted grass, which crackled beneath the feet. One could imagine the great drifts piled against the windward side. When the party reached the comparative peace of this spot it was found that the Swede was still bellowing.

"Oh, I know what kind of a thing this is! I know you'll all pitch on me. I can't lick you all!"

Scully turned upon him panther-fashion. "You'll not have to whip all of us. You'll have to whip my son Johnnie. An' the man what troubles you durin' that time will have me to deal with."

The arrangements were swiftly made. The two men faced each other, obedient to the harsh commands of Scully, whose face, in the subtly luminous gloom, could be seen set in the austere impersonal lines that are pictured on the countenances of the Roman veterans. The Easterner's teeth were chattering, and he was hopping up and down like a mechanical toy. The cowboy stood rocklike.

The contestants had not stripped off any clothing, Each was in his ordinary attire. Their fists were up, and they eyed each other in a calm that had the elements of leonine cruelty in it.

During this pause, the Easterner's mind, like a film, took lasting impressions of three men—the iron-nerved master of the ceremony; the Swede, pale, motionless, terrible; and Johnnie, serene yet ferocious, brutish yet heroic. The entire prelude had in it a tragedy greater than the tragedy of action, and this aspect was accentuated by the long, mellow cry of the blizzard, as it sped the tumbling and wailing flakes into the black abyss of the south.

"Now!" said Scully.

The two combatants leaped forward and crashed together like bullocks. There was heard the cushioned sound of blows, and of a curse squeezing out from between the tight teeth of one.

As for the spectators, the Easterner's pent-up breath exploded from him with a pop of relief, absolute relief from the tension of the preliminaries. The cowboy bounded into the air with a yowl. Scully was immovable as from supreme amazement and fear at the fury of the fight which he himself had permitted and arranged.

For a time the encounter in the darkness was such a perplexity of flying arms that it presented no more detail than would a swiftly revolving wheel. Occasionally a face, as if illumined by a flash of light, would shine out, ghastly and marked with pink spots. A moment later, the men might have been known as shadows, if it were not for the involuntary utterance of oaths that came from them in whispers.

Suddenly a holocaust of warlike desire caught the cowboy, and he bolted forward with the speed of a bronco. "Go it, Johnnie! go it! Kill him! Kill him!"

Scully confronted him. "Kape back," he said; and by his glance the cowboy could tell that this man was Johnnie's father.

To the Easterner there was a monotony of unchangeable fighting that was an abomination. This confused mingling was eternal to his sense, which was concentrated in a longing for the end, the priceless end. Once the fighters lurched near him, and as he scrambled hastily backward he heard them breathe like men on the rack.

"Kill him, Johnnie! Kill him! Kill him! Kill him!" The cowboy's face was contorted like one of those agony masks in museums.

"Keep still," said Scully, icily.

Then there was a sudden loud grunt, incomplete, cut short, and Johnnie's body swung away from the Swede and fell with sickening heaviness to the grass. The cowboy was barely in time to prevent the mad Swede from flinging himself upon his prone adversary. "No, you don't," said the cowboy, interposing an arm. "Wait a second."

Scully was at his son's side. "Johnnie! Johnnie, me boy!" His voice had a quality of melancholy tenderness. "Johnnie! Can you go on with it?" He looked anxiously down into the bloody, pulpy face of his son.

There was a moment of silence, and then Johnnie answered in his ordinary voice. "Yes, I—it—yes."

Assisted by his father he struggled to his feet. "Wait a bit now till you git your wind," said the old man.

A few paces away the cowboy was lecturing the Swede. "No, you don't! Wait a second!"

The Easterner was plucking at Scully's sleeve. "Oh, this is enough," he pleaded. "This is enough! Let it go as it stands. This is enough!"

"Bill," said Scully, "git out of the road." The cowboy stepped aside. "Now." The combatants were actuated by a new caution as they advanced toward collision. They glared at each other, and then the Swede aimed a lightning blow that carried with it his entire weight. Johnnie was evidently half stupid from weakness, but he miraculously dodged, and his fist sent the overbalanced Swede sprawling.

The cowboy, Scully, and the Easterner burst into a cheer that was like a chorus of triumphant soldiery, but before its conclusion the Swede had scuffed agilely to his feet and come in berserk abandon at his foe. There was another perplexity of flying arms, and Johnnie's body again swung away and fell, even as a bundle might fall from a roof. The Swede instantly staggered to a little wind-waved tree and leaned upon it, breathing like an engine, while his savage and flame-lit eyes roamed from face to face as the men bent over Johnnie. There was a splendor of isolation in his situation at this time which the Easterner felt once when, lifting his eyes from the man on the ground, he beheld that mysterious and lonely figure, waiting.

"Are you any good yet, Johnnie?" asked Scully in a broken voice.

The son gasped and opened his eyes languidly. After a moment he answered, "No—I ain't—any good—any—more." Then from shame and bodily ill, he began to weep, the tears furrowing down through the blood-stains on his face. "He was too—too—heavy for me."

Scully straightened and addressed the waiting figure. "Stranger," he said, evenly, "it's all up with our side." Then his voice changed into that vibrant huskiness which is commonly the tone of the most simple and deadly announcements. "Johnnie is whipped."

Without replying, the victor moved off on the route to the front door of the hotel.

The cowboy was formulating new and unspellable blasphemies. The Easterner was startled to find that they were out in a wind that seemed to come direct from the shadowed arctic floes. He heard again the wail of the snow as it was flung to its grave in the south. He knew now that all this time the cold had been sinking into him deeper and deeper, and he wondered that he had not perished. He felt indifferent to the condition of the vanquished man.

"Johnnie, can you walk?" asked Scully.

"Did I hurt—hurt him any?" asked the son.

"Can you walk, boy? Can you walk?"

Johnnie's voice was suddenly strong. There was a robust impatience in it. "I asked you whether I hurt him any!"

"Yes, yes, Johnnie," answered the cowboy, consolingly; "he's hurt a good deal."

They raised him from the ground, and as soon as he was on his feet he went tottering off, rebuffing all attempts at assistance. When the party rounded the corner they were fairly blinded by the pelting of the snow. It burned their faces like fire. The cowboy carried Johnnie through the drift to the door. As they entered, some cards rose from the floor and beat against the wall.

The Easterner rushed to the stove. He was so profoundly chilled that he almost dared to embrace the glowing iron. The Swede was not in the room. Johnnie sank into a chair and, folding his arms on his knees, buried his face in them. Scully, warming one foot and then the other at the rim of the stove, muttered to himself with Celtic mournfulness. The cowboy had removed his fur cap, and with a dazed and rueful air he was running one hand through his tousled locks. From overhead they could hear the creaking of boards, as the Swede tramped here and there in his room.

The sad quiet was broken by the sudden flinging open of a door that led toward the kitchen. It was instantly followed by an inrush of women. They precipitated themselves upon Johnnie amid a chorus of lamentation. Before they carried their prey off to the kitchen, there to be bathed and harangued with that mixture of sympathy and abuse which is a feat of their sex, the mother straightened herself and fixed old Scully with an eye of stern reproach. "Shame be upon you, Patrick Scully!" she cried: "Your own son, too. Shame be upon you!"

"There, now! Be quiet, now!" said the old man, weakly.

"Shame be upon you, Patrick Scully!" she cried. "Your to this slogan, sniffed disdainfully in the direction of those trembling accomplices, the cowboy and the Easterner. Presently they bore Johnnie away, and left the three men to dismal reflection.

7

"I'd like to fight this here Dutchman myself," said the cowboy, breaking a long silence.

Scully wagged his head sadly. "No, that wouldn't do. It wouldn't be right. It wouldn't be right."

"Well, why wouldn't it?" argued the cowboy. "I don't see no harm in it."

"No," answered Scully, with mournful heroism. "It wouldn't be right. It was Johnnie's fight, and now we mustn't whip the man just because he whipped Johnnie."

"Yes, that's true enough," said the cowboy: "but—he

better not get fresh with me, because I couldn't stand no more of it."

"You'll not say a word to him," commanded Scully, and even then they heard the tread of the Swede on the stairs. His entrance was made theatric. He swept the door back with a bang and swaggered to the middle of the room. No one looked at him. "Well," he cried, insolently, at Scully, "I s'pose you'll tell me now how much I owe you?"

The old man remained stolid. "You don't owe me nothin'."

"Huh!" said the Swede, "huh! Don't owe 'im nothin'."

The cowboy addressed the Swede. "Stranger, I don't see how you come to be so gay around here."

Old Scully was instantly alert. "Stop!" he shouted, holding his hand forth, fingers upward. "Bill, you shut up!"

The cowboy spat carelessly into the sawdust-box. "I didn't say a word, did I?" he asked.

"Mr. Scully," called the Swede, "how much do I owe you?" It was seen that he was attired for departure, and that he had his valise in his hand.

"You don't owe me nothin'," repeated Scully in the same imperturbable way.

"Huh!" said the Swede. "I guess you're right. I guess if it was any way at all, you'd owe me somethin'. That's what I guess." He turned to the cowboy. " 'Kill him! Kill him! Kill him!' " he mimicked, and then guffawed victoriously. " 'Kill him!' " He was convulsed with ironical humor.

But he might have been jeering the dead. The three men were immovable and silent, staring with glassy eyes at the stove.

The Swede opened the door and passed into the storm, giving one derisive glance backward at the still group.

As soon as the door was closed, Scully and the cowboy leaped to their feet and began to curse. They trampled to and fro, waving their arms and smashing into the air with their fists. "Oh, but that was a hard minute!" wailed Scully. "That was a hard minute! Him there leerin' and scoffin'! One bang at his nose was worth forty dollars to me that minute! How did you stand it, Bill?"

"How did I stand it?" cried the cowboy in a quivering voice. "How did I stand it? Oh!"

The old man burst into sudden brogue. "I'd loike to take that Swade," he wailed, "and hould 'im down on a shtone flure and bate 'im to a jelly wid a shtick!"

The cowboy groaned in sympathy. "I'd like to git him by the neck and ha-ammer him"—he brought his hand down on a chair with a noise like a pistol-shot—"hammer that there Dutchman until he couldn't tell himself from a dead coyote!"

"I'd bate 'im until he—"

"I'd show *him* some things—"

And then together they raised a yearning, fantastic cry—"Oh-o-oh! if we only could—"

"Yes!"

"Yes!"

"And then I'd—"

"O-o-oh!"

8

The Swede, tightly gripping his valise, tacked across the face of the storm as if he carried sails. He was following a line of little naked, grasping trees which, he knew, must mark the way of the road. His face, fresh from the pounding of Johnnie's fists, felt more pleasure than pain in the wind and the driving snow. A number of square shapes loomed upon him finally, and he knew them as the houses of the main body of the town. He found a street and made travel along it, leaning heavily upon the wind whenever, at a corner, a terrific blast caught him.

He might have been in a deserted village. We picture the world as thick with conquering and elate humanity, but here, with the bugles of the tempest pealing, it was hard to imagine a peopled earth. One viewed the existence of man then as a marvel, and conceded a glamour of wonder to these lice which were caused to cling to a whirling, fire-smitten, ice-locked, disease-stricken, space-lost bulb. The conceit of man was explained by this storm to be the very engine of life. One was a coxcomb not to die in it. However, the Swede found a saloon.

In front of it an indomitable red light was burning, and the snowflakes were made blood-color as they flew through the circumscribed territory of the lamp's shining. The Swede pushed open the door of the saloon and entered. A sanded expanse was before him, and at the end of it four men sat about a table drinking. Down one side of the room extended a radiant bar, and its guardian was leaning upon his elbows listening to the talk of the men at the table. The Swede dropped his valise upon the floor and, smiling fraternally upon the barkeeper, said, "Gimme some whisky, will you?" The man placed a bottle, a whisky-glass, and a glass of ice-thick water upon the bar. The Swede poured himself an abnormal portion of whisky and drank it in three gulps. "Pretty bad night," remarked the bartender, indifferently. He was making the pretension of blindness which is usually a distinction of his class; but it could have been seen that he was furtively studying the half-erased blood-stains on the face of the Swede. "Bad night," he said again.

"Oh, it's good enough for me," replied the Swede, hardily, as he poured himself some more whisky. The barkeeper took his coin and maneuvered it through its reception by a highly nickeled cash-machine. A bell rang; a card labeled "20 cts." had appeared.

"No," continued the Swede, "this isn't too bad weather. It's good enough for me."

"So?" murmured the barkeeper, languidly.

The copious drams made the Swede's eyes swim, and he breathed a trifle heavier. "Yes, I like this weather. I like it. It suits me." It was apparently his design to impart a deep significance to these words.

"So?" murmured the bartender again. He turned to gaze dreamily at the scroll-like birds and bird-like scrolls which had been drawn with soap upon the mirrors in back of the bar.

"Well, I guess I'll take another drink," said the Swede, presently, "Have something?"

"No, thanks; I'm not drinkin'," answered the bartender. Afterward he asked, "How did you hurt your face?"

The Swede immediately began to boast loudly. "Why, in a fight. I thumped the soul out of a man down here at Scully's hotel."

The interest of the four men at the table was at last aroused.

"Who was it?" said one.

"Johnnie Scully," blustered the Swede. "Son of the man what runs it. He will be pretty near dead for some weeks, I can tell you. I made a nice thing of him, I did. He couldn't get up. They carried him in the house. Have a drink?"

Instantly the men in some subtle way encased themselves in reserve. "No, thanks," said one. The group was of curious formation. Two were prominent local business men; one was the district attorney; and one was a professional gambler of the kind known as "square." But a scrutiny of the group would not have enabled an observer to pick the gambler from the men of more reputable pursuits. He was, in fact, a man so delicate in manner, when among people of fair class, and so judicious in his choice of victims, that in the strictly masculine part of the town's life he had come to be explicitly trusted and admired. People called him a thoroughbred. The fear and contempt with which his craft was regarded were undoubtedly the reason why his quiet dignity shone conspicuous above the quiet dignity of men who might be merely hatters, billiard-markers, or grocery clerks. Beyond an occasionally unwary traveler who came by rail, this gambler was supposed to prey solely upon reckless and senile farmers, who, when flush with good crops, drove into town in all the pride and confidence of an absolutely invulnerable stupidity. Hearing at times in circuitous fashion of the despoilment of such a farmer, the important men of Romper invariably laughed in contempt of the victim, and if they thought of the wolf at all, it was with a kind of pride at the knowledge that he would never dare think of attacking their wisdom and courage. Besides, it was popular that this gambler had a real wife and two real children in a neat cottage in a suburb, where he led an exemplary home life; and when any one even suggested a discrepancy in his character, the crowd immediately vociferated descriptions of this virtuous family circle. Then men who led exemplary home lives, and men who did not lead exemplary home lives, all subsided in a bunch, remarking that there was nothing more to be said.

However, when a restriction was placed upon him—as, for instance, when a strong clique of members of the new Polywog Club refused to permit him, even as a spectator, to appear in the rooms of the organization—the candor and gentleness with which he accepted the judgment disarmed many of his foes and made his friends more desperately partisan. He invariably distinguished between himself and a respectable Romper man so quickly and frankly that his manner actually appeared to be a continual broadcast compliment.

And one must not forget to declare the fundamental fact of his entire position in Romper. It is irrefutable that in all affairs outside his business, in all matters that occur eternally and commonly between man and man, this thieving card-player was so generous, so just, so moral, that, in a contest, he could have put to flight the consciences of nine-tenths of the citizens of Romper.

And so it happened that he was seated in this saloon with the two prominent local merchants and the district attorney.

The Swede continued to drink raw whisky, meanwhile babbling at the barkeeper and trying to induce him to indulge in potations. "Come on. Have a drink. Come on. What—no? Well, have a little one, then. By gawd, I've whipped a man tonight, and I want to celebrate. I whipped him good, too. Gentlemen," the Swede cried to the men at the table. "have a drink?"

"Ssh!" said the barkeeper.

The group at the table, although furtively attentive, had been pretending to be deep in talk, but now a man lifted his eyes toward the Swede and said, shortly, "Thanks. We don't want any more."

At this reply the Swede ruffled out his chest like a

rooster. "Well," he exploded, "it seems I can't get any-body to drink with me in this town. Seems so, don't it? Well!"

"Ssh!" said the barkeeper.

"Say," snarled the Swede, "don't you try to shut me up. I won't have it. I'm a gentleman, and I want people to drink with me. And I want 'em to drink with me now. *Now*—do you understand?" He rapped the bar with his knuckles.

Years of experience had calloused the bartender. He merely grew sulky. "I hear you," he answered.

"Well," cried the Swede, "listen hard then. See those men over there? Well, they're going to drink with me, and don't you forget it. Now you watch."

"Hi!" yelled the barkeeper, "this won't do!"

"Why won't it?" demanded the Swede. He stalked over to the table, and by chance laid his hand upon the shoulder of the gambler. "How about this?" he asked wrath-fully. "I asked you to drink with me."

The gambler simply twisted his head and spoke over his shoulder. "My friend, I don't know you."

"Oh, hell!" answered the Swede, "come and have a drink."

"Now, my boy," advised the gambler, kindly, "take your hand off my shoulder and go 'way and mind your own business." He was a little, slim man, and it seemed strange to hear him use this tone of heroic patronage to the burly Swede. The other men at the table said nothing.

"What! You won't drink with me, you little dude? I'll make you, then! I'll make you!" The Swede had grasped the gambler frenziedly at the throat, and was dragging him from his chair. The other men sprang up. The barkeeper dashed around the corner of his bar. There was a great tumult, and then was seen a long blade in the hand of the gambler. It shot forward, and a human body, this citadel of virtue, wisdom, power, was pierced as easily as if it had been a melon. The Swede fell with a cry of su-preme astonishment.

The prominent merchants and the district attorney must have at once tumbled out of the place backward. The bartender found himself hanging limply to the arm of a chair and gazing into the eyes of a murderer.

"Henry," said the latter, as he wiped his knife on one of the towels that hung beneath the bar rail, "you tell 'em where to find me. I'll be home, waiting for 'em." Then he vanished. A moment afterward the barkeeper was in the street dinning through the storm for help and, moreover, companionship.

The corpse of the Swede, alone in the saloon, had its eyes fixed upon a dreadful legend that dwelt atop of the cash-machine: "This registers the amount of your purchase."

9

MONTHS LATER, the cowboy was frying pork over the stove of a little ranch near the Dakota line, when there was a quick thud of hoofs outside, and presently the Easterner entered with the letters and the papers.

"Well," said the Easterner at once, "the chap that killed the Swede has got three years. Wasn't much, was it?"

"He has? Three years?" The cowboy poised his pan of pork, while he ruminated upon the news. "Three years. That ain't much."

"No. It was a light sentence," replied the Easterner as he unbuckled his spurs. "Seems there was a good deal of sympathy for him in Romper."

"If the bartender had been any good," observed the cowboy, thoughtfully, "he would have gone in and cracked that there Dutchman on the head with a bottle in the beginnin' of it and stopped all this here murderin'."

"Yes, a thousand things might have happened," said the Easterner, tartly.

The cowboy returned his pan of pork to the fire, but his philosophy continued. "It's funny, ain't it? If he hadn't said Johnnie was cheatin' he'd be alive this minute. He was an awful fool. Game played for fun, too. Not for money. I believe he was crazy."

"I feel sorry for that gambler," said the Easterner.

"Oh, so do I," said the cowboy. "He don't deserve none of it for killin' who he did."

"The Swede might not have been killed if everything had been square."

"Might not have been killed?" exclaimed the cowboy. "Everythin' square? Why, when he said that Johnnie was cheatin' and acted like such a jackass? And then in the saloon he fairly walked up to git hurt?" With these arguments the cowboy browbeat the Easterner and reduced him to rage.

"You're a fool!" cried the Easterner, viciously. "You're a bigger jackass than the Swede by a million majority. Now let me tell you one thing. Let me tell you something. Listen! Johnnie *was* cheating!"

" 'Johnnie,' " said the cowboy, blankly. There was a minute of silence, and then he said, robustly, "Why, no. The game was only for fun."

"Fun or not," said the Easterner, "Johnnie was cheating. I saw him. I know it. I saw him. And I refused to stand up and be a man. I let the Swede fight it out alone. And you—you were simply puffing around the place and wanting to fight. And then old Scully himself! We are all in it! This poor gambler isn't even a noun. He is kind of an adverb. Every sin is the result of a collaboration. We, five of us, have collaborated in the murder of this Swede. Usually there are from a dozen to forty women really involved in every murder, but in this case it seems to be only men—you, I, Johnnie, old Scully; and that fool of an unfortunate gambler came merely as a culmination, the apex of a human movement, and gets all the punishment."

The cowboy, injured and rebellious, cried out blindly into this fog of mysterious theory: "Well, I didn't do anythin', did I?"

THE KEAN LAND

JACK SCHAEFER was born in Cleveland, Ohio, in 1908. He studied journalism at Oberlin College and Columbia University, became interested in Western-frontier history and started writing stories about the Old West. It was not long before he fled from neon-lighted civilization to settle with his wife and daughters on a place near Santa Fe, where he lives the kind of life he wants to, writing in the mornings, horseback riding in the afternoons.

His first novel, *Shane,* is now accepted as a landmark in the development of Western fiction. He has three other novels to his credit, plus three volumes of short stories; and he has also scored as an anthologist with *Out West,* a fine collection that came out in 1955. "The Kean Land," which was published first in *Collier's* magazine in 1956, is in the form of an old man's recollection of his own life, a difficult literary task well and convincingly done.

The Kean Land

JACK SCHAEFER

It is a small city in western Colorado. The main business section is downstream about a mile and a half where the railroad crosses the river. This is upstream where the suburban area crowds along both banks pushing on up the valley. Here, on the left bank, between the valley highway and the river, out of place, incongruous in the midst of closely built homes and street-corner stores and service stations and housing developments, is an oasis of clean uncluttered fields and woodlot, a farm caught, surrounded, imprisoned by the expanding city yet still complete, intact in its own quiet integrity. It has a small barn and a low flat-roofed building that was once a feeding shelter for cattle and a small house, half original log cabin, half frame addition.

On the porch of the addition sits an old man. He sits relaxed on an old rocker in heavy old work shoes and faded levis and once-bright flannel shirt. His huge old frame once powerfully muscled, is now lean and gaunt with age but his old eyes glow with an ageless vitality. He is talking to a younger man, to a writer of tales of the American West that was and is no more.

So JEFF MARTIN put you onto me. I haven't seen Jeff in eight-ten years since he moved away but a friend of Jeff's is a friend of mine and you can drive a nail on that. Maybe I'd better apologize for speaking so sour when you pulled in here. I thought you were another of those billy-be-damned real-estate sharpers. Three of them already this week. They keep raising the ante. Can't seem to pound into their heads price doesn't mean a thing, I'm just plain not selling.

Sure, they'd like to get hold of this piece. One hundred sixty acres good land. What would they do with it? Slap together a couple hundred maybe more of those silly mod-

153

ern shacks they call ranchhouses a real rancher wouldn't
live in and make a lot of money wh'ch seems to be the
most important thing anybody can do nowadays. That's
progress. So they say. They've been putting the squeeze on
me these last years, spec'ally since this last boom started.
Raised my taxes, twice. Zoned the section so I had to get
rid of the cows. The horses too so I have to use a tractor.
But I raise some garden stuff and take hay off the fields
and with what I've got in the bank I make out. No one
but me to worry over anyway. The kids are all grown.
Getting kids of their own. Scattered from here to breakfast and all doing all right. They don't feel about this
place the way I do and no reason they should but all the
same they say stick to it, dad, if that's what you want and
try a little buckshot on those real estate boys and if you
need any bail money just holler. I promised Lettie, that
was my wife, I wouldn't sell, I'd keep it l'ke th's to the
finish and there wasn't any need for that promising because I'd always felt the way she did anyway. So I'm keeping it. When I'm laid under, the land grabbers can bid
themselves silly over it and there'll be a nice chunk of
cash out of it to be split among the kids and I won't be
around to see what happens to the place . . .

So Jeff told you there's a story in me, in my hanging on
here. Well, yes, yes there is. About this place, yes. About
how I came to be living here, in this house, the old part
there first of course. But the real story goes way back and
was over and done before I moved out here. I don't figure
in it much. I was just around and saw it happen and didn't
do much of anyth'ng that mattered myself except once
when I unlocked the jail door down in town and maybe
if I'd known what that meant I wouldn't have done it.

I haven't talked to anybody about what happened back
then since Lettie d'ed, that'll be four years th's fall. Nobody to talk to. The kind of folks crowding in around
here now aren't interested in the old days. Too busy making money or trying to and tearing up and down that h'gh-
way there in cars that aren't ever full paid for because of
always being turned in on new ones and worry'ng about
meeting installments on all the billy-be-damned gadgets

people think they have to have nowadays cluttering their houses and getting in the way of decent living. They think me a cracked crotchety old fool. Much as say so. Maybe I am—from their side of the fence. I'll say this much, in this country a man't still got the right to be cracked and crotchety if he wants to. But try to tell folks like that how it all was and why I'm keeping this farm and they just plain wouldn't get it.

Maybe you would. Seems Jeff Martin thinks you would. But I'm warning you, it isn't pretty. The right and wrong of it's hard for some to see straight. If you do anything with it you can fix the words up some, unravel them out where I get tangled. But don't you go doctoring what happened any. The trouble with you writing men is you like to have things go along neat and fitting in together the way they don't in real living. Trouble is you like to have things too fancy, twist them around so they work out slick in the end the way plenty times they just plain don't. I won't pretty this any. I'll give it to you straight the only way I can which is telling about me and what I saw happen . . .

I grew up back east in Nebraska, back in the flat country. My folks had a farm there and I was their only kid. Something happened to my mother when I was born and she couldn't have any more. That didn't slow her down in other ways though. The land was good being a piece my father had to buy because by time he came along there all the public land was gone and he went a heavy mortgage to get it but it was kind of far from the nearest settlement so we were to ourselves a lot. About all I can remember clear when I was a boy other than working twelve-fourteen hours a day when school wasn't on and I'd be hiking the miles to it is those two, my father and my mother, fighting, arguing. Over just about anything any time but mostly over me. I was good size from the start and my father figured since I was all he'd have he'd get all the work he could out of me. He believed in work anyway, always said it was the best medicine for any human ailment. Mother figured the opposite. I was all she'd have and so she was bound determined to make something of me and her idea of something was an educated man. Less work and more learning was her stand. The two of them hammered away at each other all the time, thinking up arguments and throwing them at each other. They'd get so hot over it I'd be out working with my father and see him throw down whatever was in hand and go stomping into the house and I'd know he'd thought up a new argument and was hurrying to try it on her. I was near full grown before I understood that was how they liked it, how they kept some spice and tang in a hard life. My father had a big voice and when he got going he could shout her down but all the same I noticed it was my mother usually had her way. She had her way the year I hitched rides over into Illinois with a bank draft in my pocket and to Galesburg and enrolled in Knox College.

I can't say I enjoyed that year though it started me reading some as I've done off and on ever since and I expect I learned plenty. Had to or be dropped from classes and my mother wouldn't like that. But I was big and clumsy and fresh off the farm with only spotty schooling behind me and I didn't fit in with the others. Didn't specially want to. I never was what you'd call social-minded. More I saw of the students others looked up to because they had a little money and more I listened to some of the silly guff handed out by la-de-da teachers in their town clothes and their party manners, the more I kept thinking about my father back there on the farm who'd never had a full decent suit in his life and had to read following the words with a finger and spelling them out and did two men's work every day and got peeved at himself because he couldn't do more and still found time to go stomping into the house and show my mother what he thought of her by arguing and shouting her down and ending up doing what she wanted after all. I was about ready to quit anyway, near the end of that year, when the letter came from a neighbor there was cholera back home.

I took a train far as I could and hired a horse the rest of the way but even so I was too late. They were both gone when I got there. Already buried because people around were frantic over the cholera and got rid of bodies fast as they could. That was when I found out the two of them had pushed the mortgage on the farm up to the limit to get me that bank draft. The sharper who held the paper had already stepped in and foreclosed. I checked and found he'd done it the day they were buried. Maybe I could have stirred trouble but I was too hit to give a damn. I was seventeen-eighteen at the time. I had some money left from that draft. And I had a note from my father he'd given that neighbor for me the last day. It was just a misspelt scrawl in the squiggly squarish printing which was the only way he could write. I've still got it tucked away somewhere. I didn't pay much attention to it right off but it turned out the best thing he could have left me. *dere son—bruther scott wil help—in collerado*

As I say, I didn't pay much attention to that at first except to tuck it away in my purse as a keepsake. I wasn't interested in asking anybody for any help or chasing down any relative let alone an uncle I hadn't ever seen but only heard about some the few times my father had talked about his folks that he'd split with when he sided with the union in the Civil War. I just wanted to be let alone and to hell with the whole stinking world so I drifted off by my lonesome and down through Kansas and knocked around the panhandle and over into New Mexico.

I had my full growth already in those days and looked older than I was. People took me for a grown man so I tried acting like one and began drinking more than I could hold right and bucking smalltime faro games. Didn't take long before I was flat broke. I kicked around picking up odd jobs, cadging handouts between, never staying long any one place, then I got into freighting, heavy hauling out of Santa Fe with the ox teams. I could do that. One thing I had in those days was muscle. Not much sense but plenty muscle. I'd sign on for a trip out and back and when we'd pull in again and be paid I'd quit and loaf around till the money went and go back and sign on again. Freighters in those days were a tough crew. A man who couldn't hold his quart a day and bust a barrel with one wallop of his fist didn't have a chance with them. They'd work up a fight and take a saloon apart just for the fun of it. Me, I'd hold back some because I wanted to make my pay-money last a while between jobs but then I'd get to feeling low again and I'd join in the drinking and likely the fighting too and wake up next morning in a back lot with a busted head or in jail for busting someone else's head.

It was one of those times, in the Santa Fe jail I mean, that I got to thinking. There I was coming twenty-two and not doing so well by myself any way you figured. I wasn't taking either my father's or my mother's side in that endless arguing they used to do. I was working, yes, off and on. But I wasn't working the way my father had, steady and slugging it through and aiming at some goal which for him had been paying off the mortgage and owning his land outright for once and building up his farm and though he never got there it was always there ahead of him and he was aiming at it. I wasn't aiming at anything. There wasn't even anything I felt like aiming at except maybe thumbing my nose at existence in general. And I sure wasn't learning much the way my mother had wanted me to—that is, not the kind of things she had in mind. Thinking of those two reminded me of that note. I didn't really fit where I was like I hadn't at Knox and I didn't have any notion where I would. That note was a hunch and I might as well play it. Soon as I could pull out I headed up here into Colorado looking for my uncle Scott.

I didn't know much about him except he was a few years younger than my father and like my father had headed west after the Civil War broke up the family back in the Kentucky hills. Not much on size, my father said once, and not much use with a plow but all the same a gol-damned good fighting man when the trouble came even if he did join the rebs and had to be licked. Seeing that they'd been on opposite sides in the war and kept going different ways after and neither one was a letter-writing man, how my father had managed to keep any track of him is something I never have figured out.

I didn't even know where he was in the state or if he

was still around but it didn't take long to find out. I headed up Taos way and over the line, following the Grande upstream asking questions. Right away at Del Norte I hit a man who'd heard of him and sent me on towards this Mesa country. I kept on, asking my questions, and when I got up this way I was surprised to find how well known he was. I was surprised another way too. I'd say I was looking for Scott Hammon and people would stare at me quick and sharp and check me over before they'd talk. After a while I figured what they were doing. They were checking did I pack a gun. I didn't and when they saw that they'd loosen some. But they wouldn't say much, just send me on to the next place heading here.

That's how it was when I reached this valley. There wasn't much here then, just a little settlement that was hardly even a real town yet, just a stopping-off place where a couple stage lines crossed and some stores and a few saloons and a blacksmith shop had sprung up to take care of people from the ranches scattered about and those who had come into the state in the mining-boom days and prospected around and got sense enough to quit that dream-chasing and settled here because it was nice country. No, there wasn't much here then—except the things that made it nice country. I hadn't realized how much I'd been missing the feel of good growing earth under my feet down in the dry sandy areas till I got up here where the valleys were wide and green and had trees that were trees not twisty prickly little runts. It wasn't flat and dull like over east in the part of Nebraska I'd known. Lift your head any time and you'd see the mountains ranging off into the distance telling you to stand tall with rock in your spine the way they did. It was my kind of country. It's still the same kind but it isn't the same any more. Look out there and the mountains are still all around, still standing tall with real rock thrusting through. But about everywhere in between, like here in this valley, there's the mess and clutter and meanness and littleness and frittering around that somehow blots out most of the decent when too many people get crowding together. But that's a side trail, not what I started to tell you . . .

As I say, I finally came drifting up here. I dropped off the stage I'd hooked a ride on about where the bank building is now down there in the center. It was along mid morning. First person I saw was a gent wearing a storekeeper's apron leaning against a hitching rail soaking up sun. I asked my question and he took his time looking me over and pointed at a two-story building across the road and sitting back about a hundred feet. It was fairly wide with a single doorway in the middle and a platform running clear across the front that could have been called a porch only it didn't have a roof. I went over and up on the platform. The door was open and I looked in. A hall ran straight back through and around the stairway leading up and to another door at the back. I stepped into the hall and there was a doorway on each side of me. I picked the one on the right and looked in and saw a big room, the length of the building back, fixed up for a meeting place and makeshift courtroom. No one was there. I turned around to try the other doorway and saw a sign tacked up over it: *Sheriff Office*. The door was ajar and I pushed it further and saw a small room with an old desk and a couple chairs and another door, standing open, leading to whatever was behind. This room too was empty and I was wondering whether to push in further when I heard my father's voice coming through that open inner doorway. It was my father's voice, the same flat tone with the lingering trace of Kentucky drawl, only it wasn't because it was a bit sharper, had more of an edge. "Sobered up, eh? Prove it. Walk that chalk line."

I stepped quiet over to that inner doorway and looked through and there he was. He was standing about eight feet in with his back to me and just like that as I saw him first is still how I remember him best and I knew him at once and why people were careful talking about him because there was a big handle-worn forty-five hanging in an oiled old holster at his side and he was just as my father had said, not much on size, but the bare sight of him, just the back of him, standing there straight with a kind of military erectness and a plain completeness within himself told with no mistake he was a goldamned good fighting man in any kind of trouble no matter what side he might be taking.

It was a fair-sized room he was in, the rest of that side of the building behind the little office. The back half of it was rigged for a jail with bars across and a partition in the middle making two cells. He was facing the one on the left and in there was a scrubby mean-looking man concentrating in a sort of silly mad earnestness on putting one foot after the other along a chalk line on the floor. This one was facing towards me. When his head came up he saw me and in the instant my uncle Scott was aware and was around, checking me over. He didn't know who I was or anything about me but in that one look he knew I was just a big young one and harmless. "Have a chair," he said. "Be with you in a minute." Somehow doing what he said seemed a good notion and I backed off and sat on a chair by the front window and I heard a lock rattling in the inner room and then the mean-looking man came in and stood scowling and my uncle followed and went to the old desk and pulled open a drawer. He took a gun out of it and walked over and dropped it in the man's holster and stepped back and stood still with his hands hanging limp and easy at his sides. "You did some blowing last night," he said. "About what you'd do when you sobered and had your gun again. Well, you're sober and you've got it."

The man stood rigid all over like he was frozen and couldn't move. His throat worked some and he got his voice out. "Quit it, Hammon. That was just the whisky talking."

"Well, then," my uncle Scott said. "I can't think of a single reason why you ought to stay around this town any more. Can you?"

The man took a deep breath. "No," he said.

"Right," my uncle Scott said. "Your horse is out back. It's a good day for traveling."

The man turned and faded through the outer door and my uncle went over and sat down behind the desk and looked at me. "Well, bub, what's on your mind?"

I gulped some and didn't know how to begin. "I'm Ben," I said. "Ben Hammon."

He just kept looking at me in that steady way of his. "John's boy?"

"Yes," I said.

He studied me some more. His voice was careful, not showing anything. "How is John doing these days?"

"He's dead," I said.

My uncle Scott's eyes shifted and he was looking past me, out the window. "When?"

"Four years ago. He and mother. Cholera."

My uncle Scott looked out that window what seemed a long time. Then he was looking at me again. "What are you doing here?" I fumbled in my mind and couldn't figure how to say what I wanted to say so I reached in my shirt pocket where I had it now and took out that note. I leaned over and put it on the old desk in front of him and sat back and sudden I was about ready to bust out bawling because he reached the way my father would have done and held that wrinkled old note with one hand and pushed the forefinger of the other along it, spelling out the words. "You took your time coming here," he said without looking up and there wasn't any real answer to that and we just sat there, me on my chair by the window and him behind that old desk looking down at that note and then he raised his head and about hit me with the words. "What're you after now? Money?"

That did it. That cut me loose. "Goldamn it, no!" I said. "I been taking care of myself! I'm looking for a place where maybe I belong! That's sure not here!" I was starting out of that chair towards the door when he stopped me short. "Sit down." It was about the same as if he'd caught me with a rope and put me back on that chair. He reached that note over and watched me put it in my pocket. "Your father," he said, "was a big noisy stubborn stiff-minded jackass. Like maybe you are too. He went his way and I went mine. But when we were kids and I was a scrawny little runt he whopped every big lout that tried picking on me. Maybe this is where you belong and maybe it aint. We'll just find out. I've got quarters upstairs and there's room enough for you too. You go get—"

"Wait a minute," I said. I didn't want to say this because I didn't know how he would take it but I had to say it. I stood up and looked right at him. "Maybe you," I said, "maybe you were kind of stubborn and stiff-minded too." And somehow that was the right thing for me to say and the little wrinkles around his eyes showed plainer. "Good lord, boy," he said. "Of course I was. Still am. I'm a Hammon same as your father was. Waited till he was dying before he turned to me. Likely I'd have done the same. But he knew damn well he could, didn't he? You go get your things and move in."

"Well, sir," I started in to say.

"None of that," he said. "The name's Scott."

"Well, now, Scott," I said. "Everything I've got is on me right now."

He looked at me sharp and the little wrinkles around his eyes showed even plainer. "Been taking mighty good care of yourself, haven't you? That wipes out any moving problem anyhow." He pushed up from behind the desk. "Come along. I'll introduce you around."

That's what he did, took me out and to every place near, the stores and the saloons and the blacksmith and the harness shops and the few houses close in, introducing me to everybody, nothing fancy, just telling who I was and I was visiting a while and if I liked it maybe I'd find something to do and stay around. What struck me first was how easy and friendly people were with me, how they took me as someone to be easy and friendly with and no questions asked except those meant to make me feel the same. Then I figured why. It wasn't anything about me, it was the fact I was being introduced by a man named Scott Hammon and he was backing me and that was enough for them and not because there was a big forty-five hanging in a worn old holster at his side that showed it had been used plenty but just plain he was Scott Hammon and they liked him and were proud having him as a neighbor and as their sheriff who kept things quiet in their little town so folks could be easy and friendly with each other.

I learned all about that the next days, some from him but most from other people. He'd worn a badge in one place and another for quite a while up in the mining country and made himself a name calming some rough camps. He was fast with a gun, people said. Not as fast as some of the real experts were supposed to be and he'd been winged a few times, but once he had his gun out he was so billy-be-damned thorough with it that after a while he was known around and even the best would think twice or maybe three times before forcing him to a draw. He never backed away from a showdown but he didn't go about pushing things to that either if he could avoid it. His way, when he could, when he had to arrest somebody and knew he couldn't do it peaceful, was to try to get in close and jump the play quick and lay the barrel of his gun along the side of the man's skull with power behind it and tote him off unconscious. More than one man, thinking it over after, had thanked him for doing it that way. And right too because a sore head's better than being dead any time.

Then he sort of slowed down. Not really, just in how he looked at things. Maybe that was because he got married, a woman who'd come into the mountains for her health, lung trouble, and he had a fair taste of being peaceful with her before they found she'd come too late. They settled here because it was nice country and a quiet place and he worked at the stage station and took care of her till she died and then he quit his job and sat around all day staring off at the mountains and the town people knew a good thing when they had it and got together and asked him wouldn't he take care of them now as their sheriff. He got up and took that old gunbelt off the nail where it'd been hanging and buckled it around his waist again and he only had to use it a few times on trouble-makers passing through, nothing serious, before word was around who was sheriff here and it was sensible to look for trouble other places and after that the town was even quieter.

Don't take me wrong. Not what you'd call quiet nowadays. In the old days even in a little place like this was there was always some horseplay or even brawling going on now and then and on paydays some cowboys coming in to yip and pepper the landscape just for the hell of it and get rid of their money on any sort of damfoolishness. Like the time two of the outfits that were always trying to get ahead of each other worked up a jackass and bear fight. The one was raising mules as a sideline and had a tough old jack that'd shown itself boss of their range by about killing a big stallion twice its size and they got to blowing it could whip anything and the other outfit said a bear would eat it for breakfast and some of them rode out hunting and had themselves a time getting their ropes on a bear, a big black not a grizzly because they knew they couldn't handle one of those, and brought it in. They figured to turn them both loose in the stage corral and see what'd happen. Bets were heavy and everybody around was backing one or the other. Me, I was for the jack, maybe because I'd been a farm boy, but the billy-be-damned critters wouldn't fight. Not each other I mean. They took a look at each other and lit out in opposite directions and the bear went over the rails and scattered the crowd and away and when my uncle Scott could stop laughing he had a job straightening out the bet money all around. But that's a side trail again. The point I'm after is that things happened around here now and then. People who did hard and lonesome work out in the open as plenty people did then had to blow off steam. My uncle Scott didn't mind that, knew it was just normal. He'd interfere only when somebody really stepped out over the line. All the same, alongside Santa Fe where I'd been it did seem sort of quiet.

"Scott," I said. "After all you've done and places you've been, doesn't it seem a mite dull here to a man like you?"

"Dull?" he said. "It ain't ever dull with life going on all round you—life how it ought to be lived. People living decent and being neighborly. Letting each other be and do what they want long as they don't step on any toes too hard. Not so damn many of them they can't know each other and don't have room to breathe right. Town growing slow the way a town ought with new people coming in now and then with a chance to get to be known and shake down and be part of the place. Trying to get ahead, yes, but not to make a pile fast and at somebody else's expense. I've had a bellyful of the boom places. Things here the way they are suit me."

They suited me too. As I say, it was my kind of country. Inside a week I felt like maybe I belonged. I was bunking with Scott upstairs and taking meals with him at Mrs. Morrison's, wife of that storekeeper sent me to him the first day, and already I had a couple jobs to pay my keep. In the mornings I'd go down the road and help the blacksmith with any heavy work he had. A short thick one he was, built about like a barrel and named Rufe, Rufe Martin, who'd really have been talking if he spoke as many as twenty words in a whole morning. Yep, he was Jeff's father only Jeff wasn't more than three-four then, just a little kid playing around with his mother always chasing after him for fear he'd get burnt in the shop. In the afternoons I'd be helping my uncle Scott with his paperwork. That is, I'd be doing it because if it was up to him it wouldn't be done. It was only about the second day I found him at his desk scowling at a letter he was spelling out with one finger. I took it and read it off to him and it was from a commissioner over at the county seat about seventy miles off squawking because they weren't getting any records from him and not even any answer to their letters and sometime they were going to get a mite peeved about all that. When he saw I could wrangle words enough to make sense he just plain got up from the desk and told me to wade in. I pulled open the drawers and there was the goldamndest accumulation of stuff you ever saw. He'd been shoving everything into those drawers for years.

"Records?" he said. "All the records I need are right here in my head. I jail a man for stirring trouble, why I jail him and that's that. I ain't going to hold it against him after long as he behaves himself. Any lawing we've had, well, Morrison's a justice of the peace and he takes care of that and what he's decided is all in there somewhere. People hear it at the time and they've got memories, haven't they? Any real serious business goes over to the county seat anyway so what're they hollering about? If it's records they want and you feel up to it, why give them what you can." So I waded in and I chucked out everything more than four years old and started straightening out the rest best I could. He'd sit by the window watching people go by outside and talking with those that came in to pass the time of day and answering my questions when I couldn't make out something. It was kind of pleasant in there doing that. But all the same I'd get to studying him and feeling low. I'd found him and he was all I had and he was something for anybody to have but still I'd get to feeling lonesome. He was so goldamned complete and sufficient in himself, the way his life and that stubborn stiff-mindedness had made him, it seemed to me nobody could ever get close to him. Then one day, maybe two weeks after I'd arrived, he took me by surprise. "Ben," he said. "Can you handle a plow like your father could?"

"No," I said. "He could just about plain push the thing through the ground himself. I have to have horses helping."

"I'm thinking of horses," he said. "Old Brent Kean's broke his leg. You haven't met him and you'll enjoy that. If his garden plowing ain't done soon the season'll get past him."

We went out back and he saddled his tough little gray and I put one on the big bay he'd said would be mine for fixing up his paperwork and he brought me up the trail that's now that highway out there and to this place.

First thing I saw here was a fenced pasture, that first field down there, with half a dozen cows, steers that is, and a couple riding horses in it. Then I saw the house here, the log part that was all there was then, and beyond on there, past where the barn is now, two women plowing

a good-sized plot. Trying to plow. They'd run a few furrows and those were the billy-be-damndest things you ever
saw. Zigzagged all over. The team pulling was willing
enough but it was a big plow and those women couldn't
handle it. One had the reins and was guiding the horses.
The other was holding to the plow and fighting it and
losing the fight every few seconds when the handles
bucked and pitched her around. My uncle Scott tickled
his gray faster and swung over in by them. "Now you two
quit that foolishness," he said and they stopped and turned
to look at us.

The one holding the reins was a big woman, tall and
big-boned, getting along in years with kind of wispy gray
hair. Right then she was about the tiredest person I ever
saw. It was worth seeing how her face lit up when she saw
my uncle Scott. She dropped the reins and put her hands
on her hips. "I was telling Brent only this morning," she
said, "if anybody found time to get out this was today it'd
be that little rooster Scott Hammon." She was sure glad
to see us.

The other one wasn't. Or she didn't show it any. She
was big too, about the same build, only a lot younger and
still slender the way a girl is that's going to be a real
chunk of woman someday but hasn't got her man yet and
started having a family. She was a sight right then. She
had a lot of hair, dark it was then, that'd been fastened in
two long braids wound up on her head and they'd started
falling down and unraveling and her face was all sweaty
and streaked from rubbing a muddy hand across it and
she was mad. Told me later she'd never been so mad before. Mad at that plow. Mad at her father for being so goldamned silly as to go off hunting again at his age and after
mountain goat too and fall and break a leg and have to
crawl nine mile dragging it and be toted home. Mad at
us for catching her looking like that. Mad at anything and
everything she could think of right then. "You're so
smirking smart, Mister Scott Hammon," she said. "You
tell me how we're going to plant the garden without plowing this ground!"

"Well, now," Scott said. "That's an easy one. That

ground'll be plowed. I've brought you here the best damned plower in seventeen counties and a few more acres besides. My nephew here, Ben Hammon, he's been loafing around in towns so long he's just a-aching to get hold of a plow again." And do you know, he was right. The smell of that fresh-turned earth and the sight of those work horses standing there as such horses do which are the kind I've always known best anyway, patient and waiting and ready to dig in when told, and that big old plow sticking up cockeyed out of the ground like it was daring me could I make it behave made me want to jump down and roll up my sleeves and get started. I'm not saying I was feeling like being a farmer again. That's plowing till you're sick of the sight of the billy-be-damned thing and planting and cultivating and fussing with stock and never enough time for everything that's got to be done and keep going only because it's all just plain got to be done and you started it and come hell or highwater you're going to finish it and hardly anybody with all their labor-saving machinery nowadays knows what that means any more. I was only feeling right then like a spot of plowing would stretch a few kinks out of me. But my uncle Scott was talking.

"Ben," he said. "I want you to meet Sarah Kean here who patched me up the first time I stumbled into this valley chasing a road agent from up Leadville way and he saw me first and put a bullet in me. For thirty years maybe more she's been doing the impossible which is making old Brent so happy and contented he behaves almost like a human being. That short-fused piece of dynamite there is their daughter Lettie. Taking after her father today. Hard to believe this minute but I've seen her scrubbed and neat enough to catch a man's eye." She wanted to say something and it would have been a scorcher from how she looked but he cut across her quick. "Come along to the house. Ben'll want to meet Brent before he does your choring."

We trailed to the cabin here and in, that is Scott and Sarah Kean and me because that Lettie girl faded out of sight somewhere around it, and we hadn't more than started in the doorway when a big voice that could have stood right alongside my father's was booming at us. It was coming from a man sitting by the side window that gave on up the valley on a chair that'd been padded with a couple old buffalo robes. He had one leg stretched out in splints on a little nail keg. He was sitting straight upright on the chair and he looked like a half-closed jackknife because he was long and thin, not what thin is nowadays which is spindly and brittle but thin the way a tough old timber wolf is which means lean and taut-stretched all over and made out of gristle and rawhide and not a snitch of extra weight or fat anywhere. He had big features, sharp, what you could see of them pushing out from a shock of gray hair and thick eyebrows and a beard that hadn't known a razor for years only scissors to snip it around the edges.

"Get out of my cabin, you low-bellied rattlesnake," he was booming, throwing the words smack at my uncle Scott and making a cup rattle over on the shelf by the stove. "Where'd you get the notion I'd want to see a strutting mangy little coyote like you a time like this? Couple of months and you don't get out here at all! Soon as I get laid up you come sniffing around to start crowing over me! Think I couldn't hear you powwowing out there? Do my plowing! Make me beholden to you! My rifle was in reach I'd—"

"Shut up!" my uncle Scott shouted and the cup on the shelf rattled some more and I didn't know he had that much voice. And Sarah Kean didn't pay any mind to the shouting at all except to kind of smile a little to herself and she went to the stove and began doing things with the coffeepot. "Shut up!" my uncle Scott shouted again. "I'll break that leg clean off you and whang you one with it!"

"All right, Scott, all right," this old Brent said in a surprising mild voice and that was kind of comical because the idea of Scott tangling barehanded with him, crippled and banged up as he was, would've been like a snapping little terrier tackling a lean old grizzly. "Ben," Scott said, swinging to me, "I didn't mention outside it was this moth-eaten old wreck here brought me in to be patched that time. Found me up in the hills that he knows like they were his backyard. He's been around these mountains so long that he's mostly animal but now and then a bit of human shows through."

Old Brent wasn't paying any mind to him. He was looking me over. "Big one, aint he," he said to Scott. Then to me: "See that chest over there, boy. Let's see you hyst it one." I went over and it wasn't so big but it was solid and must have had heavy stuff in it because when I took hold it felt like it was nailed down. I heard a chuckle from old Brent and I was peeved then so I squatted and wrapped my arms around it and rocked it up a little and braced it with my shoulders and got my hands under and I straightened up with it and just to show that old jackknife on the chair I heaved it on up clear over my head and held it there a couple seconds and let it down, straining hard to set it down without any bumping. "Fair," old Brent said. "Middling fair. Now why aren't you out plowing?"

I could feel the mad start in me at that and I might have done some shouting too but I noticed my uncle Scott was watching me like he was wondering which way I'd jump and Sarah Kean was pretending to be busy with her coffeepot but was really doing the same and I took hold of myself and saw that old Brent's eyes in that big sharp bristly old face didn't have a trace of meanness and something that had been tied up tight in me for a long time sort of slipped loose and I found I could do it right. "Well, now, you broken-down old misfit," I said to Brent. "Don't you go swilling all the coffee because I'll be wanting some after. I'm going out and give that ground the first real plowing it's ever had so it'll be glad you busted that leg and couldn't get to messing it up again."

That's what I did. I went out and looked that ground over. I could make out the plot lines because it'd been worked other years, but it'd been done the wrong way. It'd always been plowed crosswise, down the slight valley slope towards the river, and that meant when there was rain, water could go running down the furrow marks and off taking soil and in seedtime maybe some seed with it. I swung the team and the plow around and started slicing my furrows lengthwise. I felt fine stepping along with that big polw and the horses did too because they knew right away as horses can that they had a man behind them knew what he was doing. I'd run four-five furrows and was at the near end near the cabin and swinging around to start another when I saw that Lettie girl watching me. I could tell what she had been doing because her face was scrubbed and her hair was fixed up again and she had a ribbon holding the braids in place. I went on down the line with her watching and just to show her I let one hand drop and held the plow firm with only the other on the one handle and went strutting along. I swung and came back and she'd moved closer. "You're going the wrong direction," she said. "Oh, sure," I said. "All wrong. You're such an expert you'd know." And I went on down another furrow.

I came back and she wasn't saying a word and that should have warned me because when Lettie wasn't saying anything that always meant she was getting ready to do something and when I was swinging to start away again she picked up a stone and threw it and hit one of the horses and the horse jumped and started thrashing about some and then they were both jumping and the plow yanked over and near threw me and I had to do some hollering and wrangling with the reins to calm th'ngs down. I was stopped there and peeved and when she started in with something about maybe slow-witted as I was maybe now I'd listen I was mad and though I didn't know it then it must have been the kind of mad my father was when he argued with my mother because it wasn't really an angry mad and I just stomped over and picked her up big as she was under one arm and went stomping into the cabin here and plopped her on a chair. I looked around at the rest of them. "I'm plowing that ground the way it ought to be plowed," I said. "Anybody else tries interfering with me I'll take this whole billy-be-damned place apart." I stomped out and as I was going out the doorway I heard old Brent's voice. "Go to it, boy. But she's a neat armful, aint she?" I went out and I ripped into that plowing and did the whole plot without stopping and that was one of the times it was just plain good being alive.

There was a healthy supper waiting when I finished and we sat around talking after, that is Scott and old Brent talking with Sarah Kean chiming in some and me listening. Lettie ignored me rest of that time like I didn't even exist but she knew goldamned well I was there just as I did she was too. Then it was Brent doing most of the talking with Scott only drawing him on. He was a talker, that Brent, when he got going though there weren't many he'd do that for. I learned about him then and later when Scott and I came out so I could work the ground with an old spiked-log harrow for the women to do the planting and after that when I took to coming out some on my own.

He'd come from England, Brent had, from up in the Northumberland hill country somewhere. He wasn't much more than ten-eleven when his folks brought him to this country and he'd been here so long and out in this part that everything English had long since worn off. Except, sometimes, when he'd be real deep interested in what he was telling, he might slip into speaking in a clipped precise kind of way and pick his words neat and you'd realize that back in those early years, likely back in England, he'd had some good schooling and the few old calfbound books he had on a shelf weren't falling apart just because they were old. He had a couple Walter Scott, I remember, he swore by. He had a rifle too hanging on the wall over those books, a Winchester repeater, last of a series of rifles he'd had beginning with a muzzle-loading Kentucky long. A few books and a rifle, those summed a lot of old Brent.

His folks had settled in Tennessee but already, back in the 40's it must have been, that was too tame for him. When he was about sixteen he headed west driving team with some emigrant outfit and never saw his folks again though sometimes when he had a good reason he sent them money and he heard from them off and on till they died. He was close to seventy when I knew him and he was a walking history of a big piece of this whole part of the country. He'd hunted and trapped all through these mountains. He'd been with Captain Stansbury's outfit that made the first survey of the Salt Lake country over in Utah. He scouted some for the Army and did some guiding through the mountain passes and sometimes when he needed a stake he supplied meat to the mining camps. He'd known Indians back when they were still Indians, the Kiowas and the Comanches and the Utes and the rest, even some of the Cheyennes, and he'd fought them and he'd lived with them some and likely had a squaw a few years as plenty men did in those days because he was a lot of man and still was when I knew him.

When he was getting along in his forties he thought of settling down, what he'd call settling down, and looked around for a woman to sort of anchor him. He saw Sarah, Blanchard was her family name, walking long-legged behind an emigrant wagon herding the cows and spare mules. The outfit belonged to her sister and the sister's husband and she was tagging along because there wasn't anything for her back where they came from, Missouri I think it was, and lucky for them too because she was doing most of the work. She was no youngster herself then, not one to take an ordinary man's eye not being pretty or soft-looking or special feminine at first notice. She was big and toughened by a lot of hard work and had a tongue and wouldn't take real sass from anyone. Well, Brent saw her and went along with the outfit a few days bringing in some meat to help out. Then he went straight to her and said he'd been looking her over and maybe she just might be enough woman for him and she said right back she'd looked him over and it could be maybe he was enough man for her and he said she'd have to understand he wasn't one to give a woman fancy geegaws or sweat his guts out trying to make a lot of money and he'd expect her to trail with him and no squawking and live how he wanted to live which was simple and being satisfied with a place to stay and enough to eat and nobody bossing around and she said that suited her only any children would have to learn their lettering and he said he could handle that and why in hell wasn't she getting her things together.

They settled here when there wasn't even the beginning of a town. Just built their cabin here where there was water and grass and timber and plenty game around. He made a living hunting and trapping. After a while when more people had come in and the game was thinning they collected some cows and a few horses and he fenced in pasture and he'd cut hay for winter feed and they began depending more on their garden and even selling some off it as well as some stock now and again and they made out and were living as they wanted to live. Everybody around knew them but I can't say as everyone liked them because old rent could be cantankerous as an old brier bush and mighty short and sharp with people he thought fools and he thought most were but even those he rubbed the wrong way maybe wouldn't have had him different because he was like a natural part of the country that just bumped out and annoyed them but belonged here.

They'd had one boy, Brent they called him too, but croup took him at about five. They buried him in a little clearing you can't see from here but's behind those trees over on the riverbank. Sarah being well along they didn't think they'd have another so were surprised when a couple years later Lettie came along. They raised her right, real and straight-grained and this-is-me and you-can-be-you like themselves, and Brent gave her schooling and she thought there couldn't be a match for the two of them anywhere and in some ways she was right. Old Brent in particular. She thought anything he did just plain oughtn't be done any other way, like that plowing.

As I say, we sat around after supper and Brent got to talking. He was telling how he and Sarah covered a lot of territory and did a lot of looking before they picked this valley and figured it would be home. There were still a few Indians through this section then, mostly Utes. First people in some of the other valleys had trouble with them but he and Sarah never did. That's because he was straight with them and treated them like people which they were. He scouted first off and found some living on up the valley and came back and got an extra rifle he had then and told Sarah to come along and like always she did. She was worried so he explained they were just going visiting and that wasn't to be worried over because the last thing decent Indians ever would do was hurt anybody came calling in friendship and was a guest in their camp. He was right as he knew he would be because he knew Indians. He lugged a deer along and they all, that is Brent and Sarah and those Utes, had a feast day and they slept in the local chief's lodge and next day they had a council. He knew some of their words and was fair at sign-talk and he put across that he liked their country and wanted to live down the valley here and he wasn't one to go around killing game just for the fun of it but only what he needed and the door of his cabin would always be open to any of them passing by and wanting a meal and to show his heart was in the right place he was making the chief a present of that extra rifle. Those Utes powwowed a while, taking their time the way Indians did, and likely it helped their seeing Sarah hobnobbing with the squaws and trying to do something for a kid that was ailing. At last they told him, best as he could figure it, they'd learned not to put much faith in anything white men said but they liked the way he'd come straight to them for a talk. Since he came as a friend they wouldn't let him get ahead of them in that kind of decent doing. He came in peace and they wouldn't be the ones to change that. From that day forward, they said, he and his woman would be safe in their country. They'd pass the word around and as long as what he'd told them stayed true no one of their tribe would raise a hand against him.

"And not one of them ever did," old Brent told us. "Even along in '79 when they were being pushed out and those up north along the White River started real trouble and killed Agent Meeker who was a blundering fool with Indians anyway and troops were called out and the trouble spread down into these parts too, we never had any. Some cabins were burned not far from here. Some stock was run off and a man killed just over the next ridge. Other people were scurrying down river to the nearest fort. Sarah and me, we stayed here with the door open like always and they didn't bother us. They'd said they wouldn't so they didn't. I'd trust most Indians I've known more than I would most white men I've known. We'd got well acquainted with some of them. They'd stop by and keep Sarah hopping to fill their stomachs and do that three or four times running till I'd think they were making too much of a good thing of it only I'd remember they'd share their own last bite if we went calling, then one morning I'd find a nice skin or two on the doorstep and I'd know where that came from. It seemed a shame to me when they were all shoved over onto a reservation in Utah. This was their country first. Sarah and me always felt we got this place from them, like they gave it to us."

"Brent," my uncle Scott said. "You're the best man with a rifle I ever met but you're a double-barreled jackass in other ways. Talking about Indians like they were people when everybody knows they're just thieving skunks who had the all-fired gall to get first hold on land that really belonged to white men who just hadn't got around to discovering it yet. Talking about getting your place here from them. That kind of title won't hold in any court. I'll bet you haven't even filed on this piece."

"Filed?" Brent said. "You mean recorded my claim? I've been recording my claim to this piece of land by living on it for twenty-seven years. Everybody around knows it's mine. Besides, this country up in here hasn't been opened to homesteading yet."

"It's been opened," Scott said. "Last month. The whole county except for some mineral lands. Word came through a couple weeks back. There's a land office been set up at the county seat. We're not crowded up this way and not likely to be. Too far from markets. All the same I'm passing word to thickheaded old squatters like you to get over there and make things legal."

"Legal!" old Brent shouted. He banged a hand down on the splints on his leg and that made him wince and touched him off even more. "That's what happens when too damn many people get to crowding in! Everything's got to be legal! Everybody told what they can do, what they can't do! A bunch of fools way off in Washington who aint ever seen this country, don't know a thing about it, get to making a lot of silly rules and you think that gives a runty little packrat like you wearing a badge a right to go bossing around—"

"Shut up!" Scott shouted. "I ain't a federal marshal! Federal rules can go hang for all of me! I'm only sheriff of this district and I make most of my own rules anyway! I ain't ever tried bossing you! Far as me and the rest around here go this is your land! But you ain't going to live forever! You'll be wanting to leave it to Lettie here and that—"

"Lettie," Brent said in that surprising mild voice again. "You're sighting straight I'm leaving it to her. That's what Sarah and me want. This was Ute land once. Now it's Kean land." He stared at Scott some and then he kind of sighed. "All right, Scott. Soon as this leg's in shape I'll go over and file my claim."

There. Maybe by now you begin to have some notion what this is all about. I've been wandering on wordy about myself and my uncle Scott and those three Keans and the little settlement we had here so maybe you'll understand how it was, how I felt it all, knocking around and getting nowhere then finding this kind of country and people like that. But it didn't last long. Not the was it was then. Old Brent didn't get a chance to wait till his leg healed. Maybe, considering all angles, it wouldn't have made much difference if he had. He'd still have bumped against the law. But it was only about two months later when he was just starting to get about limping with a crutch he'd made that he was smack in the midst of real trouble.

It was the railroad changed things. The railroad people pulled a smart one. They were building into this end of the state and they were peeved at the way speculators jumped in ahead of them to grab off likely station sites and try to get fancy prices so they let on they were heading for a pass about ninety miles south and sudden they shifted and it turned out the line was coming past here, would cross the river right by our town. First we knew of it their advance men were here, snapping up the space they wanted and staking their land-grant route. Then grading crews were coming our way and camping near and a bridge outfit hit town and there was activity all over the place though it would be a while before the rails themselves reached here.

The town was booming, almost overnight. People crowded in, all kinds. Tents and shacks went up, jammed together, pushing out around. Couple of weeks after it started there were seven saloons, some just in big tents, all going full blast and trying to outdo each other with brass bands and dance girls and such. The racket never quit all night long and most of them had gambling tables too. Town lots went shooting up in price and land sharks were trading in them right and left and people were slamming stakes into the ground wherever they thought they could make a claim stick and even land that wouldn't have been rated worth taking a while before was being grabbed on the chance it would bring a price soon.

I figured it was exciting at first then I saw how it was going and was plain disgusted. What had been a nice little town was getting to be a sprawling mess of ugliness and clutter and noise. I'll admit some of the people crowding in were decent enough, just looking for a new place to settle and live. But most of them were after quick easy money and didn't care much how they got it and didn't give a hoot for the town because they'd be moving on to the next rail stop soon as the same thing started there.

My uncle Scott, he was disgusted from the first day. When the rush was going strong he talked some of turning in his badge and heading into the hills for peace and quiet but others like Morrison and even Rufe Martin who pushed himself into talking a bit asked him not to. "All right," he said. "I ain't ever backed away from anything and I'm too old to start now. A land boom ain't as bad as a mining camp anyway. The people ain't as tough, just cheaper and meaner. It'll quiet down when the rails are in and the crews move on. Meantime I'm going to make me some rules and ram them down the throats of these tinhorn sharpers." So he did and had me letter them on a chunk of cardboard and tack it up outside the office, just a few simple things like curfew on the saloons at midnight, no gunplay or be run out of town for keeps, and settle all gambling debts personal without squawking about crooks to the sheriff.

He swore me in as a deputy and told me to take care of the office because he was damned if he would with people in and out all the time asking this and that and making silly complaints. "Have to get it through their heads this town aint organized much yet," he said, "so they'll have to take things as is. Treat them decent long as they behave decent. Anybody makes too much fuss, throw him out. He gets nasty, throw him in the jail instead. I'll do the outside work." Which was what he did. He patrolled the town, not a regular beat or anything like that, just ambling around and somehow managing to be where most was happening anytime and it was right interesting to see how things would quiet down when he came along. Only real trouble he had those first weeks was over that curfew and that wasn't much. The new operators complained he was hurting business and interfering with their rights as free citizens of the state. "Likely I am," he'd say, "but if you're intending to stay around here and become part of the place, why, in about six months it'll be election time and the town'll be getting really organized and you can throw your votes around and try to elect another sheriff. Meantime I'm sitting on the lid. Would you like to make something of it?" He'd stand there ready for any move with that big old forty-five in plain view in its holster and they'd look him over and remember what they'd heard about him and subside grumbling.

There was one though named Ballard, Tim Ballard, who had a jaw and lived up to it. He didn't complain. He just kept his place open so after warning him once a few minutes after midnight and waiting a while after, Scott ambled up to the doorway and unleashed that old forty-five and shot out the four lanterns with four shots and ducked away out of the doorway and called out there was

still one bullet in his gun and more in his cartridge belt
did anyone inside want to argue. They didn't and that
was that. But Ballard sent a letter off to the county seat
protesting what he called such high-handed proceedings
and got one back from some official there saying that if
he could figure a safe way to make that little gamecock
Scott Hammon change his style of doing why let them
over there know because they never could and why not
just quit beefing and do what they did which was let him
go his way because the results seemed to be good. Ballard
came into the office and showed Scott and me that letter.
"You win, Hammon," he said. "Blamed if I don't think
I'll put up a building instead of that tent I'm using and
settle down here. I didn't know there were men like you
and a place like this left anywhere around any more."
He turned out to be a good man, that Ballard, though
there weren't many his caliber came in with the land rush.
But that's a side trail again. Point I'm making is that if
we'd had just an ordinary land boom, hitting a peak during the rail building then shaking down after, we'd likely
have made out all right. Sure, there were arguments over
land titles starting and a few lawyers from the county seat
were in town drumming up business and there'd have
been some small-scale land-grabbing and feuding over
that, but things wouldn't have got out of hand. It was
the big-scale grabbing, managed from outside, that caused
the real trouble.

The first settlers in the territory, same as almost anywhere, had the best land. That was natural, they'd had
first pick. Some had hurried over when the land office
was opened and registered their claims. But some hadn't
got around to that yet for one reason or another and even
some of those who had didn't have clear titles anyway.
The old homestead and pre-emption laws had a lot of
tricky angles like the one that tripped plenty people, the
little paragraph that said a person could make only one
entry, that if he'd ever made one on public land and gave
that claim up and moved on he couldn't make another.
Many a man who'd kept drifting west as one territory
after another was opened up, trying first one then another,

just changed his name and filed again but there was always the chance he'd be found out. So some of the big land companies that'd been getting rich picking off public land through political pull and all kinds of slick schemes figured an easy way to get hold of good land cheap was to hire men to jump claims of early settlers who hadn't filed yet or whose titles weren't clear. That way they'd be getting some of the best pieces and even some already pretty well developed. They were operating outside the law, using the law for their purpose while breaking it themselves, because it was plain on the point that homesteads were for people intending to live on them and make homes on them and who weren't acting as agents for anybody else. But a man who grabbed a claim and went along and met the legal requirements and got his patent then sudden changed his mind about living on it any longer and sold out cheap to one of those companies was acting within his rights, wasn't he? How could you prove he was really hired to do that from the beginning, specially when any proving would have to be done in courts that were under the thumbs of those companies anyway? They'd grabbed off plenty in other parts of the state and maybe other states and learned all the tricks, those companies had, and then one of them moved in on our town.

Its agents had checked the area careful and had everything planned and organized. That was plain the day the first batch of its hired claim jumpers hit town and the man in charge of them came into the office. He was one of those smooth-seeming characters that make the hair on the back of your neck rise, all smooth and easy on the outside, well dressed and even some fussy about clothes and a glib talker and underneath as shrewd and mean as they come. Scott was in the office between rounds resting and this gent introduced himself as Herbert Goss, a lawyer he said he was, and got right to business.

"A group of new citizens of your admirable community," he said, "as a matter of fact so new that they have only arrived here today, have asked me to act as their representative, their counsel so to speak. As an attorney I can assure you that their papers are in order, that they have duly recorded their claims at the land office and intend to take up residence upon them and begin improving them in accord with the law. Unfortunately some lawless squatters happen to be living on some of those claims. That is why I am here to see you."

"Even up here," Scott said. Then he didn't say another word. He just looked at this Goss and nobody knew him would have been comfortable under that look.

"Mr. Hammon," this Goss said. "I was speaking to you. I said I am acting as representative for a group—"

"You mean," Scott said. "You mean you've brought a bunch of claim jumpers to this town and they're working for you and you're working for some gypping land company."

"Oh, come now," this Goss said. "A man as smart as you seem to be knows how these things are. Suppose you happened to be right. How could you ever prove it? And why should you ever want to? Everything that shows in this is absolutely legal and airtight. We don't want any trouble. All we want is have these squatters, these trespassers, moved off with a minimum of difficulty. I have made arrangements for a deputy marshal to be sent here but he will not arrive for some days and we are in a hurry. Every day lost means a day longer on meeting the residence requirements, you know. A local sheriff who cooperated in this might find it to his profit. Others elsewhere have. I've brought along a list of the places and the squatters and if you—"

"Shut up," Scott said. He didn't shout it. He just said it but it stopped the smooth words coming from this Goss like a knife had sliced them off. "Shut up. And get out."

This Goss didn't seem to be bothered much. Maybe he'd expected that and had only been going through the motions. He sighed like he was sorry he wasn't understood right and started to leave and my uncle Scott stopped him. "Wait. Let me see that list." Goss pulled it from a pocket and laid it on the desk and Scott took it and began pushing a forefinger along it spelling out the names. Part way down he stopped reading and his head dropped lower and his eyes closed and he sat there like that for a moment then he raised his head. "I'll handle that one," he said.

"Why?" Goss said, quick and sharp. "Why just one?"

"Because the name's Brent Kean," Scott said. "You go out there and with half a dozen deputy marshals too and he'll kill you. Maybe that'd be a good thing. But not for him."

So Scott and I were saddling the horses again and coming out the trail that was getting to be a road and past the new shacks going up here and there and to this place. There wasn't any sense delaying, he said, because if anything was to be done for old Brent it would have to be strict legal, the way the company was pretending to be, and the first move was to get Brent off the place and forestall any fighting. We came out the trail and it was early summer and the grass was growing good and in that plot I'd plowed and harrowed the plants were beginning to show in green healthy rows. Lettie was out there with a hoe and came over to greet us and Sarah must have seen us coming because the coffeepot was on when we stepped inside and Brent was sitting on his chair by the side window with his hurt leg out straight, not saying anything, just waiting, because he saw Scott's face as we came in. I noticed something then, that these two, my uncle Scott and old Brent Kean, when they had something serious to talk about, they didn't do any shouting, they didn't do any name-calling. They spoke soft, almost gentle, and direct to the point and they had silences between speakings and they said about as much to each other with their eyes as with their words.

Scott didn't wait for the coffee or any small talk. He started right in and told what was happening. And Brent sat still, not a muscle moving, only his weathered old cheeks above the beard seemed to stretch tighter and his eyes seemed to sink back in deeper.

"So that's that," Scott said. "It's a man named Malley has filed on this quarter section. Hunt around outside and in some corner there'll be a stake with his name on it. I don't need to see it to know it's there. Put in some night on the quiet and with a witness too. This outfit is thorough. But this land business is tricky and there's a lot of angles. You three pack some things now and move down into town for a while so there can't be any trespassing or obstructing the law charges. Fred Morrison has room enough. He's had some law training too and lately he's been deep in these land rules. He'll figure a way for you to bust this case open and get a title."

Sarah and Lettie were tight-faced but quiet. They knew who was head of that family and had the say-so in the tight spots. And old Brent turned his head slow and looked out the window. After a while he turned it back slow and looked at Scott. "Suppose I don't feel like trusting to any law doings," he said. "Suppose I don't feel like moving. Now or any time."

"Then I'll have to do what I ain't ever tried with you before," Scott said. "I'll have to do some bossing around. I'm here as an officer of the law."

Old Brent's eyes flicked over to the rifle hanging above the shelf of old books and flicked back.

"Brent," Scott said. "There's things we both know. Even if you didn't have a game leg I could put a couple slugs in you before you even reached that rifle. You're just damned tough enough to drill me too before you went under. So we'd both be done. We'd both be out of a world that sometimes like now don't exactly seem worth living in. But there's Sarah and Lettie to think about."

"You'd use your gun," Brent said, very soft. "On me?"

"I've figured this," Scott said. "I've set a course. I'll hold to it."

Brent turned his head slow and looked out the window. He turned it back again and looked at Sarah. "Brent," she said. "I've been beside you in anything you felt like doing for about thirty years. I'm not changing now." He nodded his head a little, slow, and shifted it again and looked at Scott. "I ain't afraid of your gun," he said.

"I know," Scott said.

"Then that's enough," Brent said. He took a deep breath and sat up a little straighter and he looked at me. His big old voice came booming at me in a shout. "Well, boy! You overgrown lunkhead! Why aren't you out harnessing the team?" I jumped and started out and I could hear him booming away inside. "Sarah! Lettie! Gather some clothes together! We'll try town living for a time!"

I slapped on the harness and hitched the team to Brent's big wagon but I wasn't along on the trip in because Scott sent me to herd the stock that was in the fenced pasture over to the MacPherson place, a couple miles over there where the sharp slope starts up and there's one of those big fancy shopping centers nowadays. Mac was another early settler, that is he'd been around maybe ten years, but he'd hopped over to the county seat and done his filing in time and he was straight as a string and nobody would be trying to move in on him. He was more than willing to take the stock in with his and keep it for Brent and he was plenty peeved when I told him what was going on. "You tell the old rattlesnake," he said when I was leaving, "that if it gets to where we have to run those butting-in jumpers clean out of the country, me and my shotgun'll be ready."

It took a while, herding that stock over and swinging back into town. When I got there the Keans were already settled in with the Morrisons who had a fair-sized house behind the store. I found Scott and Brent in our office. Fred Morrison was with them. They had the door locked and I had to bang to get in. Scott and Brent must have been giving Morrison all the details because he was just starting in to figure the angles, sort of thinking out loud, when I arrived. The boom was bringing him big business at his store and he'd had to take on clerks and he was dealing in town lots too and he wasn't against the money coming his way. But all the same he was one of the old-timers and he didn't like this claim-jumping any more than MacPherson did. "That was the right move," he was saying, "to get off the place first thing. Now there can't be any loose charges floating around to confuse matters. No one can say we aren't trying to obey the law. Without digging further, there is one thing sure. We can bring suit and Brent here can collect full value for his cabin and any improvements like fencing and such. He was not trespassing when he put them up. The place had not been taken yet."

"Forget that," Brent said. "It's the land that counts."

"All right, all right," Morrison went on. "I was just talking. But there's a provision in the homestead law or one of the revisions, I forget which but it's been upheld, that when public land is opened original settlers who have been living there some length of time before the opening have three months leeway for their filing. Three months protection that means. Well, it's been a bit more than three months since this area was opened—"

"Three months and a day," Scott said. "I told you this outfit's thorough."

"All right, all right," Morrison went on. "But as I get it from you two it has been less than that since Brent here knew about the opening. From his point of view the protection is still there. Not from the law's necessarily but from his. It has not been three months since he was, in a sense, officially notified. And his busted leg adds another factor. He couldn't very well get over for his filing with a bum leg and the land office is strict about people appearing in person. We can work up a case that could sound right good. We might even win with it in land court. Given a fair shake that is. But my guess is it wouldn't come to that. We make it sound good in advance and we let word around that plenty about claim-jumping trickery is coming out in the trial and we'll worry this Malley so much—really the company but they wouldn't come out in the open, they would only act through him—that he'll just fade out and abandon the claim."

Morrison rubbed his hands together the way he did when he thought he'd swung a bargain or made a point. He turned straight to Brent. "All right, all right, Brent. I suppose you have your papers in order."

"Papers?" Brent said. "What papers?"

"Your citizenship papers," Morrison said. "You were born in England, weren't you?"

Brent just stared at him and Morrison shook his head. "Man, man," he said. "Don't you know public lands are open only to citizens or people who have started the process of being naturalized by appearing in court and filing a declaration of their intentions?"

"Citizenship," old Brent said. He wasn't shouting. His voice was soft and sort of deep and it was bitter. "My parents brought me to this country because this was where they wanted to live. Sixty years I've lived in this country and I've done my share for it. I've worked for it and I've fought for it and nobody ever threw citizenship up at me. Stansbury didn't say anything about it when he signed me on as a guide when he surveyed Salt Lake. Nobody mentioned it when they came running for me and glad to get me for the Colorado Volunteers in the Indian troubles in '64. I've led emigrant trains through these mountains. I've taken mapping crews into places they didn't know existed till I showed them. I've made one whole damn big stretch of this country mine the way hardly anybody else has or ever will because I know every rock and river in it and I've dropped my sweat and spittle on every square mile of it. Now when all I want is a little piece of it to live on and leave my daughter and that's been mine anyway for twenty-seven years, you tell me that just because some fool Congressmen way off in Washington—"

"Whoa, now," my uncle Scott said. "Didn't your father get naturalized?"

"Certainly he did," Brent said. "He told me so in a letter once."

"Then that's it," Scott said. "That covers you."

"Maybe," Morrison said. "Maybe. That depends on when. If Brent here was still a minor, yes. If he was past twenty-one, he was on his own and it wouldn't cover. All right, all right, Brent. Were you?"

"How in hell would I know?" Brent said. "That was close to fifty years back. Maybe I was, maybe I wasn't. And don't ask me have I got that letter. All such truck went when we were burned out along about the second year Sarah and me settled here. Some of those Utes helped us rebuild. Said we were fools to want a wood lodge but they helped. I told you they gave us our place. That's

title enough for me. All your legal foofarawing only
frazzles things till there's no real right or wrong left only
what you can get some side-squinting judge to say. Men
can get along together if they want and there aint too
much law mixed in. You just tell that Malley he can have
a piece of my land if he's set on it and he'll live decent
and stay out of my hair. I don't need the whole quarter
section. I'll just go back out and if anybody else comes
around claiming, well, I've got my rifle. I've trusted to it
and not to any finagling with laws most of my life now
and it's—"

"Man, man," Morrison said. "This isn't back in the
wild days. This is eighteen hundred and ninety-six. Do
you want me to help or don't you?"

"Yes," Scott said, cutting in quick. "Yes he does."

"All right," Morrison said. "All right and all right
again. I'll start suit for you, Brent, to have this Malley's
filing set aside. The land court is so jammed with cases
piled up from back along the rail line that it will be a
while before yours can come up and that will give us time
to handle this citizenship business. You write to where
your parents lived, Kentucky wasn't it—"

"Tennessee," Brent said.

"Tennessee, then," Morrison went on "Tennessee. Ad-
dress it Clerk of the Circuit Court in the county where
they lived. Find out the right date, then we'll know. Meantime, on the chance, you be ready to hobble over to the
county seat soon as the court, state court, is in session,
federal court is too far off and state will do, and file your
own citizenship intentions. We'll be on solid ground then
either way when your case comes up."

That was all could be done right then and it meant waiting, which is bad enough anytime. I don't know whether
Morrison really thought Brent could win his case or just
figured to ease him along by doing something while he got
used to the idea that he'd have to lose his land, lose this
particular piece anyway, and meantime he'd be getting
his citizenship straightened out so he could file somewhere
else later if he wanted. Anyway Morrison never said, not
to Scott or to me, not then or even later when what came

out of it was all over. He just went ahead and wrote the case up, his brief he called it, and went over to the county seat and had some trouble because the company was getting strong in politics there but he managed to wangle it onto the docket. Soon as he came back and said it was started Scott went looking for Goss and told him he'd better warn his man Malley to be mighty careful what he did if anything at the place out here. "Don't let him try living in the cabin," Scott said, "or I won't be able to answer for what Kean might do. Myself either. This case is just started."

"Just started?" Goss said. "It's already finished. Your legal shenanigans don't mean a thing. Just a nuisance. The law is behind us—beg pardon, behind Malley, since you are so sensitive on such things. The trouble with you and Kean is that you're both old-fashioned, your time is past and you're just a pair of relics walking around. A man as smart as you seem to be ought to realize that."

"There's better things than being smart," Scott said. "I'm old-fashioned, yes. Old-fashioned enough to wish you had guts enough to carry a gun and spirit enough to be crowded into trying to use it." But Goss just laughed, a mean little scratchy laugh he had. "That's what I mean," he said. "Direct action. That's your way. So old-fashioned you ought to be under glass in a museum. Manipulating the law is a lot better than manipulating a gun. Safer. More profitable. Now a man as smart as—" But Scott didn't let him finish, just swung away, and what he'd said had some effect because when I rode out checking for him I saw that Malley wasn't touching the cabin, was living in a tent he'd put up.

Meantime the boom went on booming. It spread out around because with the railroad through here shipping to market would be easy. Several more batches of claim jumpers and paid settlers came in, though the racket did let up some because the grading crews were moving on and only the bridge outfit was still in town. A temporary branch of the land office was set up in town here. Legal squabbles over town lots and building sites got to be so frequent that two days a week a judge came over from the county seat to handle cases right here too. That deputy marshal arrived and he wasn't any help at all. Maybe he was getting paid by the federal government but he was really working for Goss.

There was plenty tension in the air. The company was having things its way but most of the old-timers around and even some of the newcomers, the decent ones, didn't hold with this wholesale land-grabbing. Some of the people whose claims were jumped just faded away, ran out without putting up an argument, likely those who knew they couldn't get a clear title anyway. Some yelled and made a fuss and had to be pushed out and there were a few near-fights but Goss always had a half-dozen husky men with him when he went about notifying and after a few days that deputy marshal too. My uncle Scott took to sitting in the office a lot staring at the floor and muttering soft under his breath because it was all legal, on the surface anyway, and there wasn't a thing he could do except what he was doing which was refusing to have any part in it. Only once did he mix in and that was the time one man got so mad when Goss and his crew came to push him out that he ducked back into his shack and grabbed a gun and let fire a couple shots and lucky he missed and he slammed the door and barred it.

Those claim jumpers milled around outside and more of them were gathering and they were talking wild about stringing him up and likely that deputy marshal would have just stood aside and looked the other way but somebody got word to Scott and he went larruping out there. He made Goss and that marshal promise there wouldn't be any charges if he got the man out peaceful and he went up to the door and called out who he was and the man let him in and what he said in there was his business but in a few minutes he and the man came out. Those claim jumpers, they were an edgy bunch and mean-natured anyway or they wouldn't have been in such doings, started crowding around and talking ugly and Goss and that marshal turned their backs and went walking away and Scott got mad. He let the lid blow off and what was boiling in him come up. He cussed that crew the way likely they'd never heard before and he wound up shouting at them to go ahead start something, start something, start something. They knew he was plain itching to unleash that old forty-five of his and they backed off and he took the man and his few things into town and stuck with him till he was on the stage away.

Some of the people who'd been pushed out found places to stay in town and hung around, maybe waiting to see how old Brent would come out because they knew he was fighting the company in a law suit and if he won they might be able to do something too. That didn't make for a peaceful feeling because the men of these families were apt to be bumping into some of the claim jumpers any time and there'd be arguments. They'd have liked to look on Brent as a sort of a leader and sit around talking with him working up their mad but he wouldn't do that. He was in town but you'd hardly ever see him. He stayed most of the day in the room at Morrison's he and Sarah were using, reading in his old books or pretending to and staring at the wall like he could see right through it off into the distance and maybe he could, off into a distance that wasn't only in miles but in time too. He was one of the last of the old-time mountain men and a special breed of them at that and he had the patience they had to have, the kind that could hold them quiet under cover, for days if necessary, outwaiting danger on their trail. He'd made up his mind when Scott called him that he'd try this legal and like those Ute friends of his when he said he'd do something he'd do it. Only at night, late, when there wasn't much going on, he'd step out, hobbling on his crutch at first then later without it, only limping some, and cover miles in a circuit around avoiding houses and such and back and to that room again.

Sarah helped Mrs. Morrison all she'd let her and stayed in most of the time too. Lettie was working in the store. Sometimes in the evening she'd walk out with me but then again sometimes when I'd go for her there'd be some other young one ahead of me and we'd fuss around trying to outsit each other and I'd get mad and stomp away. Being with her wasn't what you'd call too pleasant then anyway. She took this claim-jumping hard and had to be always worrying it. She seemed to think Scott and me were somehow a part of it because we had to do with the law and it was the law that was hurting old Brent.

"That's federal law," I'd tell her. "It's only local law we have anything to do with. Can't you see it's Scott who's doing all he can and who's kept your father from getting into real trouble he couldn't ever get out of? The most he can lose now is just his land and he can always get another piece somewhere." "And can't you see," she'd tell me, "that it's not just land, it's that piece of land? If he can't have it, he won't want to go on living." "Shucks," I'd say. "He's the toughest old rooster I ever saw. He could start all over again right now and beat out any of us young ones." "But why should he have to?" she'd say and tear into me and the only way I could shut her up was ask her what in all the billy-be-damned possibles did she think we could do.

It was one of those times I made a fool move. We'd been walking and the dark had come down, only a trace of light left, and we were coming back through the trees behind Morrison's house. She'd stopped and was glaring at me and I got to thinking of those girls around Santa Fe, how you didn't talk much to them, just took, and I reached out thinking I'd kiss her and show her a thing or two. I took hold of her and she came in willing enough, her head down like she was being shy about it, and she was in close and sudden her head snapped up, hard, slamming against my chin with a jolt that knocked me loose and back a step. She was gone toward the house and I was ready to follow and maybe get really rough when I heard a chuckle off to the side. I turned and old Brent was limping up.

"Goldamn it!" I said. "What're you doing? Keeping tabs on us?"

"Simmer down, boy," he said. "I just happened to be heading out. Lettie don't worry me any. You're lucky she didn't give you a knee. Come along, stretch your legs some." He started off looking around at me and there wasn't must else to do so I tagged. Limp and all, he sure could move fast without seeming to hurry, quiet and easy like a long legged shadow slipping along. "Now you take Lettie," he said. "She ain't one of these coy things likes to tease the men. Sarah and me, we've raised her right. When she finds her man, why he won't have to coax around and try nipping a hug. If he ain't got sense enough to put it straight, she will." We went on some and I found myself trying to move the way he did, not clomping on my heels, but putting my feet down flat and letting my weight glide forward easy onto them. "See that shack over there," he said. "Past those trees. I remember shooting a bear there once. Big black. And fat. Enough grease to last us for cooking and on biscuits a couple months. Well, there's some things about what folks call progress that're all right. Like butter. Bear grease's good. Butter's better. All the same a man likes to remember he's used bear grease and brought it in himself." We went on like that, quiet most of the time with him remembering now and again, then I saw he'd taken me without any seeking landmarks on a circuit around and we were coming back to Morrison's from the other side. "Don't go rush'ng her, boy," he said. "This is a rough stretch for her right now." He stopped and looked off into the dark. "For me and Sarah too." I had a sudden feeling he was ashamed of saying that and he swung abrupt away and towards the house.

I went to our building and up the stairs. Scott was asleep on his cot and I made noise sitting on mine so he'd wake. "Goldamn it, Scott," I said. "Isn't there anything we can do, you can do anyway, about this jumping busi-.ness?" He rustled a little and I could begin to make him out lying there and staring up. "You think I ain't been beating my brains out?" he said. "I'm doing all I can see straight which is not helping it along any myself and seeing that arguments don't get growing into people getting hurt."

"That's not much," I said. "Why, the way some people are feeling, even some like MacPherson, why with you and Brent leading we could all get together and run those sharpers clean out of here."

"What's that do?" he said. "Except blow up trouble and plenty people hurt on both sides, maybe killed. We'd be breaking the law then, not a leg left to stand on. They've got the government behind them. Don't forget we're wrong too. We let things slide. Brent's wrong. Didn't file in time. I'm wrong. Didn't make him. But maybe it'll work out. The law ain't so bad. It's broad, got to be, covering so much. When you get down to cases there's got to be leeway. Maybe we can make the court see that. If a man can't have some faith in the law, how's he going to live?"

"But what if it doesn't work out?" I said. "What'll you do then?"

He lay there quiet, staring up. "I don't know," he said after a while. "I plain don't know."

That was the worst of it. There wasn't anything we could do, except wait till the case would come up and hope the judge would be decent enough to realize sometimes the strict letter of the law isn't as important as the spirit behind it. Morrison was working up every scrap of evidence he thought could help, things like details on Brent's guiding for the government and his military service, which wasn't in the regular army only in the state volunteers, but might have some effect because the law favored old soldiers in regard to public lands.

But that case never came up. Something interfered. Sarah took sick.

As we found out, it wasn't a new sickness. It was what she called a misery that'd been in her family for generations and had bothered her some, not too much, off and on the last years. My guess is some kind of internal cancer and the doctor, we had one in town then, thought so though they didn't know much about that in those days. My guess is too it hadn't bothered her much before because she was happy out here with old Brent and had so goldamned much to do taking care of him and Lettie and working around the place and enjoying it all that her system just plain wouldn't let that misery take good hold. Soon as they moved into town and she didn't have much to do, not what she'd call much, and had the land worry hanging over her and had to see old Brent staring at the wall day after day, she just plain let down and quit fighting

it without knowing that was what she was doing. It took
hold of her hard one day and after that she was in pain
most of the time and in a few days she had to stay in bed.
She began dropping away fast. She was unconscious a lot
of the time which was a blessing because the pain wasn't
letting up any now and Brent or Lettie and usual both
together stayed with her constant and one evening she
roused up and pushed herself up in the bed and spoke in
what seemed her normal voice again.

"Lettie," she said. "Don't you tell your father what I
said this morning. I didn't really mean it." She looked at
old Brent. "You ornery old scrawny hoptoad," she said.
"You've been man enough for me since the first time I
ever set eyes on you." She sort of fell back on the bed and
when they hurried close she was unconscious again and a
couple of hours later she was gone.

We buried her the next afternoon in the big lot that'd
been set aside for the town cemetery which is about the
only thing down there near the center that's still the same
as it used to be. Crowded around now with buildings
though and so jammed full of graves you can't even walk
easy in it. That's progress. Not even room enough any
more for the dead to rest right let alone for the living to
live right. But as I say, we buried her next day and Scott
had to take charge because old Brent seemed kind of
numbed. It was surprising how fast word got around and
how many people came in. I don't know whether Scott
had anything to do with this or I ought to give Goss some
credit, but he kept out of sight and kept his jumpers out
of the way too, even those who spent a lot of time hanging
around, and the town had a respectful quiet feeling during the funeral time. But what worried me was the way
Brent behaved. He moved along not paying attention to
anyone, not even answering when spoke to. He hadn't had
much sleep for days and none at all the night before. The
skin of his cheeks above the beard was stretched tight, too
tight, and his eyes were sunk way back. He wasn't really
numbed. He was aware. He was mighty aware. You could
see that in the old eyes deep in their sockets. He was just

going through with this funeral and he wasn't going to let anyone break in on his thinking and what he was thinking you couldn't tell.

Lettie was beside him and she was about the same. Her face was set and she wouldn't listen to anyone so after a while people gave up trying to sympathize with her. When I tried to take her hand and walk along with her she shook me off and looked at me like she didn't know me and didn't want to. But when it was over and Scott told her to get Brent back to Morrison's and make him rest, she nodded and did what he said. And not more than two hours later, when everything else around town was still kind of hushed and quiet, she was running headlong across the street and to our building and into our office shouting at Scott. "I can't find him!" she kept shouting over and over like she couldn't stop and Scott jumped and grabbed her and shook her and slapped her hard and she stopped with a jerk. He pushed her down on a chair and squatted in front of her. "All right, girl," he said. "Slow and easy. What's happened?"

She'd got old Brent back to the room at Morrison's and he went readily enough. Soon as they were inside he started: "What was it Sarah told you?" He kept after her and at last she told him. He quieted down right away like he was satisfied. When she said he ought to rest he lay right down and she thought he went to sleep and she sat in a chair and was so worn she slipped off too. She woke sudden and looked at the bed and he wasn't there. That startled her and then something scared her and she ran through the house and out around looking for him and then all she could think of was running to Scott.

"Easy now," Scott said. "What was it Sarah told you and you told him?"

"That she wished—" Lettie said. "That she always wished she'd be buried out home beside her boy."

Scott stood up. His voice was soft, almost a whisper. "And what scared you was that you saw his rifle was gone too."

"Yes," she said.

There. Maybe now this story begins to take some shape for you. Old Brent Kean with long memories in his mind and a rifle in his hand. That's the story. The real story. He took hold of it and it was his and clear through to the finish and that was a week later it was his.

We didn't know at first. Scott suspected and he told me to look out for Lettie and was out back slapping a bridle on his gray and he didn't bother with a saddle and went larruping bareback up the trail but the first of it was already over and those claim jumpers were gathering when he got out here. They were talking ugly and splitting into groups and starting to scour the country around. Scott didn't pay much mind to them, just to find out what he could. Then he rustled a wagon and brought the three men in, one dead, one dying, and the third, Malley himself, in bad shape. He left them with the doctor and came back to the office. From what he'd seen and heard and what he learned later the whole thing was plain enough.

Old Brent slipped out of Morrison's and headed up the trail, not on it but to one side holding to cover. He still limped some but a limp wouldn't slow him much and he moved along fast. When he reached the place out here Malley and two other men were busy cutting hay off the meadow there. His hay. Malley was driving a mower and the other two were stacking. Brent stepped out and went across the field to them. Malley saw him coming and stopped the mower and the other two did too and came over by Malley and they were all three bunched together watching him. He came up close. "Get off my land," he said. He was speaking very soft and that should have warned them but they just laughed and told him to run along quit bothering them. "Get off my land," he said again, "or I'll kill the three of you." But they just laughed again and slapped the guns they had at their hips and said if an old coot like him wanted trouble why they'd give it to him. He turned around and walked to the edge of the field, to the fence along the side of the pasture, and climbed over and turned again and rested the barrel of his rifle on the top rail. He squinted along the barrel and made his whole body relax the way he knew how so no muscle would be tense and make the gun quiver and he sighted and started firing. His first bullet took Malley through the right shoulder, low enough to rip through part of the lung, and knocked Malley off the mower seat, hurt bad but not so bad he couldn't crawl quick behind the machine. Brent grunted to himself for being so sloppy with his shooting and fired again at one of the others who was clawing at his gun and this bullet hit this one exact center in the left breast and he was dead before he even collapsed to the ground. The third man had his gun out and was ducking and dodging and sending his own bullets Brent's way but Brent sighted slow and careful and picked him off with a bullet through the belly before he'd gone far. Brent could see Malley's feet sticking out from behind the mower and he watched and there was no sign of movement. Then he heard shouting a distance off and saw some people running from the next place up and across the trail and he climbed back over the fence and headed off into the woods and faded away.

Scott hadn't much more than finished telling Lettie and me what he knew when that Goss was running into the office. He was so excited and mad he wasn't smooth-talking. He was shouting. "You're the sheriff!" he shouted at Scott. "Why aren't you out with posses after that murderer?"

"Posses?" Scott said. His voice was tired which was how he seemed to be too. He was acting like he was just pushing himself along doing what had to be done for no other reason than just plain that it had to be done. "You call those fool mobs posses? They're wasting their time."

"You just going to sit there," Goss shouted, "and let him get away?"

"I'm going to sit here," Scott said. "But I'll tell you something. Anybody brings him in it'll be me. In my own way. And you and your damned hired men'll stay out of it."

Goss caught himself then and pulled down into something of his usual style. "All right," he said. "But with you acting like this I won't be responsible for what they do when they get hold of him."

"You're not so strict law-abiding, are you," Scott said, "when it pinches you some. Now get out." Goss did and Lettie was staring after him, wide-eyed, and she turned to Scott. "Why, he means they'll—they'll—"

"Lettie," Scott said. "Brent's off up in the hills that're like his own backyard. They won't get even a sniff of him. I know I couldn't if I tried and I'm fair good myself. They won't get him."

"But even so," she said, "we've got to do something. He can't just keep on hiding and running away."

"Lettie," Scott said again. "I'll take care of him. All that anybody can now. You think a minute. You know him even better'n I do. He's never run away from anything in his life. What will he do now?"

She stared at Scott and after a minute she nodded her head slow and I couldn't follow them. "What do you mean?" I said.

"You'll see in the morning," Scott said. He took Lettie across the street to leave her with Mrs. Morrison and we had a hectic evening with the town buzzing and men riding in and out and reporting all kind of rumors. Brent was supposed to be heading off here and there and about everywhere at once. That deputy marshal was running in circles and giving orders then changing them and no one was paying much attention to him anyway. The man Brent had hit in the belly died about ten o'clock and that stirred new buzzing and more groups were forming and riding out and people like Morrison and Rufe Martin kept coming in the office wanting to know why Scott wasn't out at least to try to keep things under control if they did catch up with Brent and he just kept telling them in that tired voice to go away let him alone.

When the sun showed early in the morning the town seemed near deserted. "Come along," Scott said and we saddled and rode up the trail. It was all quiet and peaceful with the hunting way off now. The cabin here was still and silent as if nothing had ever happened. We rode right up to it. The door was closed. Scott lifted the latch and we went in and on a chair by the one front window with his rifle across his knees was old Brent. "I been waiting for you, Scott," he said.

"Yes," Scott said. "Yes. I know." He pulled over another chair and sat down slow and tired on it and hitched it around a little and the two of them sat there side by side looking out the window.

"Brent," Scott said. "A man has fool thoughts sometimes. I been thinking we could barricade the door and each take a window. You and me. We could put lead in a lot of them before they got us. You and me. There'd be some satisfaction in that." They kept on looking out that window then Scott said: "But we can't."

"No," Brent said. "We can't. I've been sitting here thinking. I lay out a while last night the way I used to in a place I know up in the hills. That's good for a man. Bigness all around and the sky wide and clean above. But you can't turn time back. I was wrong. I'd do it again but I was wrong. Men like that don't really count any more. They're only doing what they're paid to do and there's always that kind around. Always." He looked down at the rifle and ran a hand along the barrel. "Maybe I've just lived too long," he said.

The two of them sat there still and quiet looking out that window. "Brent," Scott said. "I been thinking too we ought to say to hell with the whole kit and caboodle of them and what they're doing to this country and head up north where it's still big and clean. You and me, Brent." And after a minute he said again: "But we can't."

"No," Brent said again. "We can't. A man's got to follow the trail he's started. Now mine's led to your jail." He stood up and he looked around at me and then he near tore me apart inside because what he did was call up for me something of that old gleam in his eyes and he sent that big old voice booming at me. "Well, boy! You overgrown lunkhead! Why aren't you down in town looking after Lettie?"

That was it. That was what he always did to me. He slammed at me with that big booming voice that might make some people mad and with words that might seem mean and cantankerous and what he was really doing was reaching out and taking me right into his own world with him and seeing me as another whole human be ng and saying stand up there boy and be yourself and if you can stand up to me there'll be a pair of us.

"I'm not in town," I said, "because somebody has to take care of an old crook-leg like you. I rode a horse out here. You'll be needing it to go in with Scott and I'll be hiking."

That was how we went, Brent on my horse and Scott on his riding ahead of me walking along behind. I watched them pulling on away from me towards town, the two of them riding together, not saying anything because they didn't need to, just riding along together side by side.

Things happened fast after that, or anyway they seemed to though it was really five-six days. Brent stayed in our jail, not because Scott wanted h m there or had the least little trace of a thought he'd try to slip away but because that was the safest place. Scott himself rigged a cot in the office and took to sleeping there instead of upsta rs and he was mighty particular who he'd let come into the office to see him. It was lucky the searching hadn't been organized, just haphazard bunches of men out hunting around hit or miss, because that meant they came straggling in one bunch at a time, tired and disgusted, and when they'd hear what had happened they'd blow some about what they would have done if, then they'd dr ft off for food and sleep so there wasn't many of them close around at any one time. Goss was hammering on the office door every few hours wanting to know was Scott going to help or hinder the law, was he notifying the proper authorities so a trial could get started. He was worr ed, Goss was. He wanted to see Brent at the end of a rope and fast. He didn't want what Brent had done to get contag ous, have other people taking guns and trying to chase h s jumpers off land that had been theirs. I expect that was the only thing Scott and that Goss ever agreed on, that the trial ought to be over and done quick as possible. Scott knew

Brent and knew that was all Brent wanted now and that staying in jail was hard on a man like him.

Scott sent Morrison over to the county seat right away to make arrangements. He wanted to get Brent out of our town where feeling ran high and over there where he thought the trial would be anyway. But Morrison came back and three other men with him. They turned out to be a new judge and an assistant clerk of court and a lawyer who'd been sworn in to act as prosecutor. "They're so jammed over there," Morrison said, "that it would be months maybe longer before this case could get in. The best they can do and they about insist on it is spare these men a few days so the trial can be held right here. It's irregular but it's legal enough." Scott was disappointed but after he thought it over he even perked some. "Maybe it's for the best," he said. "There's still a bit of the old-time spirit left around here."

He was right. You could almost feel it in the air around town. The most talk, the most noise, was made by the claim jumpers and those who sided with them, who figured the old days were gone and maybe a good thing too because they were poky and not much money around so let's go along and make things boom and make money too because that's the most important duty a person has and anybody who gets in the way ought to be shoved aside and we can't have old soreheads going about shooting people anyway. But here and there were those who'd lived here longer and known what it was like once and who looked on old Brent as one of them, something that had belonged to them in a special peculiar way like an old landmark and the big rocky quietness of the mountains around, and even if they didn't mind the town getting bigger and more bustling they still didn't hold with having a bunch of newcomers pushing people out and taking over and beginning to run things. Arguments were plenty along the main street and in the saloons. That makeshift court-room across the hall from the office was packed to the limit when the trial started about the fourth day.

I'll say this, the judge was fair. He didn't like the assignment much but he was fair and he knew his law and he had a sharp dry I'm-in-charge-here manner of speaking that helped keep reasonable good order. Picking a jury took all morning. Morrison was acting for Brent who just plain wouldn't hear to hiring a special lawyer. "I don't want any legal trickery or finagling," he said. "All I want is an old friend and an honest man and Fred here's both." Morrison and that prosecutor had some wrangles over jurymen but when it was finished Morrison had what he was after. He had five of the old settlers on that jury.

After noon recess Scott and I brought Brent in and the real business started. It took longer than was needed, most of the afternoon, because that prosecutor insisted on calling as witnesses just about everybody who'd hurried to the place here soon after the shooting. He even wanted to have Malley carted in on a stretcher to testify, but the doctor was firm against that. Malley was still in bad shape, touch and go with that ripped lung, and the doc wouldn't let him be moved. The prosecutor didn't know old Brent or he'd have known that wasn't needed, there wouldn't be any contesting the facts or twisting what happened. There'd be straight truth-telling and no dodging and no whining. And that's what he got when Brent took the stand.

Brent had been sitting there while the rest went on, Scott on one side him me on the other, sitting still and quiet as an old rock, looking across the room, over the heads of the jury facing him, right through the opposite wall and off into the distance. When he was called he stepped up on the little platform and sat on the chair there and when that prosecutor started on him he bent his head forward a little and focused straight on him. He answered the first questions polite enough. Then he saw how that prosecutor was winding around and he was a bit peeved. "Son," he said. "What you're after or should be is to show what happened. Your way'll take all day. Shut your yap and I'll tell you." The prosecutor began burbling something and the judge cut in, sharp and dry, with the comment that might be a good notion. So Brent told what had happened out here, straightforward, simple, and it tied in with what some of the witnesses said Malley'd said when they got to him. Listening to Brent you knew, everybody knew, that was exact how it was.

The real wrangling came when Morrison took over. He couldn't explain away what Brent had done but he could aim at showing why. He kept Brent on the stand quite a while, bringing out the background of the whole business and digging into the claim-jumping and just about every question he'd ask, that prosecutor would be on his feet shouting objections and there'd be cracking back and forth whether it was pertinent or not and the judge would have to rule and mutterings and remarks were breaking out all through the room. It was Brent shut it off. "Quit fussing, Fred," he said. "You mean well but you'll only tangle things more. Everybody on that jury knows all that, knows why I did it, or they're more stupid than they look." Most of the jury sat up straighter, staring at him, and the room quieted and he went right on. "Let's get this over with. I killed those two men. It was just my sloppy shooting didn't make it Malley too. The only question now is does that jury think I had reason enough. Likely not. They don't look like much to me."

The judge was staring at him, eyes narrowed, like he'd never bumped against Brent's kind before. The whole room was quiet and in the quiet there was a sudden sound, a sobbing catch of breath. It was Lettie, on one of the back rows of seats between Mrs. Morrison and Mrs. Martin fighting hard not to cry. And old Brent looked out at her. "Lettie," he said. "None of that. Ain't I always told you how a man should be? When he decides to do something, why do it and face up to what it means." Brent turned towards the table that was the judge's bench. "Judge," he said. "You been acting square, according to your rules. Can't you hurry this thing along?" He stood up, stretching tall, and he stepped down from the stand and came and sat between Scott and me and nobody made a move to stop him.

The judge hurried it but he didn't have to do much urging. That prosecutor kept his remarks to the jury brief and to the point. He figured it was a cinch now, that Brent had clinched it himself by admitting everything right out and then ruffling the jury. Morrison was just as short. He knew by now that what would happen would happen regardless of what he said and if he'd done anything it was when the jury was being picked. Then the judge gave his instructions, brief too, and he sent the jury upstairs to our living quarters to do their deliberating and the waiting began.

We could hear them moving around some up there and now and again we'd hear voices, not clear enough to make out words, just enough so we'd know they were arguing. It got to be suppertime and most people drifted off to eat and some came back and wandered around, inside and out, waiting. The judge and those other two officials went out and came back and Scott and I took turns. Old Brent was back in the jail and ate there. Lettie brought him food as she always did, going past Scott and me like we didn't exist, in and out without a word, and we left her alone in there with him as we always did too.

About nine o'clock the foreman came down. He was red-faced, peeved. They were having a time, he said, and that prosecutor snorted at that and the foreman went on, couldn't they knock off for the night and go at it again in the morning. But the judge said no, his time was running out, he'd keep them up there till they reached a verdict. He couldn't stop them flopping where they could and napping some and he'd have food sent up but that was all.

We worried through that night and no verdict. The judge said call him if and he and the other two went and got some sleep somewhere. Scott and I made out in the office. All the next morning and the same. The whole town was waiting. People were milling up and down the main street, talking and arguing and wandering around. The saloons did mighty good business. Goss and his special crew were camping in the courtroom, trying to or pretending to play poker in one corner and getting madder by the minute, and most of his paid settlers were around town somewhere. The judge was getting impatient. He'd planned to leave by the evening stage. He sat at his table-bench playing solitaire and near wore out his cards. And

old Brent sat sometimes on the chair in his part of the jail
and lay sometimes on the bunk, still and quiet as an old
rock, staring right through everything around him off into
the distance.

"Goldamn it, Scott," I said. "Why aren't you in there
talking to him? He seems so all alone."

"No," Scott said. "He's off where I can't follow. He's
been farther and done more than I ever did. He's best
alone now."

So the waiting went on. Along late afternoon the whole
jury came stomping down the stairs. They looked like
they'd been having a time all right. They were all red-
faced and they wouldn't look much at each other. The
foreman didn't even wait for the judge to get in a peep.
"We're quitting!" he said. "We had it seven to five for a
hanging at the start and we got it down to nine to three
and we're stuck and we're quitting!"

The judge looked them over, disgusted, and took hold.
"All right," he said. "We ought to have the prisoner in
here and make this formal but I won't bother. I'm dis-
charging you as a hung jury. I'm declaring a retrial. Date
to be set soon. You'll get your duty money in a few days.
Now clear out, I have a stage to catch." It happened so
fast word hadn't got outside yet and not many people were
in the room. Those jurymen straggled out. Other people
followed them, hurrying to spread the news, and that left
only Goss and his crew. They'd dropped their cards and
were standing in a bunch looking mean, specially Goss.
His law-manipulating wasn't going according to schedule.
And the judge showed then maybe he knew more about
what was behind all this than I'd figured before. "That
means you too, Mr. Goss," he said. "I'm clearing this
courtroom." And there wasn't a thing Goss could do, not
then, except go out and his crew with him.

The rest of us, that's Scott and me and the judge and
those other two officials, went into the office so they could
fix up their records. I ducked back to the jail part and
told Brent and all he did was raise up a little on the bunk
and say: "So it ain't over yet. They didn't look like much.
Couldn't even make up their minds." He lay back again

and I hurried out because I wanted to get across the street and tell Lettie. I had to plow through people milling around in the street because the word was spreading fast. I pushed right into the house and she had the room door closed where she was and I hammered on it and shouted something about the jury and then I shouted didn't she hear me. Sudden she yanked the door open and she really looked bad, all worn and tired and red-eyed. "They couldn't agree," I said, "so the judge discharged them." Her face lit up like a match when you strike it. "Does that mean they'll let him go?" she said. "No," I had to say. "It means there'll be another trial." Her face got hard and she glared at me. "You and your law," she said. "You're just playing with him. Dragging it out. Making it worse." She slammed the door shut and all I could do was go back to the office.

The judge was just leaving, the other two with him. "Don't get me wrong," he was saying to Scott. "I was dragooned into this job so I'm doing it. I don't care a hoot whether he hangs or not, except how, though he does have a lot of pepper in him and we don't seem to have too much of that nowadays. It's for a jury to say. But I'll do what I can. I'll see about a transfer right away and let you know." They left, heading for the stage station, and Scott closed and bolted the front door of the buliding after them and came back into the office and settled on a chair by the front window.

"Ben," he said. "I ain't your father and I ain't built right to be, maybe not even a fair substitute. I don't know how to put things. But you're getting a strong taste of it. The way it is sometimes. The law I mean. Being a sheriff ain't always making people behave decent and strutting some with a badge and getting a name. It's being the middle sometimes with the right and wrong of things all mixed and all you can do is set a course that seems right to you and hold to it. There's that Goss that's first cousin to a rattlesnake and I wouldn't trust with a nickel walking around free as air. There's Brent that I'd trust my life to anytime anywhere in the jail waiting for another trial that can mean his neck. You could pull out of this, Ben. A young one like you with everything still ahead. Maybe that's one thing would make sense."

I looked at him sitting there, not much on size but all the same with that clear and almost lonesome completeness within himself a goldamned good fighting man and I don't mean just fighting with a gun or muscle but fighting straight and steady and maybe bullheaded and stubborn but still straight and steady through all the doings big and little and decent and mean alike of all the days of living and I thought of old Brent back there following the trail he'd started and Scott sitting here holding to the course he'd set and I saw that pulling out wouldn't make any sense, not for me, and that maybe one of the few things that do make sense is sticking to what you've come to believe in no matter what and seeing some purpose in living other than just getting through the days pleasant as possible and even if I didn't have any yet nobody could stop me going on looking.

"No," I said. "I'm not pulling out. But not because I like what I've seen of the law much. Likely for a lot of reasons. Maybe one's because my father whopped people that tried picking on you once and I know why he did."

He looked at me. "Thank you, Ben," he said, simple and quiet. "That pays for a lot. I guess you're a Hammon all right. Now get upstairs and clean things some. Likely they made a mess."

They had. They'd made a real clutter. It took me a while cleaning up and when I went down again Scott was still by the window. "I don't like it," he said. "Trial's over and they know how it came out and the new one can't be for a while but the crowd ain't thinning out any. Not much anyway. They're staying away from this building and that's good. But they're hanging around."

"You want me to go out and circulate around some?" I said.

"No," he said. "Neither one of us is leaving here. Maybe I'm just jumpy but we'll sit tight."

I watched out the window with him and he was right. Too many people were out there. They were staying away from the open space in front of the building but we could see them going up and down the street, wandering around and talking in bunches and drifting on down toward the saloons and out again and around, and too many of them were men that'd come into our territory taking orders from Goss. But they were staying away from our building. They'd look over towards it and a couple times I saw some pointing but that was all.

We sat by the window and the sun was low, throwing long shadows outside, ready to drop behind the mountains to the west, and then Lettie was coming across the street with her tray of food. I unbolted the front door for her and bolted it again. She marched into the office, not looking at either of us and maybe the reason she wouldn't and wouldn't speak was she was afraid she'd break down but you couldn't be sure, not the hard way her face was set, and she put a plate with a couple fat sandwiches on Scott's desk. "Nice of you, Lettie," Scott said. "That's Mrs. Morrison," she said and went right on with her tray into the back room and pulled the door closed after her. We ate the sandwiches and after a while she came out, still not looking at us, and headed for the outside door. "Lettie," Scott said and she kept on. "Lettie," he said again, sharp, almost mean, and she stopped. "Quit acting a fool," he said. "Soon as you get back you tell Fred Morrison to move about some and come here the back way and tell me what's doing." She just nodded and I unbolted the door for her and she went on and across the street.

It wasn't much later when Morrison rapped on the door at the rear end of the hall. I was waiting for him and let him in. That door had a good bolt too and I fastened it soon as he was in. He was uneasy and worried, but not too much. He started talking right there in the hall. "Well, Scott," he said. "Well. I'm glad you sent word. I was so busy catching up accounts at the store I wasn't aware. But I don't think you'll have trouble. There is considerable talking. Yes, yes. What you would expect. The law is too slow. It is not certain. Perhaps something should be done. With the usual cuss words and foul language for trimmings. But no one is steamed up enough to touch things off. There has been one ruckus. One of those jury hold-outs was fool enough to stay around and just a while ago several of the others jumped him and he took a beating before he got away. That was tough on him but maybe it was a good thing. It's something new to talk about and it blew off some of the steam."

"Goss," Scott said. "What's he doing?"

"Yes," Morrison went. "Yes. That is the real trouble spot if there is one. He is buying drinks. He is buying all they will take for those talking against Brent. I don't know what he is saying because he kept his mouth shut when I was by. I am not so certain he would really like to get something started, though he was mad enough earlier. It isn't as if Brent were acquitted."

"Maybe," Scott said. "But he was after a hanging and he hasn't got it. He ain't absolute positive now he will. And he knows his jumpers ain't going to be feeling safe till he does."

"Well, yes," Morrison said. "Well, yes, perhaps. But just a delay is not enough to push things. He is not getting anywhere. He is only getting them drunk. In a short while now they will barely be able—"

Morrison stopped. He jumped a little. I guess we all did. There was another rapping at the rear door. Scott's old forty-five was in his hand. I don't know how but sudden it was there. He motioned me to go unbolt the door. I did and the person outside pushed in. It was Tim Ballard, that saloon man Scott tangled with when the boom first started. He nodded around. "Hammon," he said. "I thought you ought to know. Malley's just died."

There was silence in that hallway and faint, far off from down the street outside, we could hear some yelling and that faded out and the only sound was the soft slither of metal on leather as Scott slipped his gun back in its holster.

"A man came legging into my place with the news." Ballard said. "I saw how the boys were taking it. Then Goss came in talking big and he looked too blamed pleased to suit me. So I came here."

Morrison sighed. He looked older all at once and kind of sad. "So I was wrong," he said.

"Hammon," Ballard said. "You cut down my profit with your damn curfew. You busted four lamps for which nobody's paid me a cent yet. I don't know why that puts anything up to me but somehow it does. My bartender can take care of the place. If you don't mind I'll stay here a while with you and see what happens." He reached a hand into the side pocket of the jacket he had on and pulled it part way out, enough to show he had a gun there. "I'm not too good," he said. "But I've used this a little in my time."

The back door was opening again. It was Morrison, going out. That shook me. I hadn't figured him that way. I hurried and bolted the door after him. "Stay there," Scott said. "Watch that door. You never can tell." And he and Ballard went into the office where they could watch out the window.

I stayed there by the back door and faint I could hear the yelling again and the quick dusk of this mountain country dropped and it was dim and growing dark in that hall. Then I heard, not a rapping, just a scratching on the door. "Who's there?" I said. On the instant I could hear Scott and Ballard coming into the hall behind me. "Morrison," a voice said outside, low and not much more than a pushing whisper, but it was his voice and I opened the door and he came in and he had an old shotgun in his hands and right behind him was the thick barrel-shape of Rufe Martin. "Bolt that door," he said and I did. "Scott," he said, "Lettie is safe at the house. I told the wife to keep her there no matter what. Rufe and I thought perhaps we could slip Brent out. But they are posting men around."

A cold shiver hit me, thinking of us cooped up in that building with men around watching to keep us there for whatever would happen, and then it was gone because my uncle Scott was speaking. "Going to play it rough," he said. He didn't say that at all worried. There was even an edge of eagerness on his voice like he was glad how things were because maybe at last he'd have a chance to cut loose. "They don't know what rough is," he said. "They'll find out."

He took us into the office stumbling some in the growing dark and he lit a lamp and set it on the floor in a corner behind the desk so the light was just spread out dim through the room and enough into the hall so we could make out to move around. He went to the old cupboard in the opposite corner and unlocked the padlock on it and took out a rifle and loaded it and handed it to Martin and another for me. "No shooting," he said, "unless they rush us. I've bluffed out these things before."

That was when he heard the yelling again, louder, coming closer, fading out again only now in front of us, across the way. Out the window we could see them, dark shapes across the open space and in the street, a whole crowd of them, more than a hundred I'd say because somehow people who aren't really in on a mob still go straggling along sort of fascinated and blood-hungry and eager to watch and maybe are even stampeded into taking part. There was one bunch, about fifteen of them, close together and pushing out some and they were the ones to watch and a half dozen of them came cautious across the street and the open space and up on the porch. "Hammon," someone shouted. "We want to talk to you."

"Go ahead, talk," Scott shouted.

"Where we can see you," the voice shouted.

"Talk is it?" Scott whispered to us. "That's a good sign. They ain't screwed to the point." He stood up from where he was crouching by the window. "I'm going out," he said. "In the doorway. Got to show them I ain't afraid of the whole caboodle. Let them see too we're ready for them." He posted us in the hall backing him where the dim light from the office would show on us. "Stand back from that door," he shouted. "I'm coming out." He unbolted the door and the second the bolt was slipped they pushed from the outside, swinging the door in and shoving him back, and two of them crowded into the doorway and in the same instant Scott's old forty-five was in his hand bearing on them and they saw us all facing them with guns ready and they froze where they were. "Talk fast," Scott said.

"What the hell?" someone said. "That's Ballard."

"The blacksmith too," another one said.

They were some surprised. They fidgeted around but they didn't back off.

"Thought you wanted to talk," Scott said.

"Hammon," a voice out on the porch said and it belonged to Goss. "I'm not speaking for myself. I'm just speaking for these men here who—"

"Quit that, Goss," another voice said. "You're in this too. All we want, Hammon, is for you to clear out. You chuck in your badge and clear out and you'll be all right. We ain't waiting for any elections. We're taking over."

"A bunch of drunks like you?" Scott said. "I ought to lock you all up but I ain't got the time. You thought there was only two of us here. There's five good guns waiting if you start anything. You won't. Now clear that doorway."

"This is a public building, ain't it?" someone shouted. "We got as much right here as anybody."

"Say something," Scott whispered to Morrison and that Morrison, quick on the talking trigger, began spouting something about being a justice of the peace and as such ordering them to disperse and go home think things over. But I didn't hear much because Scott was whispering to me. "Any gunplay now the whole town'll bust loose. Can you clear that doorway?" And sudden I felt good. I'd been trailing along thinking I was useless because even with a rifle in my hands I couldn't do much being as I never was good with guns. I was just a big overgrown lunkhead. But I had size. I had muscle. I reached over in the dim light and leaned my rifle against the wall. I put my head down some and sudden I drove forward and I curved out both arms to take in those two in the doorway and I carried them right off their feet and on out through and smacked them and myself into those outside and I heaved the way I'd spent years heaving on big old plow handles when I was growing and the whole bunch of them went sprawling this side and that and some even off the porch and I ducked back in fast and Scott slammed and bolted the door.

"All right, Rufe," he said. "You and Ballard take the courtroom windows, front and side. Fred you take the back door. I'll take the office window. Ben, you be ready for wherever you're needed. Keep an eye on the front door but that's likely safe. Anybody comes close'd be in crossfire from the windows." The others scattered to their places and he crouched by the office window and raised it open a bit. "Every door and window's guarded," he called out. "Better call it a day and go home."

Those who'd been at the door had scurried back to the street, maybe thinking a bullet or two'd come after them, likely mad as hornets. There'd been some satisfying crunching when I hit. Across the way there was a lot of racket, people talking and shouting and milling around. More of them seemed to be out there even than before but they were staying away from in front of the building.

"Too much light in here," Scott said. "Makes me an inviting target at that window. But we got to have a little." He took the lamp from the corner and opened the door to the back room to set the lamp on the floor inside and to one side so only a little light would come through the doorway. That lit up the blank-walled big inner room and back in the jail part we could see old Brent. He was sitting on the edge of the bunk watching us. As the light hit his deep old eyes you could tell that he knew, that he knew everything. His keen old ears had been hearing things through those single-partition walls and he knew. "Scott," he said and it was sort of funny, him telling us who'd been out front in it. "Scott. There's bad weather brewing. A real storm."

"Nothing we can't handle," Scott said. "Don't you worry."

"I ain't worrying," Brent said. "Not about that." And Scott swung around, hurrying again to his window, and Brent caught me with a little flip of his head. I went closer and he beckoned me right up to the bars. "Boy," he said "Where's Lettie?"

"Over at Morrison's," I said.

"Good," he said. "This ain't for her. Her time's ahead. I've had mine. This is me alone again the way it ought to be with Sarah gone. The way it was before I knew her, when it was mostly just me and the bigness of this country around and now and again——"

"Shucks, Brent," I said. "You're not alone. There's——"

He stopped me with a hand up. "Think I don't know?" he said. "It's a crazy fool world, boy. There's a lot of men out there working themselves up and plenty will get their fool head shot off if they start something and this whole section'll get split apart worse than it is already and there'll be bush-whacking and dry-gulching and fighting around for a long time. There's that damned little coyote Scott who'll maybe get his fool head shot off too though that'll take doing. There's you, boy. And those others. That Ballard now. Who'd have thought it of him? And it's all over what'll only be a pile of old bones at the end and soon enough anyway. That's me. It ought to make me feel important. It don't."

"Brent," I said. "It's not just you."

"Don't try to blow it up, boy," he said. "Right here and now it's me." There was a new burst of yelling outside and he looked past me towards the front. "Go see what's happening," he said.

I hurried to the office and crouched down by the window with Scott. They'd started a fire in the street, down a little ways, and were piling wood on it. A wagon came up and the man driving swung it sidewise near the fire and stopped the horses and another man climbed up on the seat and stood up there and started talking. We couldn't hear him but we could hear shouts rising off and on and we could see pretty well in the firelight. "I'll be damned," Scott said. "They've got a body in that wagon. Must be Malley's. And that's Goss talking."

The crowd was thick around the wagon and Goss up on the seat was having to raise his voice to be heard but even so we couldn't make him out because the men swarming around were raising what reached us as just a mixed angry yelling. Then one voice climbed above the others: "Burn 'em out!"

Scott pressed closer to the window and something pulled me around to look into the back room. Brent was up, standing close against the barred door to his part of the jail. He was beckoning to me. I slipped away and Scott was so intent he didn't notice me go. "Well, boy?" Brent said. "They're planning to burn us out," I said. He looked at me and that look held me there, still and waiting, and then he said, soft, very soft: "All right, boy. Unlock this door."

I've wondered countless times why I did it. Maybe I figured that if they were going to try set fire to the place it wasn't right for him to be penned in there. But I don't remember any figuring. I only remember doing it. I think it was just plain because old Brent Kean told me to. I think it was simple as that. I leaned the rifle I was carrying against the side bars and I reached in my pocket for the big flat key that was the same as the one in Scott's pocket too and I unlocked the door.

He pulled the door open and came through. He moved swift and easy as a big lean old cat despite his limp. He reached with one hand and set it for a tiny tick of time on my shoulder as he passed me and with the other hand he scooped up that rifle. He stood there in the open a few seconds checking the load with quick experienced old fingers then he was moving towards the office and as I say, that's the story, the real story, old Brent Kean with long memories in his mind and a rifle in his hand.

He slipped into the office, quiet, and the rifle held at his hip was bearing on Scott and the first Scott knew he was there was he said: "Hold it, Scott. Don't move." And Scott froze still, crouched down by the window, only his head moving so he could look around and up, and Scott's eyes flicked over at me following Brent into the inner doorway and narrowed some and back to Brent. "I'd use this gun," Brent said. "On you. All I want is one minute. One minute for myself before you do anything at all."

Scott looked up at him. It seemed to me Scott just plain

wanted to cry, wanted to put his head down and bawl. "I ain't afraid of your gun," he said and then his voice broke and the words came shaking. "Or any man's. Or anything they think of trying."

"I know that," Brent said and they looked at each other and then Scott's voice was steady again. "Then that's enough," he said. "Have it your way." And old Brent turned and was out in the hall and we heard him unbolting the front door and we heard Morrison's voice from the rear end of the hall saying something in surprise and the front door opened and Brent was out on the porch.

I jumped to the window by Scott and we both peered out. He loomed up there on the outer porch edge, lean and tall in the faint far edge of the light from the fire out in the street. Then they saw him. The yells climbing told they knew who it was. He stepped down and out some into the open space and he raised that rifle and fired once, twice, and the first answering shot was an echo of his third and more guns were blazing from out in the street and he staggered and dropped to his knees and collapsed slow sideways and lay still.

The silence that shut down outside was sudden and complete then there was the sound of running feet and all of us in the building were out on the porch and those men in the street were scattering, scurrying off into the darkness, and the wagon went clattering off fast, and its sound faded and there was only a fire out there lighting the emptiness. We looked down at the body of old Brent, limp and still on the ground. "The damned old wolf," Tim Ballard said. "He wanted to go down fighting."

"No," Scott said.

I stared at him because I didn't get it at first.

"He could pick off a running deer at three hundred yards," Scott said. "There was a whole crowd out there. Maybe a hundred twenty feet. Look sharp. You see anybody hit lying out there?"

We looked. There was only an empty street and a fire lighting some of it and sending flickering shadows along it.

"Fred," Scott said. "You go over to Lettie. Rest of you take him inside." And Scott stepped down off the porch and started away. I hurried after him. "Where you going?" I said.

"Goss," he said. He went right on. He went right past Brent's body without stopping. I hesitated then I followed and I picked up the rifle lying beside Brent's body as I passed. All kind of wild notions were pounding in my head and I was fed up with the whole goldamned world and I kept thinking that even if I couldn't do much with that rifle as a gun I could do plenty damage with it as a club. But I should have known. He was Scott Hammon. He couldn't be anything else. He made his own rules and he held to them.

We stopped at the first saloon and looked in. There were quite a few men in there but not as many as I thought there'd be. They were crowded by the bar and they were being unusual quiet. They saw Scott in the doorway and looked at each other and away and fidgeted around. But Goss wasn't there. It was in the fourth place that we found him. We went in and Scott went up and took his stand about ten feet from him and the population in that saloon dwindled mighty quick.

"Now, Hammon," Goss said. "Don't you go—"

"Shut up," Scott said. He didn't take his eyes off Goss and he spoke kind of slow and cold. "A man smart as I seem to be knows what happened can't be pinned on anybody. Technically Kean was breaking jail. Impossible to prove whose bullet got him anyway. But there's one piece of my old-fashioned law I can still make stick. I'm running you out of town. Disturbing the peace. Inciting to riot. I'm giving you one hour to get out. I find you here then or any time after I'll shoot you on sight."

Goss got out. We never saw him again.

Of course the company just sent in another man but he was wary, he only stopped by every so often to check and he didn't push things. Claim-jumping in our section slowed down. No more jumpers were sent in and some of those first ones quit and left though most of them finally got title and collected before they left too. The company did all right, got most of what it was after as such outfits about always do.

We buried old Brent the next morning, next to Sarah in the town cemetery. There was one thing funny about that. Lettie didn't show at all. "Staying in her room," Fred Morrison said. "She doesn't want to see anybody." But she was a Kean, Lettie was. She had old Brent's blood in her and Sarah's too and she could take hold.

It was early afternoon the same day and we were sitting in the office, Scott and me. He was by the window and he wasn't saying much, not even about my unlocking the jail door. He never once said a thing to me about that, not once even in the years after which weren't too many for him though the kids did get to know him some when they were little before the big blizzard and he was out helping open the way to snowed in families and froze a foot, the one that didn't have good circulation because he'd been winged in that leg once, and gangrene set in and took him in just a couple days. I figure knowing him even that little helped the kids turn out right.

But as I say, he was by the window and I was by the desk, about as low as I ever was. Even with Scott sitting there, a Hammon like me and not really so complete and firm within himself that once in a while he wouldn't break down and let me know it, even with that I felt like I didn't belong anywhere at all, not even around here. I wasn't going to stick around that office any more, not after what had happened. It had the smell of law about it even though maybe only Scott's kind of law and I'd had enough of any kind. I didn't have anything to be doing, to be aiming at, and couldn't even begin to think of anything. And then I got to thinking when I was plowing that patch out there and how it was, doing what I really could do right and Lettie watching me and making me mad, the kind of singing-inside mad my father must have had when he was arguing with my mother, and that made me even lower because what I'd done had finished that. And Scott said: "There's a wagon outside."

I looked out and there was Brent's big old wagon with

his team hitched to it and it was stopping out front and Lettie was up on the seat driving.

All I could do was stare and Scott said: "Get on out there."

"I can't," I said. "Not after what I did."

"Ain't you learned anything yet?" he said. "There's people and there's people. That's Lettie Kean out there. Brent Kean's girl. Now you jump."

I went out because there was something I had to tell her and I didn't want to but I had to do it. She sat there looking down at me and she was in pretty bad shape. She couldn't keep the tears out of her eyes and some would slip over and run down and she'd been wiping at them with a hand dusty from the reins and that'd left dirt streaks.

"Lettie," I said. "I'm the one let him out."

She looked at me and her eyes didn't waver any. "He wanted you to, didn't he?" she said.

AS 299—Great Short Novels of the American West   64

"Yes," I said.

She looked at me and she nodded her head a little and then it hit me, her being there on that wagon.

"Where are you going?" I said.

"I'm going home," she said. "He wanted it to be Kean land. He wanted a Kean to be living on the place. Malley's dead and no relatives and the claim's open. I'm a citizen. I was born here and I'm past twenty-one. I've been at the land office and I've filed on it."

"Lettie," I said. "You can't do that. A woman can't handle a farm all alone."

"I thought," she said, "I thought maybe I wouldn't have to do it alone." And then she fixed me for life. She raised her voice, not a real shout, just an echo of a big old voice we both had known. "You overgrown lunkhead," she said. "Why aren't you climbing up on this wagon?' '

I stepped up on the near front wheel hub and to the seat and sat beside her. I reached and took the reins from her and we drove on out home here.